THE OTHERS

ANNETTE MORI

Affinity
Rainbow Publications

2021

THE OTHERS

ANNETTE MORI

The Others
© 2021 by Annette Mori

Affinity E-Book Press NZ LTD
Canterbury, New Zealand

1st Edition

ISBN: 978-1-99-004916-3

All rights reserved.

This is a work of fiction. Names, character, places, and incidents are the product of the author's imagination or are used fictitiously and any resemblance to actual persons living or dead, businesses, companies, events, or locales is entirely coincidental

Editor: Angela Koenig
Proof Editor: Alexis Smith
Cover Design: Irish Dragon Design
Production Design: Affinity Publication Services

ACKNOWLEDGMENTS

A huge thank you to all of my beta readers: Emily Cubbage, Erin Saluta, Ameliah Faith, Carrie Camp, Dana Holmes, and Danna Micoletti, who made brilliant suggestions to improve the initial draft. I would also like to express my gratitude to Affinity Rainbow Publications and the wonderful trio: JM Dragon, Erin O'Reilly, and Nancy Kaufman, who continue to provide feedback to tighten up manuscripts that need assistance and to publish my unconventional work. I am eternally grateful for the opportunities they give me to let my stories see the light of day. I always enjoy working with the beta editor, Nancy Kaufman, who helped tighten my story. Thanks to Angela Koenig for her magic as the final editor to tighten the story even further. She is a delight to work with. Inevitably, there are those pesky final errors that slip through, and I am thankful that the final proof editor, Alexis Smith, catches those before the book goes to print. Thanks to Nancy Kaufman for the final cover. Nancy is also a promoter extraordinaire. A huge thanks to all the other readers and fellow writers who have sent personal emails, written reviews, and posted nice things on Facebook (you know who you are). The Affinity authors are an especially supportive group and often share posts or send words of encouragement. Finally, my wife, Jody, continues her support even when it interferes with our time.

DEDICATION

To all those brave men and women who continue to fight for democracy and decency. And of course, as always, to my beautiful wife.

TABLE OF CONTENTS

PROLOGUE

I remember my first kiss. Although the kiss was with a boy, I still count it as my first. Now that I know I'm a lesbian, I wish the kiss had been with a girl. But no matter how much I want something different, you can't change history.

Parry Admirer. That was his name. No kidding. We were ten years old, and he was my boyfriend. Although Parry had shaggy blond hair, the kids called us Sonny and Cher because of my long black hair and eyes the color of dark chocolate. I'm not Native American, but my Italian heritage was close enough for the ten-year-olds to make the comparison.

Parry's bold suggestions shocked me. When he said we should hold hands, my eyes grew to the size of saucers. He laughed. He knew what a good Catholic girl I was. But I was also curious and wanted to have new experiences.

Across the street from my house was an enormous field that separated my childhood home from the primary school. In the middle of that field was an old bomb shelter. Parry grunted as he lifted the massive cement square that closed off the shelter from the rest of the world. I was scared as I climbed down the metal rungs. An orange stain appeared on the palms of my hands from the rusty steel leading to the dirty cement below. I ignored the cobwebs hiding in the dark corners. Parry had to reassure me he would leave the trap door off and let the sunshine in.

I blinked in the sliver of light, sitting across from Parry with my legs folded like a pretzel. He mirrored my pose.

CHAPTER ONE

I was in another bomb shelter. But this time, I was about to experience a different first. We couldn't stay inside any longer. It had been several months, and all of our food and water was gone. It was time to take a chance that not every living thing in the world had expired in the craziness.

In the aftermath of the US election, the US president had raged against the results and gone on a firing rampage. Every national security advisor, FBI director, or CIA chief who could have made a difference was replaced with his loyalists. The entire world paid rapt attention. The aggressive rhetoric had led to an eventual conclusion. The great superpower that was the USA was vulnerable to all of our enemies. Russia was eager to take advantage of his hissy fit. After all, Russia had sown the seeds of mistrust, and zealously harvested the rewards. They made the first strike, and we scrambled below before the devastating dominos followed, and the nuclear fallout rained on our heads.

Em paid attention and had predicted that North Korea and Russia would align again to defeat the US. Both countries had enough firepower to wipe the US from the face of the earth. Our allies had long since abandoned us. We were on our own.

I didn't doubt that others survived. I shuddered to think who they were. I wagered the president endured with his entire family and all the other crazies in his administration. The other likely survivors were undoubtedly the conspiracy theorists and survivalists. They had been licking their chops for this moment to arrive.

How did I come to be a survivor with my wife and our two cats? My wife, Em, is a seer and a brilliant scientist. She was the lone voice in our little corner of the world, stating that the unlikely presidential candidate would win. Everyone thought she was crazy. I didn't. I'd seen her make other predictions that seemed impossible.

Six months before the current sitting president won the election, we made our plans. Neither of us was mollified by the light at the end of the tunnel with his loss of a second term. His behavior and rhetoric only worsened with each passing day that brought him closer to when he'd lose power.

†

Em and I methodically pulled together supplies and built an airtight shelter we could live in for several months. Our friends thought we were overreacting to the gloom-and-doom hyperbole from the left. I hate that we couldn't convince them otherwise. Em didn't have family, and I was estranged from my sister and nieces—my only remaining loved ones after my parents had died in the car crash that was entirely preventable. My father's propensity for Irish whiskey finally resulted in his downfall, and Mom was collateral damage. The winding road didn't help. At that point, we were so estranged I hadn't learned about their deaths until months after the funeral.

I hadn't broached the topic of trying to find my sister and nieces with Em, but in the back of my mind, I wondered if they had survived. Surely an apocalyptic event might change everything, and we'd let bygones be bygones. Yet, even if they had survived, how in the world would I find them?

Our shelter was comfortable. I pretended we lived in one of those tiny houses, and that was acceptable to me. Em had engineered ingenious systems that would enable us to push waste outside of the shelter without letting the radiation inside. Without those systems, the smell would have been unbearable, especially with the cat poop.

I'd never gone a single day in my life without a shower and insisted that our tiny house allow me to wash my hair daily. Em adapted a solar camping shower to hang from the rafter, using recycled water. I don't know how she connected the panels without letting in radiation, but she was gifted and had somehow managed that feat. She had attached a shower drain to a pipe that drained far away from the shelter. I became proficient with my use of water. Em had informed me we couldn't take a chance that piping in water from above wouldn't also bring in radiation or other harmful particles.

Em helped me set up a hydroponic system for fresh vegetables. I wasn't a big meat eater, and Em was always more adaptable to change, so protein in the form of legumes supplemented with canned goods provided plenty of food to keep us healthy. We knew the first thing we would run out of was water, and then batteries for the items not connected to our solar panels. There is only so much room in a shelter, and we always recognized we couldn't hide underground forever. Em didn't even believe it was prudent to stay close, opting to find a society we could integrate into with ease. Toward the end of our stay in our cozy cement domicile, I broached the topic I was most afraid of.

"What do you think we'll find out there?" I asked. There was a noticeable tremble in my voice.

Em pushed my bangs aside. "Lise, I do hope a hairstylist survived because you're way overdue for a haircut."

I used my arm to wipe the tears away. "Nice try, Em. I need to know what you believe waits for us on the other side. I can handle the truth." The quiver in my voice betrayed my false bravado.

Em quirked her eyebrow and grabbed my hand. "Oh, Lise, I know you're scared, and that makes you angry because you think you're weak. You're not. I know you can handle the truth. There may be armed militias settled into distinct territories, but I hope most squabbles are already resolved."

"I don't know how to use a gun, and neither do you. How will we fight the crazies?"

"Don't worry, Lise, we won't have to because we'll find our people. We have a lot to offer."

"You have a lot to offer. Every single dystopian novel I've ever read reveres the brilliant scientists."

"Oh hon, plants mock me as they shrivel and die—no matter what I do. You have a green thumb. You'll be invaluable to whatever new society we fold ourselves into," Em soothed.

"Can we look for a hippy commune with lesbians, please?"

"Of course, but you need to be the one to judge when we've found nirvana. You know I don't have a single strand of gaydar in my DNA."

I laughed. Em was right. If it wasn't for the fact that I was a militant lesbian who wore T-shirts and rainbow bracelets proudly announcing my love of women, she might not have made her move. Although my finely tuned gaydar had been intact, I dismissed her repeated attempts to woo me with offerings of lemonade, and lunches she happened to prepare too much of. I assumed she was merely a friendly sort who offered those things out of kindness and exceptional manners while I worked on her place in Seattle. I was so enamored with Em that I eagerly accepted her hospitality. She finally had enough of my total oblivion and made her move.

Back then, I had a great deal of bravado and swagger at the bars, especially after several drinks. Alcohol was my saving grace to enable me to step out of my shell. But not with Em because, deep down, I couldn't believe this accomplished woman would want to become involved with a lowly landscape artist who worked part-time for a garden center to make ends meet. I suppose opposites attract, and we fell in love despite our differences. Em always made me feel a lot smarter than I am. Next to her genius, I felt profoundly unintelligent. I was so far beneath her. I had no business conversing with a genius. Em insisted I had a unique perspective on life, and not all learning happened in college.

†

I underestimated the brightness of the sun. Squinting to protect my sensitive eyes, I got my first look at the outside world. I breathed a sigh of relief when I saw the greenery. Before settling into the shelter, I had spent several days clearing the brush around the entrance before spraying chemicals and covering a twenty-foot radius with gravel. I hated using the poison on any plants, even weeds, but the hard work paid off. We quickly removed the heavy cement door without the excess foliage making it impossible to push aside.

"The plant life survived," I exclaimed with excitement.

"Did you know that after Hiroshima, the first plant to bloom was an oleander? Mother Nature has an amusing sense of humor since the oleander is also one of the most poisonous plants on the planet."

"How do you know that? For someone who kills plants by looking at them, I am constantly amazed by your vast knowledge of so many topics."

"Book knowledge is a far cry from real-life experiences." Em lifted her shoulders in that familiar way she had when she tried to pass off her braininess as no big deal.

"Do you think it's safe?" I asked.

"I do. We've allowed for enough time. Remember when I explained how radiation dissipates more rapidly than reported? The recent growth shows how life survives despite the insanity of humans."

"It's just so hard to push away those old notions from the horror movies back in the fifties. I still remember that movie, *Attack of the 50 Foot Woman.*"

Em laughed. "Only you, Lise, would think of that movie. As I recall, it was aliens, not radiation, that caused her to grow."

I shrugged. "The doctor thought it was radiation. Do you think we have enough supplies in our packs?"

She nodded.

I stood half out of the shelter, my waist leaning against the opening. I set one pack on the ground and then pivoted to peer into the hole and accept the other bag from Em, placing it next to its twin in the tall grass. Finally, I was ready to take Sonny from Em's hands as she lifted him to me. He was squirming, but of the two, Sonny was more malleable than Cher. Cher could be a right pain in the ass when she was scared. Who wouldn't be frightened? Cher could sense my mood and would follow suit.

"You better bring Cher outside. She's more likely to mold into your shoulder and not scratch the shit out of you than me."

"Good plan." Em retrieved the sling and placed Cher inside. At first, she meowed pitifully, and then Em kissed her head. "It's okay, my sweet little baby. We're going to see the world together, and you'll end up loving the adventure."

I wasn't sure if Em said that for Cher's benefit or mine. Probably both of us.

Em surfaced and crawled from our temporary sanctuary. I looped the other sling she had handed me over my head and placed Sonny inside. He lifted his head and looked at me with such admiration and trust.

"Your idea to use those baby slings for Sonny and Cher was so inspired. They'll be happy to cling to us while we adapt to the new world order," Em said as she reached into my sling and scratched Sonny's head.

Sonny and Cher were our cats, and there was no way we would leave them behind. They'd adapted well to the shelter, but would they do okay now that we were emerging from our tiny home?

I was glad we saved our babies.

CHAPTER TWO

"We'll look for water first," Em said as we hiked through the forest. "Most people think starvation gets you, but that's not true. People can survive longer without food than without water. I'm trying to remember where that stream and the runoff from the mountains was in relation to our shelter. I think it was less than a half a mile to the east."

"Maybe I shouldn't have insisted on keeping clean because we'd have plenty of water to last longer." A wave of guilt flowed through me.

"Nonsense. We'll find that water source again. Don't worry about that. After we treat the water, it'll be the finest tasting beverage we've ever had. The runoff from the mountains is fast-moving water, and it doesn't pick up too many microorganisms that these tablets won't take care of for us."

We continued our trek through the forest for another fifteen minutes until Em tilted her head.

"Do you hear that?"

I shook my head. I focused more on keeping my eyes peeled for any aggressive militia groups and was oblivious to every sound in the dense woods.

"I believe we've found our water source." She grinned like a fool, and I couldn't help myself; I smiled in return. When I grabbed her, I inadvertently smashed our kids in the process as I kissed her with gusto.

Two simultaneous, meows broke us apart, but I kept ahold of her hand.

We walked on until we came upon the small waterfall flowing into the narrow stream we'd scoped out before setting up house in the shelter. I was excited when I saw the flash of silver.

"Do you think the fish will have four eyes now?"

Em laughed. "Now that is fake news. The four-eyed fish in the genus Anableps has nothing to do with radiation exposure. In 2011, an angler caught a three-eyed fish near a nuclear reactor in Argentina, but the scare was without merit. They weren't even sure the bump in the middle was an eye versus a tumor. Ridiculous." Em shook her head.

I smiled again at my walking encyclopedia. Em was my wife, the love of my life, and someone who knew so much about so many things. I wondered if the controversy over same-sex marriage survived the new world order or, if like everything else, the rumpus wouldn't come close to rising to any level of importance.

I remembered back to before the time our president and the North Korean leader showed whose penis was bigger through their arsenal of nuclear weapons. Hurricane Harvey hit, and my hope for humanity improved as Muslims, Christians, and Jews stood side by side, helping one another. The only person who had seemed to perpetuate the hate was our current president. He held onto his hardline stance on immigration. Officials made a public statement clarifying that they would not suspend the laws. Enforcement agents would remain vigilant. They would not allow criminals to take advantage of the disruptions caused by the storm. The president continued to display the worst of humanity amongst so many who showed the best of the human race.

"This looks like a good spot to hunker down for the night. I must say, I'm grateful it's summer. The warmth is a welcome relief to my old bones," I admitted. "I can set up the tent and babysit our furry babies if you know a way to catch one of those fish I see swimming in the stream. I'll even clean them."

"Deal." Em shrugged out of her pack and then let a squirming Cher go free.

The petite feline stalked around the bag, sniffing it as if the damn thing would come to life and bite her.

"Cher, it's just our much-needed supplies. Stop eyeing the pack like it's your enemy," I chastised.

"She's fine. Let her check it out." Em met my eyes. "How are you doing? Change is hard."

"You're here, my personal service animal."

Em quirked her eyebrow. "Service animal?"

I wiggled out of my pack, setting it on the ground, and then I released Sonny from the confines of his baby sling. "It was the only thing I could think of. You know how sometimes people get cats or dogs to help with anxiety and call them service animals. Besides, you're an animal in bed." I grinned before grabbing Em and planting a big kiss on her lips.

After my spontaneous demonstration of affection, Em threw her head back in laughter. She turned her attention to the pack on the ground and dug inside, finding a fishing line and lure. She swore that when she was young and couldn't afford fishing poles, her father taught her how to fish without all the fancy equipment. I believed every word she said when she told the story. Em could do anything. She wasn't just my personal service animal. She was my heroine.

Tying the line to a long thin branch, Em headed to the stream with her makeshift pole and our collapsible water skins. Tucking the water purifying tablets into her cargo shorts, she blessed me with a parting smile. Cher followed her, perhaps wanting to try her paw at fishing alongside her favorite human.

Sonny sprawled on the grass next to the packs and promptly closed his eyes. It was nap time. I pushed my fingers through his soft fur before turning my attention to the three-person tent and getting to work setting up for our first night out of the shelter in over 300 days.

†

Em had her talents, and I had mine. After pitching the tent, I gathered an impressive amount of firewood. The fire spit out tiny embers as it crackled in a healthy blaze. Left alone, I couldn't help letting my mind wander as I thought about my sister and the last time we'd talked.

Juggling the two bags of groceries, I knocked on the weathered door of my sister's manufactured home. Paint chips floated to the ground, and I wondered if her asshole husband would let me bring paint to spruce up the place. I could easily paint the small home in a weekend if they'd only let me help. I waited patiently, knowing Kim was home with the kids. I'd waited until his truck was gone. He always went out with his drinking buddies on Saturdays, so the coast was clear. Kim didn't answer the first knock, and I heard scuffling noises and fervent whispering.

"What the hell, Kim? Open the door. I know you're home, and he's gone."

After a few more minutes, Rylee, my youngest niece, opened the door. She had a frown on her face, and I knew right away, something was wrong.

"Mamma's sick. She told me I should send you away so's you don't catch it."

I smiled at my niece and said, "Well, if your mama is sick, then I guess I'll make her soup or something and take care of you guys while she gets her rest. Good thing I came by, huh?"

"She'll be mad I let you in."

"No, she won't. Kim," I called, "I brought you groceries. Hopefully, you have soup. If not, I'll make another trip to the store and be back in a flash."

Kim shuffled into the kitchen while I was putting away the items requiring refrigeration. "I wish you would stop buying us groceries. He gets mad thinking that I'm telling you he doesn't provide for us. You should go before he gets back."

I glanced in Kim's direction and noticed her concealing her face. I knew my sister, and she was definitely hiding something. I closed the refrigerator door and stepped close, gently turning Kim's face. Her left eye was swollen shut, and a small trickle of blood leaked from her split lip.

"That son of a bitch—"

Brook and Rylee had both quietly entered the kitchen, stopping me from continuing my rant. Brook quickly went to her mother's side, clinging to her like she was a buoy in the middle of a raging ocean. Rylee remained a few feet away, with an almost resigned look that was far too mature for her age.

"You can't keep letting him do this to you." I lowered my voice. The kids were already traumatized, and I didn't need to add to their fear.

Kim stroked the hair of her oldest daughter and instructed, "Brook, please take Rylee to your room to play while I talk with Aunt Lise. Okay? You be a good girl for mommy."

Brook nodded her small blonde head and reached for her sister's hand, but Rylee was having none of it. She crossed her arms and shook her head, declaring, "Daddy hit Mommy. He's a bad Daddy." Her eyes pleaded with me to do something about this.

I kissed the top of Rylee's head and tried to reassure her. "Let me talk to your mommy. I promise everything is going to be okay."

"Come on, Rylee, I'll read from your favorite book."

Rylee dragged her feet, following her sister while looking over her shoulder at me until I smiled back at her.

"If you don't come to live with me right now, I'm calling social services. I'm not letting that bastard use your face as a punching bag while your kids watch. When you stop being his entertainment for the night, he'll eventually turn his rage toward Rylee or Brook."

"I'd never let that happen. How dare you say a single thing about my life? Clean up your own backyard. Mom and Dad kicked you out for a reason. Do you honestly think I would let my kids see you bring home various women and expose them to your sinful life? I let you visit because I'm always here to supervise, and they adore you. Get out, and don't you ever come back." Spittle flew from her mouth. I'd never seen her so angry before. "You are no longer welcome in our home. If you ever come near me and my kids, I'll take out a restraining order on you. How dare you threaten me with social services?"

My mouth opened to respond, but no words would come. Calling social services was an idle threat, one made in haste and anger, but apparently, Kim was genuinely rattled by my warning. I wanted to take the words back and find others to replace them. Words that would finally convince her to leave, but they never came, and I left without a fight. At barely twenty-one, I didn't have the strength or maturity to stand my ground.

I heard Em's footsteps, thankfully jarring me from this unpleasant memory. She approached carrying two large trout, and the surprise must have shown on my face. I stood and accepted her offering, laying them on a rock. Em had already gutted and cleaned them.

"You look surprised. Oh, ye of little faith."

"I knew you would be successful. I just didn't think the trout would be so big and that you'd catch two."

"I had a wonderful accomplice. Cher would chase the fish in my direction, and after a few of my special jigs, they couldn't resist my charms any more than you can."

I laughed and kissed her on the cheek. "You must have had your Swiss Army knife with you. It's amazing that little thing can do such a good job filleting a fish."

"I thought it would be better to clean the fish by the stream. That way, I could wash my hands."

"Good idea. I found berry bushes. While you were playing the hunter, I was gathering. I wish I'd come across someone's old garden, bursting with a fresh bounty of vegetables."

"You'll get the seeds you took from the shelter to grow. I've never seen a greener thumb from anyone else. You should make sure I steer clear of the new shoots when they start growing."

I must have pulled a face because Em crouched down and touched my cheek.

"Do you think any structures have survived? I can't imagine winter will be a whole lot of fun in a tent," I lamented.

"I do. We just need to find the right ones, so we don't end up joining some overzealous survivalist unit where they believe women are only put on earth to bear their children and ensure the continued existence of the human race."

"I'll bet the president survived and hopes his base made it through his colossal mistake. I guess this was one way to avoid conceding to his epic loss," I said bitterly.

"I have faith we'll find the right group to align with."

"Do you think our home in Seattle survived?" I ventured into that dangerous territory.

On the one hand, I hoped our home was still there. On the other hand, I didn't want to see the damage. With a large navy base across the sound, Seattle by location had become a target and was on the list of cities to hit. I knew it was unlikely to have survived intact.

"I always wanted to live in a rural area, and now we will." That was Em's answer.

"Em, if radiation dissipates as quickly as you said, why did you want to stay in the bomb shelter so long?"

"I wanted to avoid the squabbles over dominance. Lise many things will have survived, but not the infrastructure. Without a means to deliver supplies to people who are used to running to the grocery store, there will be chaos. That is the real danger of war. Internal fighting will kill more than the original bombs. When resources are limited, true human nature rears its ugly head. I had a vision we would find our place closer to the mountains. I wanted to ensure our survival by avoiding the initial pandemonium. Neither one of us possesses fighting skills. Coming late to the game ups our odds."

"I could kill someone who threatened you." I puffed out my chest.

Em gave me a sad smile. "Oh, babe, no, you couldn't, and that's why I love you. If you were put into that untenable position, a death by your hands would change you in ways that…" She shuddered. "I wasn't willing to take the risk."

Her assessment deflated me, but she was right. I didn't have the temperament for aggression. War changes people, and sometimes a person doesn't know what they're made of until facing a horrifying position. Whether or not I wanted to, that was a lesson I would learn in the not-too-distant future.

Mashing wild berries on the fillets, I placed them in the grilling apparatus designed for fish but adapted to other items. The fish was the best I could remember. I suppose my comparison to ten months of canned food with limited fresh food offerings had colored my appraisal. We had cans of tuna, salmon, and chicken to supplement our small garden in the shelter, but there was nothing like freshly caught fish.

I didn't notice Em's keen eyes focus on the spot above my head or the snap of a branch until it was too late. Em set the trout carcass on the ground for Sonny and Cher to pick at the bones. She folded her hands in her lap before greeting our visitor.

CHAPTER THREE

"You're in our territory without permission," the gruff voice declared.

"We were simply passing through. If you prefer for us to pack up and move along right now, we can do that," Em calmly responded.

"You're unaffected. Are you one of the government deserters or from a survivalist camp?" he asked.

At that point, I glanced in his direction and saw the stranger's partially disfigured face and arm. Radiation burns traveled down his jawline, changing his otherwise flawless, chiseled lines to something less than perfect. His appearance was far from grotesque. I had the odd notion that this flaw gave him more character. I didn't turn away and met his eyes—two small granites. I shivered at how cold and impassive they were.

"We were in a bomb shelter until today. Not exactly survivalists, but prepared," Em answered.

The eyebrow unaffected by radiation lifted. "For ten months?"

Em nodded. I was too scared to engage in any conversation with this man who carried an assault weapon as casually as an executive might hold his briefcase.

He pointed the weapon at me. "Is she mute?"

"No," I croaked.

"Come with me," he ordered.

I tried not to panic. Em touched my arm to reassure me. "May we bring our cats?" she asked.

"Only if they can catch their own food. Supplies are not wasted on animals."

"It won't take us long to pack up the tent." Em made the plea.

"You have five minutes."

He hadn't made a move to kill us or do other unspeakable things. I took that as a good sign. For some ridiculous reason, this man with his Hollywood good looks, despite the scars, pinged my gaydar. He hadn't leered at either of us. He had merely observed us as if we were an interesting new species of bug. I suppose my idea of the post-nuclear world after total chaos included a great deal of raping and pillaging. His actions suggested neither had happened. Yet, there was a lack of emotion in his manner that was unsettling.

†

We reached a nasty-looking fence with barbed wire curling on top in an intricate, impressive pattern. Another scar-faced man with a pronounced limp opened the sturdy metal gate, and then waved us in. He wasn't carrying a gun, and for that, I breathed a sigh of relief. The mixture of natural stone and wood dwellings looked a lot sturdier than what I suspected was more common in these parts before the war. The plentiful wood in the forest showed signs of distress, but I doubted radiation was the cause. Thankfully, there were still plenty of trees standing.

I squinted to make out the expressions on the faces of those people in the far distance who appeared to go about their business, not giving Em or I a second glance. So far, the only gun I'd seen was slung over our escort's shoulder. No one else appeared ready to start a war. The corner of a large garden peeked out from behind a copse of trees. I desperately needed to check it out, but we were clearly being escorted somewhere.

I had an absurd thought that perhaps this colony, or whatever they called themselves, had an affinity to the story of *The Three Little Pigs*. I wondered who was the Big Bad Wolf in their eyes. Smoke drifted into the sky from the chimneys of no less than forty dwellings in this complex. They were attractive enough. I wondered if they were new or a special place that had somehow survived the blasts.

Soldier Boy led us to a mid-sized home and knocked on the door.

A feminine voice answered, "Come."

We entered the home. The coziness of the place surprised me. Sitting on an overstuffed couch was an average-looking woman who appeared to be tinkering with an electronic device. Noticing her short, spiked hair in a shade of mousy brown, I wondered if this woman could be "family." A tall, thin woman with long blonde hair walked into the living space. Unlike the other woman, she was striking in appearance and could have been a model in a former life. Her finely chiseled features came together much like a work of art that crowds fawn over. She stopped when she saw the three of us standing in what I suspected was her living room.

The woman on the couch lifted her head and looked at us. With her square jaw, stormy gray eyes, and nonexistent smile, she had a harsh, masculine appearance that scared the shit out of me.

"Daryl? What have you brought us?"

"Possible new recruits. They were by the stream. Eating trout."

"I see. Let me have a conversation with the trespassers. Thank you for your dedication. Give my best to Sam." She glanced at the tall woman and patted the spot next to her.

With a nearly imperceptible nod, the striking woman dried her hands on the towel she carried and sat next to the imposing presence who had beckoned her. How this average-looking person commanded the room surprised me.

"I am Trina, and this is my wife, Hannah." Setting the device on the table, she then pointed to the empty love seat. "Please sit. I see you have cats. I must admit to a weakness for the small felines. Practicality has limited our ability to accept them into the fold. However, we have made a few exceptions."

Reluctantly I sat, and Em joined me on the love seat. Without looking directly at Trina or Hannah, I found my voice and pleaded with Em, "We're not letting Sonny and

Cher fend for themselves." There was no way in hell we were giving up Sonny and Cher as I clutched Sonny tightly to my chest.

Em touched my arm to calm me as Cher remained in the sling we had fashioned for our babies. "If joining this... I'm not sure what you call yourselves—"

"Alternate society," Trina supplied. "You can let your cats roam. I don't think they'll harm anything, and it will help with their transition to the outside."

"We aren't anarchists, soldiers, or religious nuts. If you have an expectation that we'll carry guns or live anything other than a peaceful existence with others, no thanks. We'll pass and quietly move along to another place," Em declared with authority.

"You are together?" Hannah asked.

Em nodded. "Yes, we were legally married several years ago." Her hand found its way to the wedding band, and she twisted it around her finger until the Australian opal in the flush setting was back on top.

Trina smiled and pointed to herself and Hannah. "We don't always carry guns. That's not our primary contribution to society. I'm an electronics expert and possess unique facilitation skills. I suspect I'm regarded as a wise elder, although others in our society are much older." She shrugged. "I sort of fell into this leadership role. Having individuals who possess fighting skills is a necessary evil. Aggression is a last resort, but not out of the question when protecting what we've built here. Don't be naïve enough to forget there will always be others who wish to trample you to stand at the top of the pyramid. In this new world order, that means fighting over supplies and other valuable resources, including knowledge."

"Knowledge?" I asked.

"Yes, anyone who holds the skills and knowledge to help us survive. What did you do before the war?" Trina asked. "May I also ask you to provide your names, first names? We don't have much need for last names anymore."

"Emma, or Em. I was a research scientist, and I suppose an amateur inventor of sorts. I liked to tinker in my spare time."

"I'm Lise. I was just a gardener."

Trina and Hannah looked at one another, and their smiles grew. "Those are much sought-after skills," Trina noted.

"Lise is a virtuoso with plants. We brought seeds with us, and I hoped we could plant a small garden." Em glanced at me, and the love shone on her face.

"You were planning to go it alone? I wouldn't advise that. There are factions still at war." Hannah's face adopted a pinched look.

Trina's eyes softened, turning lighter shade of gray as she grasped her wife's hand. "As you may have already assumed, after the bombs, the real war began. They targeted all the major cities. Millions of lives were lost in the initial attack. But it was the aftermath that caused the greatest loss. Medical care for those affected by radiation was limited, and a fair number expired. Others survived, but lost their remaining humanity…"

"They resented you for surviving unharmed," Em finished.

Trina nodded. "We were in a remote section of the mountains and unaffected by the initial blast. Those who were intelligent enough to act raided the rural areas for supplies untouched by the spreading radiation. Squabbles began shortly after. When we first came upon Daryl, he was not much more than a rabid animal. He tried to reach his family in the city. They didn't survive. He had a two-year-old daughter and a husband." Trina looked away at a blank spot on the wall, appearing to remember something and trying to compose herself. "Hannah has a special gift with men and women who are…mentally wounded. Forgive his flat affect. Trust me, he has come a long way. We collected other like-minded individuals and—" Trina gestured to their surroundings "—created our own society. It hasn't always been easy to remain independent. We sometimes fight out of necessity and survival, not by choice."

"You won't make it on your own. We tried with only ourselves and Daryl. There is strength in numbers unless you plan on remaining hidden in the deep woods forever. Even when you select remote areas, sometimes *the others* find you," Hannah added.

†

I wondered if I'd fallen into some dystopian nightmare when Hannah said something about *the others*. The ominous nature of how she had tossed out that word caused the hairs on the back of my neck to stand at attention, like obedient soldiers.

I looked at Em for direction. She was so much smarter than me and unflappable when facing disasters. It was as though dealing with chaos was in her preliminary design.

Em smiled and took my hand, squeezing it before responding. "I suppose there's a lot to learn about the challenges we'll face now that we've emerged from our shelter. I always like to keep my options open in case our core values don't align. For now, I propose we remain. Let's call it an orientation period. If, after a few weeks or months, either of us determines this is not a good fit, we'll move on. No harm, no foul. In the meantime, I believe we can contribute at least enough to earn our keep, so to speak. Does that work for you?" Em looked at the device sitting on the table and pointed at it. "May I?"

Trina smiled. "Of course, I can't get the damn thing to work. It helps to maximize our solar power."

Releasing my hand and carefully removing the sling, Em set Cher next to me before kneeling in front of the table. She turned the device in her hand. "It looks like it's missing a small spring. An easy fix if you have the basic tools and a spring that will work. I worked on a solar-powered car back in college. If you need to re-engineer a vehicle, I can help with that."

"I hope you choose to remain with us. We didn't want to rely on gas-powered vehicles. Human-powered machines don't allow us a large range when we go on scouting missions. In the beginning, we secured most of our resources with a large diesel truck. We converted our trucks to biofuel, but it's still rather dirty, and other means of transportation would be highly sought after. *The others* use gas-powered trucks and cars. Without aid from other countries, that resource will become obsolete soon enough."

"I'm assuming the United States was the only country affected by this war, and we weren't provided any aid to help rebuild, most likely because the president hadn't played nicely with others?" Em returned to sit next to me, apparently satisfied that she had diagnosed the device's problem.

Trina nodded. "There was a lot of fear about not only radiation but the experimentation with nerve gas. When the World Health Organization sent small contingents of medical professionals and others to help in the most affected areas, it was clear a new nerve agent had been used, and then the aid abruptly ended. China and Russia are now the remaining superpowers. Although North Korea and Russia became allies, North Korea remains inconsequential in the whole scheme of things. Our democracy hung by a thread anyway, so the larger global community never stepped in to avert the catastrophe. From the little we've learned, NATO was able to hold off aggression in Europe and other parts of the world, leaving only the US to fight our own battles."

"How do you know all of this? Surely the media was decimated in the attack and the aftermath of destruction," Em asked.

"It was, but there are a handful of small tribes, territories if you decide to be generous in your description. Some of them have operated long-wave radios. The information is spotty, but it's all we have. Also, every few months, the president addresses what is left of this country. He finagled that outlandish outcome because, in all the chaos, he remains president. There wasn't much of a government left to fight his declaration of a national emergency. There would never be a peaceful transfer of power, but the war dictated no transfer. I suspect he'll be a lame-duck president for quite a long time."

"I suppose we are like an island now," I interjected.

Hannah nodded. "Our incompetent president got his wish. Only Americans remain in the states now. Other countries refuse to take in our refugees. Ironic, huh? Canada and Mexico have both closed their borders, and the president got his wall. Mexico ended up paying for it, and his campaign promise was fulfilled." Trina laughed.

†

As I took in the additional information Trina provided, I heard the distinct sound of gunfire. Although it seemed to come from a distance, I was unnerved by the *rat tat tat*. A loud explosion seemed too close for comfort, and I thought I could smell the acrid smoke, though that might have been my overactive imagination. Sonny, who had so far remained in my arms, wriggled from the sling, jumped down, and began looking for a place to hide. Not to be outdone, Cher emerged from her own cocoon of protection and followed suit. Truth be told, I wanted to join them. Instead, my leg began to bounce. Em grabbed my hand and placed our joined hands together on top of my thigh to calm me. Her gaze tracked our babies as they found their way behind the overstuffed couch.

Daryl had quietly entered the room. If possible, his expression was even dourer than when we'd first met. With his hands clasped in front, he stood rigid, waiting for Trina to acknowledge his presence.

Trina lifted her eyes to Daryl and nodded.

"*The others* breached the outside perimeter, but they don't have the firepower to continue their assault," Daryl reported.

"How do you know?" Trina asked.

A hint of a smile reached Daryl's face when he answered. "Sam was patrolling the perimeter, and you know how inconspicuous he can be. He's like a tiny mouse."

"Injuries?"

"Minor. We haven't fully engaged."

"Don't. Let *the others* run out of ammunition and then return fire to scare them back. We'll need them far enough from the outside perimeter to rebuild our first line of defense."

"I thought you would say that. I've already given those preliminary orders but wanted to make sure you concur." Daryl nodded and then pivoted as he left the room almost as quietly as when he'd arrived.

I found my voice. "Do these attacks happen often?"

Hannah and Trina shared a look I suspected reflected their indecisiveness over how much information to provide.

Trina sighed. "Often enough. So far, we have a spotless record. We've never lost, and not one person has died in any of the skirmishes. Our dear president vowed to 'make America safe again,' but he's lost all control over *the others* so far. Most don't recognize his authority. We live a peaceful existence until we're forced to protect our way of life."

"How can he claim to be the president in the aftermath?" Em shook her head in what I recognized as exasperation.

Trina quirked her eyebrow. "You remember what he was like, don't you?"

"Well, he wasn't my president before, and I'll bet we're now in the majority to claim, 'Not my president,'" I declared.

Trina nodded.

"How many times have *the others* attacked since the bombs hit?" Em touched her wedding band. Whenever she was stressed, her fingers found their way to the symbol of our love.

"This is the tenth attack," Hannah answered.

"We're in grave danger if we try to go it alone, aren't we?" Em's posture straightened and became rigid as she confirmed her fears.

Trina closed her eyes and then slowly opened them. "Yes, I'm sorry."

Em had done most of the talking, but I felt the need to let these strangers and my precious Em know what I was thinking. "We'll stay then and contribute. I will fight alongside you," I declared with the false bravado I knew Em recognized. "Em is my life, and I won't let anything bad happen to her. She has a lot more to offer than me. I offer my loyalty to this new family. Is everyone, um, gay or lesbian or uh, you know, not straight?" I asked.

"Mostly, yes, but there are some gay-friendly people here, and we don't discriminate." Trina grinned.

"We don't have the temperament to fight," Em declared. "Perhaps instead, I can offer to fortify the outer defense with nasty traps that will give anyone pause who tries to infiltrate. Lise can multiply the output of your gardens."

"Wonderful. Welcome to the family. I hope that since you're now family, I can be rude and excuse myself for the evening. It's late anyway. Hannah, can you please find a place for Em and Lise in our temporary lodgings until we're able to build a new house?"

Hannah leaned forward to kiss her wife. "Absolutely."

CHAPTER FOUR

After we'd cajoled our babies from their hiding place, Hannah led the way to our new lodging. It wasn't anything special, but to us, it was like a mansion after living in a cramped shelter. I guessed it was about 500 square feet with a cozy loft. Lined with pine, the small space had an airy feel to it. I thought a stone fireplace would have provided a perfect heating source and created such a lovely romantic ambiance, but the woodstove looked like it would do the trick. I supposed a post-apocalyptic world wouldn't be too concerned about the atmosphere. Functionality was higher on their priority list.

"This is quite nice." Em's eyes were roving as she took in her surroundings.

I was sure she was cataloging ways to improve on whatever amenities the cabin offered. Em always looked for opportunities to make anything and everything more efficient. I, on the other hand, appreciated the more aesthetic elements of a home. I noticed the fluffy rug in the middle of the small living room and what looked like soft, worn fabric on the loveseat and recliner. Bonus points for how well they matched. There was what I assumed to be a handcrafted wooden table in front of the love seat. The wood looked as smooth and soft as a baby's bottom, and I couldn't resist running my hands along the finely sanded wood grain.

"If this cabin is up for grabs, it doesn't have to be a temporary place for us. I love it already." I knew the sun would shine through the large windows and looking out on the massive old-growth trees every day was a bonus.

Hannah didn't respond to my comment, and I wondered if this was a top-of-the-line domicile in this unknown world—intended for dignitaries and anyone they were trying to convince to join their merry band of survivors. We'd already agreed to stay, so I wasn't sure why she didn't respond.

Em jumped in, sensing the awkward silence from Hannah. "We've been living in a bomb shelter for a long time. We don't require much. If there is some other place you'd rather we stay, I'm sure that will be more than sufficient for our needs."

As if shaken from a trance, Hannah shook her head. "Oh no, I'm sorry. If this place is where you'd like to settle, we can always build another guest cabin. I'm a little surprised at how malleable you are given the recent events. Most newcomers are warier. Trust is not a commodity in great supply these days. I would have expected more…uh…fallout from the attack, even though it was relatively minor by our standards. Neither of you seems unsettled."

Hannah didn't know Em like I did, or she would have recognized the subtle signs of stress. As for my odd reaction, I think I might have still been in shock. Maybe Em was as well. The reality of our circumstances hadn't nestled inside our brains yet. Extraordinary events often generated astonishing reactions.

"I typically save the losing-my-shit response to when Em can soothe my tattered edges. Or, I dig in my garden. Don't worry. The more stressed I am, the more success I'll have with the harvest. I can already tell we're going to have quite the bounty."

Sonny squirmed in my arms, letting me know I needed to let him down to check out his new digs. It was almost as if he knew this was going to be his new home. As soon as I'd released Sonny, Em let an agitated Cher follow. Cher wasn't about to let Sonny have all the fun. Our babies started sniffing around the unfamiliar territory—their way of acclimating. Apparently, the earlier drama was forgotten.

Hannah cracked a smile. "I'm not the greatest with helping people assimilate, but Trina is a lot worse than me. Crap, see, assimilate sounds so cultish. While I have a special talent for assessing people, my skill doesn't extend to helping them adapt. There are others a lot more sensitive to the emotional needs of new recruits. I can hook you up if you need that."

"Thanks, Hannah. We're good." Em tried to smile and then clasped her hands together.

I noticed the small shake before she caught herself. I thought she might squeeze her hands so hard they'd turn white to stop the tremble.

I was sure Hannah noticed and took that as her cue to leave us alone. "We're in the main house if you need anything."

After she left, I took Em's hand and led her to the loveseat. Our hands locked together like two puzzle pieces, and I searched Em's eyes, for what, I wasn't sure. Reassurance? Strength? Or maybe I was trying to discern how freaked out she'd become since Daryl brought us to this fortress. Gunfire, explosions? Was this the revitalization we expected after emerging from the bomb shelter? I never imagined this would be our new life. Perhaps Em hadn't voiced her predictions to save me from completely losing my shit.

Em squeezed my hand. "I'm okay. Trina appears to be an accomplished leader. I think we lucked out. We adapted easily to the bomb shelter. How hard can it be to live within the boundaries of this pseudo commune?"

"I'm not sharing my wife." I pulled Em into an embrace and held on. It was a joke, but I still felt the need for her warm body against my own.

Em pulled away and gifted me with that irresistible impish smile she saved for me. "Damn, Hannah is sexy in that apocalypse warrior kind of way."

"That is definitely not funny. I know you're attempting to calm me, and I'm not trying to push anything disturbing under the rug, but can we find the bed and turn in for the night?" I craved the closeness of Em's touch. She had a way of soothing me like no other.

Em's fingertips brushed my cheek as she pushed a strand of sweat-soaked hair away from my face. "You'll always be my heroine. I love you."

Her words floated on a lazy puff of air. It was just the right volume to calm me. It was funny how we always traded places and could turn off our own stress to lull the other. Em must have recognized it was my turn to be calmed.

Before we made our way to the loft, I opened every cabinet, looking for additional blankets to place in front of the woodstove. I knew that, eventually, the cats would make their way to the bedroom, but I wanted them to be comfortable for now. They'd been outdoor cats before entering the bomb shelter, so the transition might be a little tough on them, but they would learn to adapt again. Hopefully, they'd do it without accidents in our small cabin.

†

With the moon glowing through the small loft window, I let Em take me to a different place. Her fingertips adeptly skimmed my skin as she found her way to the spot where my arousal pooled. I loved this woman and how she knew exactly how to touch me. Tonight, I wanted slow and steady. Needing to savor every moment, she answered my need.

"Thank you," I whispered. "After all these years, you still know exactly what to do to make me forget the rest of the crappy world exists."

"Shh, you're distracting me." She giggled. "We have to christen our new digs properly. Forget the saying: I licked it, so it's mine. I like this place, so I'm going to declare: our juices christened it, it's ours."

My laughter filled all the crevices of the tiny house. "I double-dog-dare you to say that to Trina tomorrow morning."

"Mmm, this is serious. A double-dog-dare, huh?" She moved her mouth to my neck and began kissing my pulse point as her fingers slid inside around my opening. Arching my back, I met her insistent request for entry.

Even though I wanted desperately to return the favor, she had turned me into a puddle of mush, incapable of stroking her the way she liked. Feebly, I attempted to reach her clit but gave in to the building sensation as I opened my legs for her and shifted to my back.

"Oh, that is so good. Don't stop."

"I wouldn't dream of stopping right now. That would be cruel," Em whispered. "By the way, I think we're far enough from any other cabin, so scream all you want."

The decibels on my moaning continued to climb as my climax hung on the precipice. Finally, my walls pulsated, and I cried out my release.

Panting, I turned to face my wife and brushed a strand of hair from her grinning face. "God, I love you so much. What I can't understand is why you chose me?"

"Now, you know, I'd never survive a post-apocalypse world without you. Sure, I realize your declaration to fight alongside scary Daryl and Hannah was mostly bravado, but to protect me, you would do almost anything. Remember, I'm a kind of a seer. You would risk your life for me without blinking an eye. I've never felt one-tenth of such love from anyone else. We fit. We always have and always will."

I ran my hands over Em's body and then climbed on top to kiss and lick my way down to her center. It didn't take long for Em's hips to rise and meet my mouth. Em was equally vocal with her reaction to my touch, and I hoped she was correct that we were too far away for anyone to hear.

CHAPTER FIVE

The light from the window in the loft spread slowly in the tiny space, and my eyes opened to sunshine. I guessed it was still early by the placement of the sun. Em remained asleep with her arm draped across my middle. She hadn't let go and was almost in the exact position we had settled into the previous evening.

Our clothes lay in a heap beside the bed where we'd discarded them. No matter the temperature outside, Em and I always preferred to sleep skin to skin, regardless of whether we'd made love the night before or not. It wasn't sexual, but more like a need to remove any layers between us. Barriers of any kind never worked for us.

Stirrings from the camp made their way into the cabin. I assumed the members of this fine establishment started their day early. That wasn't a surprise to me. When a person had to rely on growing their own food and remaining self-sufficient without the luxury of a famous coffee place on every corner, farm life prevailed. I was okay with that.

"Fuckity fuck, fuck. Piece of shit." I heard Daryl's voice above the sputter of a motor.

Em's eyes fluttered open, and she smiled at me. "Oops. If I can hear him grumbling, I wonder what they heard coming from our cabin?" Em chuckled as she stretched her arms above her head. "Perhaps I can earn my keep and see what's frustrated our escort from yesterday."

I laid my hand on my embarrassed face and said, "God, I hope not. Do you think they'll tease us?"

Em shrugged. "I would think they have better things to do than worry about two vocal lovers."

My stomach growled loudly. "Well, I suppose we better find a way to earn our keep. I'd like to get a better look at their gardens, and I'm hungry. Perhaps we can trade your expertise for breakfast. Hopefully, Sonny and Cher were able to hold their bladder last night."

We each grabbed our clothing and dressed quickly, bounding down the stairs like it was Christmas morning. The sun had started to warm the day and felt good on my skin. I opened the door to let the cats do their business and stepped outside. Em followed and lifted her face, hovering for a second while she let the sun caress her skin. I knew her thoughts mirrored mine. After months without feeling the sun, we would take the time to relish this glorious sensation on our second day in the outside world.

I stifled a laugh when I saw Daryl kick what looked like a cobbled together generator. I was sure this one did not run on gas. Both cats were sniffing the ground but stayed clear of the strange man hurling profanities.

Em began a decisive stroll in Daryl's direction. "Morning. Can I take a look? Perhaps I'll be able to help."

Daryl snarled. "Be my guest. The damn thing works only half the time. Is it too much to ask to get a hot shower occasionally? This always happens on my day to take a shower."

Well, that answered the question about bathroom facilities. I wondered how often they would allow us to bathe in luxury or relative luxury. There were always lakes and rivers that could do the job in a pinch.

"Do you have any tools? A spare parts shed or something?" Em asked.

Daryl grunted and walked toward an aluminum and wood structure that seemed cobbled together with superglue and duct tape. It wasn't exactly ready to crumble, but a slight listing to the left side suggested a needed repair. I wondered if the group lacked a decent carpenter in their midst. I'd learned a few things over the years and thought I could lend a hand with basic structures.

When we entered the building, I realized my rushed assessment was off. The inside was filled with a variety of parts and tools, meticulously organized. As I looked around, the structure was more substantial than I thought. This was another lesson in not judging a book by its cover.

"Wow! There's a lot of stuff here." I was impressed.

Em's eyes scanned the large shed. I'd always been amazed at her ability to size something up and know exactly what to do to solve a problem. Her hobby of tinkering with a multitude of mechanical devices would serve us well. She'd passed on a successful career as an engineer to pursue research. She was the very definition of a Jill-of-all-trades and grandmaster of most.

Flipping open a large metal toolbox, she nodded in appreciation. "This will do."

Her eyes landed on a collection of nuts and bolts, then swiveled to what looked like a table full of car parts with a smattering of rust. But what did I know? Rusty old parts were rusty old parts regardless of where they came from.

Her hands deftly picked through the various hunks of metal. Before leaving with her bounty, she spied the table with solvents and rags and grabbed a few items, juggling everything in her arms. She looked like she needed help, so I grabbed the toolbox. Em made a beeline for the generator and began working. Her efficiency was a kind of poetry in motion, and she'd gathered a crowd of onlookers as she worked.

Out of the corner of my eye, I saw Daryl crack a smile when the generator sputtered to life and purred like a kitten.

"I've made a small modification that should allow you to connect this to multiple locations. Do you have other water heaters that need power?" The nonchalant nature of Em's question was so Em-like. She didn't register the gaping mouths as ten other camp residents looked on.

"We do," Trina answered. "I could use the help to hook them up. You'll be the heroine of the camp if you're able to increase the number of hot showers allotted to everyone. Follow me."

Em nodded and stretched after emerging from her squatting, then sitting position, after she'd made whatever brilliant repairs and enhancements caused the generator to rumble with renewed life. "My wife's stomach has been growling so loudly I almost couldn't concentrate. Do you suppose this has earned us a hearty breakfast?"

Trina guffawed. "This has earned you an endless supply of breakfasts cooked to perfection. Not my strong suit, but Hannah makes a mean omelet. Or, if you prefer something else, she is very creative with our supplies." She touched her wife's arm and asked, "Hannah, would you please ensure Lise receives that hearty breakfast? We'll join you after we've modified the other generators." Trina glanced in Em's direction. "How long do you think it will take?"

"How many water tanks do you have on the compound?" Em asked.

"Ten."

"I believe I spied some wire—" Em began.

"I'll get it," Daryl interrupted.

"A ten AWG wire or larger should do," Trina answered.

"Yes, perfect. It shouldn't take more than an hour with both of us working together."

"If you show me what to do, I can help." For the first time since I'd met Daryl, he sounded tentative. Unsure of himself. It made me like him just a little more.

†

I didn't notice the chicken coop when we'd first arrived. No big surprise since, at that moment, I had been too busy gawking at the razor wire fencing. I did, however, notice the scrumptious flavors in the omelet Hannah made for me. There was nothing like the taste of farm-fresh eggs. The cheese she'd added had a tangy zest that was unmistakably goat cheese. Fresh garden herbs added that extra boost that had me moaning with pleasure.

Em grinned at my response and shoved her own forkful of goodness into her mouth. She had enough decorum to chew thoroughly before asking the question on the tip of my tongue. "Will you explain how this camp, or whatever you're calling this collection of talents, works?"

"Alternate society," Trina gently reminded.

Em set her fork down. "My apologies. I forgot. Seems a bit bland for a name."

That earned Em a hearty chuckle from Trina. "We leave the innovation to the running of our society and not unimportant notions of naming conventions."

Em nodded thoughtfully. "If there is a strict schedule for us to adhere to regarding the assignment of chores or job duties, please let us know what that might be. Otherwise, I'm likely to roam around the place and see what needs fixing. I have a tendency to stick my nose into things that you might not appreciate. It's one of my less appealing traits. I can follow the rules if they make sense to me, otherwise," Em shrugged, "I tend to go off the rails and was considered a bit of a rebel in our old life. I assume you have rules."

Trina steepled her fingers below her chin and nodded. "Yes, we have rules. I would be most interested in your opinion on them."

I watched with interest as Em, my little genius, and this obviously commanding woman, assessed one another. I hoped that Trina would be too distracted with her focus on

Em to notice how I pushed a small amount of the omelet into one of the cloth napkins. The cats could catch their own prey and survive, but they'd not been doing that for quite some time, and I wanted to provide enough food for the transition. I knew I'd failed when a tiny smile appeared on Trina's face at the split-second glance in my direction. Before Em responded, she looked at my lap. Apparently, I wasn't as wily as needed to remain undetected.

"Never been one to keep my mouth shut. Go ahead, list them," Em said.

"All right. Keeping the peace within our property is paramount to our survival. Fighting others, while not optimal, is a necessity, but infighting is strictly prohibited. We manage this with rule number one. All opinions and perspectives matter. We are all equal here. Disagreements are handled through discussion, never violence or bullying. Each of us seeks to understand rather than be understood. More listening and less talking. Hostility of any kind, verbal or physical, is forbidden. Sometimes we must carefully navigate the definition of hostility. The definition is different for all, but when one crosses the line, it is always evident. Is that an acceptable rule?"

Em nodded. "So, who makes the final decision?"

"I've agreed to accept that responsibility."

Em raised her eyebrow. "You sound like that was a job you were asked to take on."

"It was. If our society decides another is more suited to the task, I will happily relent, which leads to rule number two. After a decision is made, even if it turns out to be the wrong decision, there is no blaming, only an evaluation for future use. We debrief and talk about how we could have done better. Tearing down others for any reason is also barred in our alternate society."

"Sounds reasonable. How do the tasks and duties get assigned?"

Trina smiled. "That brings us to rule number three. There is no assigning, only volunteers. You will contribute in whatever fashion you believe would benefit our society most. In my experience, each person ultimately knows best what they are capable of. Schedules don't exist, except for our rotating hot showers. Although, we may have to revisit that with our increased capacity for hot water. We simply contribute what we can, when we can. Em, you're more than welcome to poke around anywhere you wish and fix anything you believe has enhancement potential."

"Don't you ever have slackers?" I asked.

"Survival has a way of fundamentally changing societal rules. Oh, and we screen those invited to remain with us. Hannah has an uncanny way of assessing strangers. Her record is perfect."

I glanced at Em, who seemed to relax with every word spoken.

"Is that it?" Em asked.

"One final rule we all adhere to."

"What's that?" I asked.

"There is a difference between carving out space for you and your loved ones and collecting unnecessary wealth. Every person takes what they need, balanced with what is available, no more, no less. Needs differ greatly. We understand that, but survival for all depends on the absence of greed. While it may appear as though the lodgings Hannah and I occupy are more opulent than other dwellings, the main house is used for other purposes. We've agreed to relinquish a certain amount of privacy for the good of the whole. I'd happily exchange places with anyone. So far, no one has taken me up on that offer. By the sounds emanating from your cabin, I don't anticipate the two of you will volunteer." Trina winked.

While my face turned twenty shades of red, Em laughed. "Hmm, good to know. We thought we were too far away."

Trina waved her hand in the air. "Those are sounds most don't mind hearing. They are preferable to gunfire and bombs, giving us hope for the future. Love has a way of lifting all our spirits."

"I'll be honest, the barrage of bullets and loud explosions more than unnerved me. Keeping busy will also help my sanity," Em responded with seriousness.

Occupying myself with work was something I could definitely lean into. I took this as the perfect opportunity to ask about the gardens I'd seen from a distance.

"Will I be able to work in the gardens?" I was itching to dig in the rich earth. I was happiest in my garden.

"As much or as little as you wish. I trust you and Em to decide how much time you put into those tasks each day. We recommend balance, but none of us have the time nor the inclination to be your mother or father. As adults, you decide." Trina slapped her thighs and stood. "It's time for me to tinker unless someone needs me to weigh in on something or we have unexpected company. Em, you're welcome to come with me to see my latest project or wander and poke around as you suggested previously. Hannah spends part of her day in the gardens and would be happy to show you around, Lise."

Em and I responded in stereo. "Sounds good to me."

I decided I could wait to take my hot shower after I was covered in dirt.

"Oh, and if you'd like to provide scraps to the cats until they can fend for themselves, just ask. I don't believe we want to start off not trusting one another." Trina smiled to take the edge from her words.

"Sorry," I mumbled. "Daryl made it clear that we wouldn't be able to feed the cats with resources intended for people. They'll be able to fend for themselves, mostly, but it might be hard during the transition. They aren't used to finding their own food yet."

"I realize that, and I believe we've already established you aren't parting with your babies. With your garden expertise, we'll have enough, and I presume your contributions will be worth much more than a few scraps for the cats. Hopefully, that is now settled, and you won't feel the need to deceive anymore."

"No, ma'am," I replied sheepishly. I felt like I'd received a dressing down from the principal.

Em chuckled. "Lise, you'd never make it as a spy."

"Good thing that isn't a talent they're looking for," I responded with a fair amount of petulance.

†

Em gave me a quick peck before following Trina. That was her way to soothe my ruffled feathers at having been caught pilfering food. She probably would have gotten around to asking about food for the cats because that's who Em is—blunt and straight to the heart of any matter. She never tolerated bullshit in any form. Trina seemed a kindred spirit in that respect. I felt a small amount of jealousy regarding how the two seemed to understand each other instantaneously.

I could tell by the tiny bounce in her step she was excited to see what Trina was working on. The more complicated the project, the better. This camp would keep my love challenged, and that was important after being cooped up for so long with limited opportunities to literally and figuratively stretch ourselves.

The gardens were vast compared to what I had envisioned. There were three, large, open areas, each easily the size of half a football field. Two massive greenhouses stood across the length of the fields, and when we stepped inside, I found them overflowing with starter plants and vegetables thriving in the warmer environment. I wondered about the possibility of building a third that would house plants from the seeds we had to offer. Perhaps we could experiment with hydroponics. Using less water and space had to be an advantage worth exploring. I opened my mouth to suggest this as we reached the first greenhouse, but Hannah beat me to the punch.

"You're probably wondering why we haven't developed a hydroponic system."

I grinned. "You read my mind."

"We haven't had anyone with that level of expertise. A trip to the library wasn't at the top of our list when we first began collecting supplies. Besides, I wasn't sure we'd be able to find what we'd need, anyway. And, it's not like I had the knowledge to develop our own liquid nutrients without a biochemist."

"We had a hydroponic garden in our bomb shelter. Em knows how to set one up and how to make the liquid nutrients."

After waving me inside, she stated, "It seems we hit the jackpot with both of you."

"With Em, yeah, me, not so much."

Hannah's kind eyes captured mine. "It's tough to be the other half when aligned with someone who shines so brightly. I've learned a valuable lesson from Trina. The men and women who live here follow her so effortlessly because she doesn't simply espouse the philosophy that everyone is equal, she believes this in her core. No contribution to our society is too small. We all have special gifts to share. You will shine as brightly against the bounty of our gardens. Of this, I have no doubt."

I fingered the leaves of a tomato plant and then stuck my finger in the pot, bringing the wet dirt to my nose for a quick sniff. "This soil is good, but it doesn't contain the right nutrients needed for hydroponics. It's easiest to use the Masterblend 4-18-38 powdered fertilizer with calcium nitrate and magnesium sulfate. If there are still gardening stores intact that haven't been decimated or tainted, we could grab whatever is on the shelves."

"We collected as much fertilizer and other supplies that were left behind. To our delight, *the others* placed a greater priority on canned foods and weapons. They foolishly left the nurseries alone. We don't have any powdered fertilizer or the other chemicals you cited. How important are these supplies?" Hannah's narrowed gaze told the story of the seriousness of her question.

"If you want to set up a proper hydroponic garden in the most efficient manner, they're essential," I answered after wiping my finger on my shirt.

"Scouting missions are dangerous but necessary. We leave at first light tomorrow." Hannah's no-nonsense declaration shocked me out of my temporary stupor.

"Wait? What? You want me to go with you?"

"Do you have alternate plans tomorrow? Perhaps a dinner date with your wife?" Hannah grinned. *So, the woman could lighten up.*

"Um, no, but I'm not a skilled fighter. What if we run into *the others*?" I tried not to let my voice quiver, but I wasn't successful.

"There's a better than fifty percent chance we'll cross paths with those who wish us harm, but I'm confident you will do what is necessary. When pushed into a corner, people do a lot of things they never think they're capable of."

"I suppose if Em's life was at stake," I declared, leaving unsaid what I was thinking. I didn't believe I could pull the trigger to save a relative stranger.

Hannah sighed. "I understand. You've only just met me. I don't rise to the level of worth as much as your beloved wife. We'll take Daryl and a few other fighters if that will assuage your fear."

"I'm sorry. Like I said before, my skills are limited. I don't mean to be such a wuss. I'll go with you. There may be other materials you didn't think to pull from the shelves that will prove invaluable to us. Can I see where you store your gardening supplies?"

Hannah's smile was genuine as she gestured with her hand for me to follow her. "Right this way."

CHAPTER SIX

I could hear Em's laughter before we entered the room. It seemed she'd found a kindred spirit in Trina as the two women tinkered with a piece of machinery that was beyond comprehension to me. She'd certainly seemed to settle in quickly. When Hannah and I approached, Em quirked her brow. She could always recognize the lines on my forehead when something worried me.

"Lise, what's wrong?" Em asked.

I shook my head. The last thing I wanted to do was worry Em. I tried to remove my telltale wrinkle and grinned at my wife.

"Nothing. We're going on a foraging mission tomorrow to secure all the ingredients for a hydroponic garden," I answered as nonchalantly as I could manage.

Em caught my eyes and held them as if to challenge my statement. She always knew when I wasn't telling her the whole story. "And?" she prompted.

"Lise is worried about running into *the others*. We'll take Daryl and two more of our best fighters with us. We leave at first light tomorrow morning. It'll be fine." Hannah shared a look with Trina.

"Oh. Is it vital to make the trip to a nursery? I assume that's where you intend to go." Em pushed the device she was working on away from her hands. She gave me her undivided attention.

"I know you can make the Masterblend from scratch, but that would require too much effort and extra time to extract the chemicals. Besides, I doubt they have a full lab with the equipment needed to accomplish that task." I stuck my hands inside my pockets and waited for her reaction.

"Lise is correct. We don't have a lab. We could develop one, but that would require a scouting mission to obtain the necessary materials. Perhaps something to consider for a future trip outside of our boundaries." Trina clapped her hands and stood, signaling the discussion was over. "Hannah, would you like me to help with lunch?"

I looked between Trina and Em, expecting a protest from my stubborn wife.

Em frowned and stood with her arms crossed. "If you don't mind, I'd like to talk about this some more before the decision is made to put my wife in harm's way. Perhaps I don't believe the reward is worth the risk."

Uh oh. An early battle between the two imposing women was about to ensue, and I wanted no part in the tussle.

"All right. Let's sit and look at this from all angles. Hannah and Lise, your opinions are relevant to this discussion, considering you're slated to make the journey."

Hannah glanced in my direction, shrugged, and sat in the chair opposite from her wife. I kept my eyes at my feet and only sat after Em and Trina resumed sitting on the couch.

"Lise is a more accomplished and knowledgeable gardener than what we've made do with so far. Her expertise on the supplies will be critical when selecting any remaining items on the shelves," Hannah explained.

"Can't you make a list of what to look for?" Em suggested.

All eyes shifted to me, and I reluctantly answered, "I could, but then I can't gather other treasures that could help. I'm not likely to remember everything. I might miss something that would be valuable. Besides, I won't know what is left from the previous foraging unless I go along with Hannah, Daryl, and the other fighters. I admit, at first I was a little reluctant, but I think this is important, Em."

"How often do you run into *the others* on these little excursions? I assume you've made numerous trips outside of this compound." Em turned to Trina, and the intensity of her look would have made the strongest woman shrink under her scrutiny.

"I understand your concerns. I won't try to diminish the danger. It's a rare day we don't come across *the others*. However, Hannah is very skilled at avoiding them. Rarely does she engage with them. Fighting is only a last resort. What will ease your concerns?"

Em ran her fingers through her hair. "I don't know. This is all new to us. After what happened yesterday, I'm very skittish about putting Lise in harm's way. We've never lived in a city where carrying a gun is normal. Nor have either of us ever owned a weapon, shot a gun, or heard any gunfire. Before yesterday, the closest we've come to gunfire is on the television, which will usually result in one of us changing the channel. We both have an intense aversion to violence. That's not to say I expect the rest of you to accept the risks while we reap the benefits." Em pinched the bridge of her nose. "I don't know what I would do if something happened to Lise." Tears formed in the corners of her eyes. "I know I need to trust you, Lise, to make the right decision. You want to go, don't you?"

I nodded. "I do, Em. Not only do I think these supplies will help us through the winter, but I also need to see for myself what remains of the world."

"Okay, thank you for indulging my need to raise my concerns. What's for lunch? I'm starved." Em grinned at Trina, and I could see the tension dissipate between the two natural leaders.

I wondered if they would tussle again. As a newbie, I didn't believe that Em would assume the leadership mantle, but she definitely was a major contender. If Trina was as wise as I suspected, she would always provide Em the respect she deserved.

†

The day was still early after we finished a simple lunch of sandwiches. Someone in the compound made fresh bread daily, and the roasted turkey was undoubtedly from either something wild or contained within a pen I hadn't seen yet. I'd forgotten how good fresh, organic foods tasted. Enough time had passed that I was sure any possibility of radiation exposure had already dissipated. Without the preservatives, the purity of the flavors burst through. I'd always believed that additives muted the taste, and the evidence was now in front of me to prove my theory. I'd suspected that even when we'd chosen organic, free-range chicken in the grocery stores, they always snuck in a few chemicals to keep the meat fresh.

"This was delicious. I'll be happy to garden and harvest if someone else does the baking, cooking, and processing." I wiped my mouth on the cloth napkin, balling it up and placing it on the scarred wood table.

"I've set aside some turkey for the cats. Although, I believe I saw the male with a mouse this morning." Hannah popped the last of her sandwich into her mouth.

"Thank you. That's good to hear. Sounds like Sonny and Cher will be fine. I saw a few other cats on the premises. Do you save scraps for them as well?" I asked.

Trina smiled lovingly at her wife, who grinned back at her. "She does. Hannah is a softy. I suppose we both are. I've been known to offer a few bites here and there. Believe it or not, Daryl is the worst. Don't let him fool you. While he doesn't claim to own any of the cats, he's made friends with all of them." She set aside her fork and changed the trajectory of the conversation. "Hannah, what time will you depart tomorrow morning?"

Hannah finished chewing the strawberry she'd plucked from the bowl in the center of the table. "First light. If we leave early enough, we may avoid any unwelcome skirmishes."

Although Trina's expression was impassive, there was something about the way she leaned forward that let me know she worried more than she let on. "Will you be able to avoid passing by their main camp?"

Hannah shook her head. "We'll find a path that gives a wide berth to their camp, but lately, we've discovered bands of men farther from their base. I believe they are running out of supplies, which is why they've stepped up their attacks, not only on our compound but against other smaller fringe groups."

Trina began tapping her index finger on the table. "I see. As they become more desperate, we'll need to increase the security around the perimeter. Their weak attempts at entry haven't gotten them very far, but if they were to secure more impenetrable transportation, we might be in for a greater fight." Trina stopped tapping and laid her hand on Hannah's knee. "How far away is the closest military base? And, have you learned anything more about any possible military support for this area?" Trina removed her hand from Hannah's knee, and her tapping resumed, which ratcheted my nervousness as they discussed issues entirely outside my wheelhouse.

"The base is farther than they've been willing to travel with the other militias to contend with that are in between. And those militias have greater firepower than our neighbors. They believe that as a 'queer camp,' we're undermatched for them, and they'll eventually prevail." Hannah grinned. "The base in Yakima was abandoned by the military. I've heard they've chosen to consolidate their resources around the president and other members of our failed democracy. For now, the mountains remain in the hands of *the others* and other small camps similar to ours."

"I don't like how close they came yesterday. Have you been able to secure other volunteers for perimeter patrol for the time you'll be away?" Trina stopped her tapping when Hannah's eyes traveled to her nervous hand.

"Daryl has been working with a few of the older teens." Hannah held up her hand before Trina could protest. "I don't like it any more than you, but several are eager to contribute. Connor is strong, smart, and competent with a weapon. He hates the garden where he's been working until now. At eighteen, we have to respect that he's an adult who can choose where to contribute. Those are the rules we've established. We can't change them now."

Trina sighed. "Connor may be strong and even mature for his age, but the other young men and women are not. Don't let Harley or Bruiser badger you into letting them volunteer for patrol. I've told them not until they both turn eighteen. Can we keep that in mind when accepting volunteers for dangerous duty?"

Em and I watched the exchange with interest. I felt increasingly uncomfortable that my recommendation on a type of fertilizer leading to the scouting mission would result in putting children in harm's way.

"Um, maybe we don't have to take as many fighters with us. I don't feel comfortable knowing we might leave the compound underprotected because I'm a wuss," I interjected.

"Moving around the pieces on the chessboard is what Hannah does best. Please don't misinterpret the conversation. I trust Hannah implicitly. Often, it is helpful to look at every decision from multiple angles. We've survived this long despite blistering odds because we carefully review every contingency." Trina stood and kissed Hannah gently on the mouth. "I'll make my way to the perimeter tomorrow to lend an additional hand."

Hannah chuckled. "Ah, so you've missed being in the middle of the action, have you?"

"Perhaps." Trina smiled.

CHAPTER SEVEN

The knock on the door startled me. I guessed when Hannah said first light, she meant it. The sun had barely risen as I peeked through the window and saw the orange haze. I wanted to ask for her definition of first light.

Em groaned and rolled over. After opening her eyes, she leaned in to peck me on the lips. "You better get dressed. I think your wake-up call is at the door."

"Ugh. It's too early. There's too much orange. I want to see a lot more blue before I'm ready to greet the day." I rubbed my eyes and reluctantly swiveled my body to let my feet touch the icy floor. Even in the summer, the mornings were nippy.

Grabbing my jeans, I quickly stepped into them, hopping around like a crazy person while I pulled them over my butt and zipped up. Forgoing a bra for the moment, I donned my sweatshirt and padded down the stairs to open the door to a smiling Hannah. The cats rushed outside. I suppose they were eager to find a place to pee, or their hunting success from the previous day had reignited their instincts. Either way, I wanted to ask about installing a cat door, so they could come and go as they pleased.

"Morning, Lise. Are you ready for a quick breakfast before we head out?"

"Oh, right, breakfast? Yeah, that would be good, huh?"

Hannah's eyes traveled to my disheveled appearance. "Or not." She laughed. "How about if I pack your breakfast while you finish getting ready?"

"Thanks, I'd appreciate that. I'll definitely take some coffee to go if that's possible."

I stretched my sore back. Digging around in the garden the day before had reminded me of muscles I hadn't used since before hiding inside the bomb shelter.

"It is. By the way, if Em is available, Trina would love to show her a few things to get her opinion on how to improve our systems. She wanted to do that before she heads out on patrol. Would that be possible?"

I imagined my grin had an evil tilt to it when I answered, "Oh, I'm sure Em would love that. We'll both head to the main house as soon as we're ready."

"Great." Hannah gave a small wave and began walking the path to her house.

I closed the door and bounded up the stairs to rouse Em from her slumber.

Em wasn't the friendliest in the morning. Not a morning person was an understatement. The grimace on Em's face was comical as she sat up in bed with the covers at her waist, exposing her breasts. The chill of the morning created pebbles on her nipples, and I groaned at not being able to take advantage of the glorious sight before me.

"I heard," she grunted. "You're having entirely too much fun this morning at my expense. There better be a pot of coffee waiting at the end of this little rainbow you've painted."

I chuckled. "I think if I have to get up this early, you should have to join me. I'd love to convert you into a morning person. I've been trying for years. I suppose all it took was a nuclear disaster and joining the illustrious 'queer camp.' I'm sure *the others* meant it as a slur, but I kind of like the name. You know, reclaiming queer and all."

"I wonder what Hannah and Trina think of that?"

I shrugged. "Don't know, maybe I'll ask Hannah."

"You do that." Em held out her hand. "Okay, hand me my clothes."

I bent to retrieve Em's jeans and sweatshirt from where she'd tossed them the previous evening. Feeling a twinge in my back, I began rubbing the area above my tailbone after tossing Em her clothes.

"Ugh, I think I'm getting too old to spend so many hours in the garden, even if that's where I find my higher power. I've gone soft in that damn shelter."

Em quickly donned her clothes and pointed to the bed. "Why don't you lie down for a few minutes, and I'll rub your back. I'd rather you not traipse around in enemy territory hunched like an old woman."

Stretching from side to side and back and forth, I answered, "I don't think we have time. Hannah and Trina are waiting for us."

"Good thing we took our showers last night. I'm sure it won't matter if we're fifteen minutes late."

"Okay, you win. I really am sore. Spending the entire afternoon in the garden totally kicked my ass," I admitted.

Knowing I would need to layer up today as the day warmed, I'd donned both a sweatshirt and T-shirt. I removed both before climbing on the bed. Lying on my stomach, I felt her strong hands press against the small of my back. She knew exactly where my old injury caused the most discomfort. I had to admit, her magic hands made a big difference.

Lightly smacking my bottom, Em declared, "All done."

I flipped onto my back and smiled contentedly after she placed a relatively chaste kiss on my lips.

"I love you. Be careful today," she said.

"Yes, ma'am. You have fun tinkering. Show them your brilliance."

The back rub Em had given me gave us both a tiny burst of energy. I pulled an underlayer from the small dresser in the loft and slipped it over my head before adding my warm sweatshirt. I didn't know if we would need to do any hiking or if the entire trip would be in their old truck modified to run on biofuel, so I grabbed a pair of light wool socks and my sturdy boots. It was better to be prepared. Em didn't bother to select new clothes since she would be tooling around the complex. She could return to the cabin anytime she wanted to change into lighter clothing as the sun warmed the day.

After we descended from the loft, I opened the front door and nearly ran into Hannah who, I imagined, was getting ready to knock on the door.

"Oh, good, you're ready." Hannah lifted her hand to show me the burrito. I swear I could see steam emanating from it in the crisp morning air.

"That looks good. I assume there are farm-fresh scrambled eggs and cheese inside." Greedily I took her offering, wanting to gobble it down before the eggs turned cold and rubbery.

Daryl was behind her with a to-go mug of coffee. His crooked grin made him look less menacing as he held the cup out for me.

"Thanks, Daryl, you are a king among kings." I grabbed the coffee with my free hand.

Em peeked over my shoulder and exclaimed, "Hey, where's mine? How come I don't get door-to-door service?"

"Trina has a full breakfast at the main house for you. I've never seen her so excited. She can't wait to pick your brain. I think she might have a little crush on you," Hannah answered.

I frowned. "I'm not sure I like the sound of that."

Hannah laughed. "It's strictly intellectual—more like immense respect for a colleague that shares the same passions for tinkering. You don't need to worry because we aren't a commune. We don't engage in wife swapping or swinging. Not that we would make a rule against that for others who might prefer a polyamorous relationship, but it isn't our thing."

Em propped her head on my shoulder. "You're cute when you're jealous."

"Okay, chop, chop. We have to go," Hannah said. She was all business now. "Lise, you and Daryl will ride with me, and Sam and Karl will be in the other vehicle."

The old beat-up trucks weren't very attractive, covered in large swatches of discolored paint, but they looked sturdy enough to get from point A to point B. Next to the other truck, Daryl spoke quietly with an attractive short, muscular, Hispanic man, who looked in my direction and waved like we were best friends. I wondered what Daryl was saying to him. It was a little unnerving. He touched Daryl's arm in what looked like an intimate gesture before climbing inside.

I followed Hannah to the truck and looked back to see Em wave at me as she made her way along the path to the main house. Hannah always carried a sidearm, but it was the surprising amount of nasty looking weapons laid side by side in the extended cab that caused me to gasp as I climbed into the back. There was enough room for me to sit beside what I assumed were AK 47s. I'd never seen this kind of gun up close and personal.

"That's a lot of firepower," I said, not even trying to quell the shake in my voice.

"There's more in the back. It's strictly a precaution—additional insurance. Do you know how to fire a semi-automatic?" Hannah asked.

"No! I've never even seen one, except on television or the movies. I hope you aren't expecting me to contribute to a battle if we run into *the others*." I gulped. Shit was getting real now.

Hannah glanced at Daryl, who'd taken a seat in the front. "There's a small handgun on the floor. You should at least know where that is, in case you need to grab it and use it.

Just don't blow your foot off. They are all loaded. Pick it up, and Daryl can show you how to remove the safety."

"Is that really necessary?"

"Yes," Daryl and Hannah both answered.

I lifted the gun from the floor like it was a dirty diaper and handed it to Daryl, who had turned around, ready to give me a quick lesson. Hannah had already started the truck, and we were moving to the reinforced gate.

Daryl accepted the gun. He pointed to a small lever at the butt of the gun and said, "It's very simple. Sweep this lever forward on the Beretta. Like this." He demonstrated deactivating the safety, then returned the lever to its original position. Handing me the gun butt first, he said, "You try now. Don't forget to put the safety on before setting it on the floor."

With trembling hands, I duplicated his actions and received his crooked smile.

"Good. After you turn the safety off, aim at your target, and squeeze the trigger. If you have to use a gun, chances are the target will be close, and you'll have no choice."

"Okay, but if it's all the same to you, I'll stay hunkered down in the truck."

"Yes, you will," Hannah answered. "The gun on the floor is in case someone gets through and searches the truck."

As we bumped along the side road, I tried not to worry too much about what we might encounter along the way.

CHAPTER EIGHT

"Smoke at two o'clock, Hannah." Daryl pointed to the right, where a wisp of smoke curled into the air, creating a kind of corkscrew shape.

We'd only been on the road for ten minutes. I assumed this was not a good sign.

"I see it. It's probably a small group of scouts. Grab the radio in the glove compartment. I want to warn Trina," Hannah directed.

"Why don't we just take them out? They're too close to camp and in our territory."

"No, I promised Trina we would never be the aggressor. You know, we only fight as a last resort. Besides, we have Lise with us. Em would not be happy with us if we didn't do everything in our power to avoid confrontation." Hannah glanced in the rearview mirror, possibly to gauge my reaction. I was sure I looked like a deer caught in someone's headlights.

I heard the click of the glove compartment pop open before Daryl handed Hannah a walkie talkie. She held the radio in front of her mouth and pressed the button to talk.

"Hannah to base."

The telltale hissing sound emanated from the small radio, and then Trina's crystal-clear voice answered, "Trina here, go ahead, love."

"Small scouting team spotted about five miles from the compound. Make sure you stay vigilant as you patrol the perimeter today. By the look of the smoke, they aren't on the move yet."

"I assume you're going to take a detour now?"

"Yes. We'll take an alternate route, giving them a wide berth. A little four-wheeling will add to the adventure." As Hannah turned her head to Daryl, I could see the mischievous grin on her face.

"Just be careful, okay? We need all of you to return unharmed. Trina out."

"Bye, love."

After Hannah handed the radio to Daryl, he quipped, "Yeah, no playing in the mud, getting stuck, and twisting your ankle again."

"I wish we had quieter vehicles. Converting to solar or electric can't come soon enough. It sure would make these missions a lot safer if *the others* weren't able to hear our motors."

Daryl grunted affirmation in response.

Hannah made a sharp turn to the left, and the bumpy road dwarfed my previous assessment that the journey would be a little rough.

My voice vibrated as I asked, "How long until we reach the nursery?"

"If we're lucky and don't run into any obstacles, maybe another hour to the first location. If we don't find what we need there, we can travel farther to the larger abandoned town, but I'd rather avoid that store. It seems like *the others* return to that location more often than the one off the beaten track."

Our small caravan finally made it to a gravel road that wasn't any smoother than the dirt roads Hannah had taken us on, but I breathed a sigh of relief, believing that at least we wouldn't get stuck in the mud. Four-wheel drive did not guarantee we would be safe from this fate if the soil was thick enough to swallow the massive tires.

In horror, my body slammed against the cache of weapons as Hannah swerved to miss a deer that had suddenly appeared in our path. Tires spun in the gravel, spitting rocks when Hannah returned to the central portion of the road. Two seconds later, the loud explosion caused the truck to shudder in response. Hannah slammed on the brakes, causing more gravel to fly from the tires. My head swiveled toward the second explosion, and through the smoke, I saw the other truck safely stopped on the far side of a massive hole in the road.

Hannah was in motion before I had a chance to feel any gratitude for the other truck avoiding catastrophe. "Daryl, grab the automatic rifles. That was a booby trap intended to snare anyone traveling on this road. They won't be far behind. We need to find cover, fast. Lise, can you climb a tree?"

I froze in fear as the surrounding scene registered. I couldn't form any words and remained mute.

"Lise! Time to move. Grab the Beretta and climb the closest tree, now," she ordered.

Daryl was already out of the truck, handing several rifles to Hannah. The other men in our caravan had joined Hannah and Daryl, grabbing the rest of the guns from the back. Daryl plucked the Beretta from the floor and slammed it into my hand. I stared wide-eyed into his grim expression.

"Get out and put the gun in your pants while you climb the tree. Snap out of it, Lise, because if you don't move now, we're all doomed. Let's go." He reached into the cab and grabbed my arm so hard I thought it might leave a bruise.

I blinked once, trying to make sense of the situation as he tugged me to the edge of the forest where the massive pine trees hovered above us.

Finally, sensing the imminent danger, I jammed the gun into the back of my pants and ran as fast as I could into the woods on the heels of our scouting party.

I saw Hannah point to a large tree to the left. "That one looks sturdy enough. Start climbing, Lise. I'm right behind you."

I tried to shut out the rustling sounds that meant our enemy was close and pulled myself up, reaching each new branch by using muscles I no longer possessed after being cooped up so long inside the shelter. Grabbing a spindly branch that wasn't sturdy enough to hold my weight, I heard the snap. Before I tumbled gracelessly to the ground, I let my hand grasp wildly for another option and wrapped my fingers around a sturdier choice. I swung precariously from the new limb, nearly running out of energy to continue my climb. Hannah had to provide a small push to enable me to reach the next stable branch.

When we'd climbed high enough to satisfy Hannah, she whispered loudly enough for me to hear, "Lise, you need to tuck into that crevice and remain as quiet as you can. Hopefully, they'll focus on the trucks and leave us alone. There isn't much for them to salvage, but we also can't afford to lose our primary mode of transportation for scouting missions. If anyone tries to hotwire our trucks, I'll have no choice but to take them out."

I nodded to let her know I understood her order.

At first, I had no idea how Hannah carried a pack and three rifles as she climbed the tree. Then I registered how the straps on what I assumed was a sniper rifle and the automatic weapons seemed tailor-made to attach to her body.

Although I heard the snapping of small branches as she ascended, there were no major mishaps. I wondered if she practiced this at the compound. Did they engage in war games exercises that would prepare them for every contingency?

Hannah inched forward until she was so close, I could feel her breath against my neck as she whispered again in my ear. "I need to see what's happening on the ground. When I turn my body enough, can you quietly unzip the front pocket on my pack and retrieve the small binoculars?"

I nodded again, too afraid to speak. Like a graceful acrobat, she maneuvered her tall body enough so that the front pouch was inches away. My trembling hands reached for the zipper as I eased it to the left. The buzzing in my ears from stress drowned out any noise I made as I opened the compartment and found the small binoculars. I prayed that I was quiet enough.

After Hannah turned again, she touched my arm and murmured, "Good, that's good. If we're lucky, they'll sniff around the trucks and move along."

Balancing on the sturdy branch, Hannah brought the binoculars to her eyes and remained immobile, only slightly moving her head toward our abandoned vehicles. I could barely detect male voices but couldn't make out any of their words. Wishing I had a set of spy glasses, I strained my eyes to see anything through the thick trees. I scarcely made out six figures in camouflage clothing. They were swarming the trucks like a horde of worker bees inside a honeycomb.

When Hannah handed me the binoculars, I thought she had offered me a chance to see what was happening below. Instead, needing both hands, she loosened her strap and carefully removed the rifle with a scope, then rebalanced herself on the limb. I had no idea how she accomplished this feat. Hannah straddled the thick branch and twisted her body so that the rifle pointed in the direction of the beat-up trucks.

"Shit," she hissed as she looked through her scope. "They're going to try to hotwire my truck. Holding the rifle against her chest, she signaled to the three men balancing precariously on their own tree limbs. I watched as everyone engaged in a kind of sign language I didn't understand.

After furiously gesturing back and forth, Hannah raised the rifle again, took aim, and several shots rang out in perfect synchrony. Since I was so close to Hannah, I thought her rifle had started the precisely timed assault, but I couldn't really tell. It was over in a matter of seconds.

Tired of balancing precariously in a massive old tree, I shifted, signaling I was ready to get the fuck down. The adrenaline from earlier had subsided, and restlessness took its place.

Hannah shook her head. "No, Lise. We need to stay here for a few moments. Sometimes scouts have back up. We can't take the chance. To be on the safe side, we'll wait here for another thirty minutes." Although her words no longer came out in a whisper, there was a quiet seriousness to them.

I gasped, and before I responded, she had placed her finger against her mouth.

After gesturing again to our colleagues, Hannah returned her attention to me. "You're doing great, Lise. I promise everything will be fine. This isn't our first rodeo. The mountains and trees have been our savior for a long time, and we've adapted well to their bounty. It's been hard for the *others* to combat an attack they aren't prepared for. Trees are almost as good as rooftops or the battlements on the upper walls of an old castle. We practice these drills all the time. The men are adept at climbing trees in full battle gear."

"I'm not sure if I want to practice that skill. I don't want to join you in another scouting mission if that's all the same to you."

"I might suggest practicing, just in case. We've made a game of who can climb a tree the fastest. The little ones enjoy it."

I let myself relax as the minutes ticked by, and Hannah seemed unperturbed by anything that might happen below. I had to admit that when I was a child, I loved climbing trees. To have an excuse to return to this silly activity had a certain appeal.

74

I wasn't fooled by Hannah's attempt at distracting me as her eyes continued to scan below for potential threats, but I answered her questions.

"What was it like living in the bomb shelter for so long?" she asked.

"I'm not going to lie and say it was all rainbows and unicorns, but I couldn't have picked a better person to spend ten months with, locked inside a tiny space. Em is the love of my life, so it wasn't all hardship. We had a lot of time to make love." I grinned.

"Were you happy to emerge and find the world hadn't disintegrated after all?"

"Happy, yes. Surprised, no. Em explained about radiation and how long the harmful effects would remain. She was more worried about infrastructure and all the internal struggles. Looks like we may have emerged too soon. They're still happening."

Hannah shrugged. "Unfortunately, that is human nature. If you wanted to avoid that, you would have needed to spend your entire life in the shelter. However, Em was correct in her assessment regarding the first few months. The territorial squabbles resulted in a massive loss of human life."

I realized I still had the binoculars in my hand and offered them to Hannah. She smiled as she accepted them and held them loosely in her hand.

"Tell me your love story. Where did you meet?" There was a softness to Hannah's voice that I didn't expect.

"Em hired me to landscape her new house in Seattle. She was a highly sought-after scientist, with companies knocking on her door all the time. She had a ton of money to blow and wanted to surround her home with beauty. Not having the tiniest skills with plants, she wanted someone who would create a garden of Eden for her and maintain it. I was besotted the minute I laid eyes on her."

"She's a striking woman. You're a beautiful couple."

I smiled. "Yeah, she is, but Em's real beauty is who she is on the inside. I didn't think I stood a chance with her, not to mention that I had no clue she was a lesbian, which was so bizarre since I have very refined gaydar. Oblivious me did not pick up on how many times she would invite me inside for coffee, lemonade, whatever she'd prepared. Soon, that evolved to lunch and dinner. We'd talk for hours, and she didn't treat me like some lowly gardener. She acted like I was someone with as many different degrees as herself."

Hannah chuckled. "Trina had to make the first move, too. Her intelligence was intimidating enough, but you know how she has that self-assured presence about her. That was equal parts turn on and positively terrifying."

I eyed Hannah strangely after she'd confessed that to me. "But, you're like a model. I mean, you had to have women chasing after you."

"Not the ones I ever wanted. Modeling is not as fun as you might think it is." Hannah looked away for a second, and when her eyes returned to meet mine, there was a split second of dullness before returning to her usual brightness.

"Wow, you were a model?"

"I was. It's not an occupation I'm terribly proud of now. There's a very seedy side to modeling, especially if you start when you're young and naïve. There are far too many predators who take advantage of young girls with stars in their eyes. I was happy to get the hell out with a modicum of sanity." The dimness in Hannah's eyes returned, and then just as quickly disappeared when she redirected the conversation. "So, I assume Em made the first move."

"Yup, she came out and bluntly asked me, 'Are you ever going to pick up on my gestures at romance?' I was so damn shocked, I began to stutter, and then she kissed me. Like really kissed me. I felt a tingle in every single one of my limbs. I squealed like a pig after that and told her I was hopelessly in love with her. Succinct as always, Em merely said, 'good,' and then dragged me to her bedroom. That same evening she told me she'd fallen in love during one of our quiet moments."

We continued to chat like old friends for thirty minutes, and the time seemed to go quickly. Hannah glanced at her watch and then signaled to the rest of our party. Making sure all her rifles and weaponry were secured to her body, and the binoculars were safely tucked inside her backpack, Hannah scrambled down the tree as gracefully as she had ascended. She motioned for me to follow.

Of course, I panicked as I looked down and realized how far I had climbed. I mapped out my descent, taking deep breaths to calm my already frazzled nerves, despite the friendly talk with Hannah. This time I knew I had ample time to plan. I also felt every scrape on my hands and arms from the rapid climb to the top. Making the jump to the ground resulted in a clumsy landing as my butt hit the packed earth. Hannah offered her hand, and I took it, rubbing my sore behind.

Everyone except me continued to scan their surroundings as we made our way to the trucks. I wasn't prepared for the six dead bodies that Daryl and the others quickly dragged into the woods. My eyes focused on the blood splattered on the side of the truck. A warm hand on my shoulder did little to calm me as I hyperventilated.

"Deep breaths, Lise. I know it's hard to see this, but we had no choice," Hannah soothed.

"They were men trying to survive, like us."

"No, Lise. The black band around their arms says differently. Those men are responsible for atrocities that you cannot imagine humans capable of. The different factions are all marked by the colors of the bands they wear. We refuse to identify ourselves in any manner, but these men wear their bands like a badge of honor. Unfortunately, *the others* closest to our territory wear the black bands—religious fanatics who view women as nothing other than broodmares and playthings. Their other teachings are frankly too distasteful to discuss. Trust me, they are not merely men struggling to endure." Hannah opened the truck door and waved me inside.

Daryl remained quiet as he restacked the guns.

After all the remaining rifles were stored away, Daryl asked gently, "Did you want to keep the Beretta tucked into your waistband?"

I should have felt the gun as I leaned back into the seat. However, with the carnage front and center, I hadn't registered the uncomfortable sensation of something poking the small of my back. I leaned forward and pulled the gun from my jeans, wordlessly handing it to Daryl, who ensured the safety was still on before setting it on the floor.

I tried to wipe the memory of those dead eyes staring into space. Hannah had grabbed a rag from the bed of the truck, and as unobtrusively as possible, she'd wiped the sides where the blood had splattered. I would thank her later for removing the evidence of our one-sided skirmish. Later, I came to understand just how lucky we were. If Hannah had not swerved to avoid the deer, those explosives might have done real damage to not only the truck but to the human cargo inside.

†

I was immensely grateful that we hadn't run across more trouble before reaching the long gravel driveway into the nursery Hannah had selected to check out. Like I imagined most other stores, this one looked completely abandoned. Without proper care, many of the trees and bushes that were still in neat rows looked unhealthy. However, I glanced at a few fruit trees I thought might do well enough and turned to Hannah to make a plea.

"Do you think we would have enough room to grab a few of those fruit trees? Usually, I prefer replanting smaller trees, but having the option of a first-year harvest is more appealing at this point."

"We'll make room. Fruit is always a welcome treat." Hannah climbed from the truck and waved over the other men in our small caravan. "Lise, point to the trees you want the guys to load up."

After selecting the healthiest fruit trees, we made our way inside. Like a kid in a candy store, I picked through what was left, happy to learn that not only were there stacks of the Masterblend 4-18-38, but the other chemicals were equally plentiful.

I pointed to the bounty. "Grab the entire supply of this and also the calcium nitrate and magnesium sulfate."

I screamed in delight when I saw the liquid plant food and directed the gang to grab every bottle they had in stock, along with some seaweed extract which was the most challenging ingredient to make for a portion of homemade liquid plant food. I considered our haul an enormous success. This nursery probably tailored its inventory to organic farmers and gardeners.

I couldn't resist returning to the rows of fruit trees and bushes. I had the insane desire to save every one of them. Touching their leaves and breathing in the earth and sweet aroma of budding fruit brought me back to my happy place. I'd located several scraggly blueberry bushes that needed tender loving care to survive. I would make it my mission to baby them to health.

Hannah approached, and I sensed she was almost hesitant to interrupt my perusal of the plants. "Lise, we have to go soon. Staying too long presents unnecessary risks."

"Sorry. I hope we have room for these blueberry bushes." I pointed to the bushes that weren't completely dead.

She nodded.

After adding the ten pitiful plants, I made one last trip inside the nursery for bat guano. Nothing beats bat shit as fertilizer for blueberry bushes.

By the time we rolled away from the nursery, we had ample supplies for increasing our harvest tenfold. I was giddy with excitement until we left the relatively wide-open space and entered the back roads traversing through the woods. I wondered if we would run into *the others* again.

Hannah broke the silence inside the truck. "I think it's best if we give the northeast route a try."

A single nod and a grunt was Daryl's answer. After a minute of silence, he added, "Try the forest road six miles to the east of our compound. The last mile into the back is a little rough, but may be worth it. Sam has been exploring the east a little and removed enough brush to make our way back to camp. He's yet to come upon any scouting groups. Probably because he just finished clearing the path for a truck to pass through."

"Good to know," Hannah answered.

Bumpy was an understatement as we made our way through the narrow path to the camp. The last mile felt like the longest part of our journey, but at least we didn't run into *the others* on the way back. That gave me hope that perhaps we could use this back road again to forage for additional supplies. Compost could take from a few months to years if not properly tended. I'd already noticed ways to encourage a faster breakdown in their compost bins and piles, but that didn't help us in the short term.

†

Hannah stopped at the back gate and waited for Daryl to jump from the truck. He opened the gate wide enough for both vehicles to pass through. I was eager to unload the supplies and decide the best location for the fruit trees.

Trina and Em greeted our caravan, and the smile on my face was genuine when I saw my love approach. Em quickly gathered me in her arms, and I melted into the embrace. She held me for several minutes before finally letting go and placing a gentle kiss on my lips. Forgotten were the six men whose wide-open death stares would haunt me for days. We made quick work of unloading the trucks, and then Em's eyes landed on the bloody rag Hannah had used to wipe the evidence of our skirmish from the side of the truck.

The smile slipped from her face, and Em asked, "What happened?"

Hannah and Trina shared the look of two lovers who knew how to communicate without words. The rest of our merry band stood to the side, almost frozen in anticipation.

"Where?" Trina asked.

"A fair distance from the compound. Thirty miles, give or take. A deer saved our lives. We'll have to remember that the next time one of the men wants to go hunting. The improvised explosive device was crude but would have done the trick had I not swerved to avoid the poor thing. The gravel that spit from my back tires activated the bomb before Sam's vehicle was too close." Hannah provided the details in an almost monotone voice.

She hadn't yet embraced Trina, and I wondered why not? Was this an ordinary mission and not worth the level of worry that Em and I felt?

"And the blood?" Trina's eyes had also landed on the bloody rag.

"Theirs. We took to the trees and used the sniper rifles to take six men out. We had no choice. They were about to hotwire my truck, and I couldn't let them take that valuable resource."

Trina quirked her eyebrow. "A truck can be replaced."

"They wore black bands," Hannah stated, as if that were explanation enough.

Trina clenched her jaw and nodded. The rest of our caravan waited patiently until Hannah made her way to her wife, and they finally embraced. Trina whispered something in Hannah's ear, and I only caught two words. Trust and love. *What else was there?*

A shift in the wind seemed to parallel something else in the atmosphere. I imagined a higher power turning a switch as everyone moved at once, excited chatter following. It was as if the group had needed both respected leaders to reconnect and do a quick debrief before regular activity returned.

Em must have decided it wouldn't help to dwell on what had happened and began her teasing, "I see you convinced them of your ability to save those wretched bushes and trees. I certainly hope you can do your magic because I miss pie." Em licked her lips. "It figures you saved the ones that bear your favorite fruit."

I grinned. "Who doesn't love apple pie? There are pear and plum trees, too, you know. I did think of others. The place was a goldmine. We have enough fertilizer to last a long while, plus additional supplies to make our own. We should be set for years if I can get the compost bins to produce more quickly. I even found some bat guano for the blueberry bushes. I see blueberry pancakes in the relatively near future."

"Why can't you use the chicken manure?" Em asked.

"Oh, we can, but I've already seen evidence of burning. That means it hasn't been composted correctly."

Em nodded. "Ah, too much nitrogen, huh?"

"I do believe you'll be our garden savior, Lise," Trina noted. "Have you decided where this orchard of yours will reside?"

"I think I'll take another stroll around the property, including the edges. Can I get back to you on that?"

"Of course. I'll bet all of you are hungry. Sam, Daryl, will you join us?"

The short man who had waved at me before leaving the compound grinned. His boyish charm was a perfect contrast to Daryl, who remained dour most of the time. As if a light bulb had just gone on, I realized this was Sam, and he and Daryl were a couple. An unlikely pair, but opposites attract. I imagined Sam was the reason Daryl had come a long way, as Trina had shared with us when we first arrived, because he'd found love again. I wondered if, behind closed doors, Sam was able to tease a smile out of him now and again?

"Well," Sam drawled, as his playful light green eyes danced with mirth. "I suppose that depends on what's on the menu."

"Chicken and dumplings. After making some adjustments to the power grid, Em and I did a little cooking. I'm finally able to make the one dish that Hannah taught me. I'm not much of a baker either, so Em made the blackberry cobbler."

I tried not to let my jealousy prevail again. I had assumed that while we were gone, Em had her own mission, and that did not include baking cobbler with Trina. She was supposed to be improving the systems at the complex, and I thought Trina had volunteered for perimeter patrol. I knew deep down that Em loved me, but I didn't want her getting all domestic with Trina, a woman who had such a commanding presence and intellect to match Em's brilliance.

I was about to suggest that Em and I rustle up our own dinner because we'd been having all our meals with Trina and Hannah since our arrival, when Sam responded, "Sold. I'm looking forward to getting to know Em and Lise. I think we'll all be great friends."

Daryl tried to keep the scowl on his face, but I could see the corner of his lip turn up. What else could I do? I was being ridiculous. Anyone could see the love bursting between Trina and Hannah.

Em's brow furrowed as she caught my eyes, silently asking what was up with me. I knew I would spill the beans as soon as we returned to our cozy cabin. The damn woman had x-ray vision in her ability to suss out my feelings. Em didn't have only one superpower. She had many.

†

I tried to relax after our early dinner. But when we returned to our cabin, I was still a little wired. Em built a fire in the wood-burning stove. Although the night air had not yet cooled the living space, the warmth of a fire seemed to settle me as much as digging in the earth.

Em didn't waste any time as she jumped right in and asked, "So, what was that strange look on your face when Trina invited us for dinner? Does Daryl still make you nervous?"

I slumped on the love seat, and Em joined me, taking my hand. "I don't want to say. You'll think I'm being ridiculous, and I am."

"Lise, I would never diminish your feelings. Come on, spill."

I bit the corner of my lip and confessed. "I'm happy that you and Trina have common interests, but I guess I got a little jealous about you making the cobbler with her. Stupid. I know."

Em shook her head. "Not stupid. If I'm totally honest, you going off on a dangerous mission with Hannah, the very definition of a runway model, caused a minor twinge in me that I am reluctant to admit to."

"You know, she really was a model, but it didn't seem like she enjoyed the lifestyle that went with the job. Believe it or not, Trina had to make the first move, too. Hannah said she was totally besotted with her, but Trina was so intimidating to be around at first. She told me their love story." I grinned.

"Hmm, an unlikely pair like us. Trina went to Stanford for her degree in mechanical engineering. She's done an amazing job with cobbling together the basic systems in the compound," Em said with a touch of awe as she turned my hand over and started making small circles on my palm.

"A brainiac like you." I figured that Trina graduated from a prestigious college and couldn't help it when my body responded to this new piece of information.

She must have felt me stiffen and stopped making circles, turning her body to look directly at me. "Lise, I admire her knowledge in the same way that I am awed by your incredible skills with plants and your ability to make me laugh. Not to mention so many other of your wonderful traits. You are the only woman who can make me laugh and tease out my lighter side. Even though change is hard for you, I am constantly amazed by your ability to adapt and evolve." Em began stroking my palm again. She knew how much I enjoyed those light caresses. "While it's very foreign for me to be jealous, I understand you connect with Hannah in the same way I connect with Trina. She's more on the quiet side and hides her talents, like you."

"Admitting you're jealous, really?" I grinned, and then I remembered how Hannah had helped me up the tree and couldn't resist teasing Em just a little. "Then I probably shouldn't tell you that Hannah had to push on my butt to help me climb the tree. I tried not to let her assistance offend me." I batted my eyes.

"You are bad." She bumped against my shoulder playfully.

"I promise I've never let another woman touch my ass since the day you and I got together, but I was close to slipping and falling and couldn't worry about propriety at that moment."

Em laughed. "Yup, that ass of yours is mine and vice versa. I believe I need to give that very fine butt of yours some special attention tonight. Time to forget about everything that happened today except acquiring those fruit trees and bushes." She leaned in to kiss me, and our kiss turned passionate. After we broke apart, Em stroked my face. "I hope you know that you are the only woman I will ever love. We fit."

"I do, and yes, we do. I love you." I grabbed her hand and led her to the loft, eager to reconnect and find the peace that only Em could provide. Digging in the earth didn't even do that for me in the same way as Em's soft caresses.

CHAPTER NINE

The next day, I left the cabin a little later than usual to spend time with Mother Earth, even if that meant digging holes for the trees, which was my least favorite thing to do. Although our lovemaking did a lot to settle me the previous evening, I still needed to dig in the earth to further ground me after the disturbing events on the previous day.

When I heard the excited voices as I dug my fourth hole for the orchard, I saw a group of older kids carrying an enormous fish bounty. Apparently, the kids had ventured outside the compound gate. I assumed they had traveled to the place where Em had wanted to camp on our first day outside the shelter. Fresh fish sounded good to me, and I wondered if the rules allowed anyone to fish in the stream.

"Hey." I set my shovel on the ground and waved my arms in the air.

A girl of about fourteen or fifteen years sauntered confidently in my direction, followed by the rest of the small group. She squinted one of her eyes and tilted her head at me.

"I heard that we recruited new people with skill. You're the gardener, right? Rumor is you're some kind of virtuoso with plants." She pointed to the tree sitting next to the large hole I'd dug. "That looks pitiful. Sure, I see the small fruit trying to grow, but I doubt you'll save it. The shock of replanting will surely doom the poor thing."

I laughed at her assessment. She wasn't entirely wrong, but I was confident in my skills to save the tree. I wondered who had taught her about trees and plants. She might be someone I could toss around various ideas with.

Ignoring her blunt appraisal, I asked, "Can anyone go outside the gate and fish in that stream? That's some nice-looking fish you have there."

She narrowed her eyes. "You gonna tell Trina?"

"Nope." I crossed my heart. "I promise. I guess that means you weren't supposed to go fishing. What's your name, kid?"

"I'm not a kid. I turn seventeen next week." She didn't look seventeen, but I was glad my surprise didn't seem to register with her as she rambled on. "Next year I'll be old enough to patrol. I can take care of myself." She pointed to the wicked knife attached to her belt. "I did fine before Daryl caught us. Who do you think suggested climbing the trees? The dumb bastards in the black-band camp still haven't figured that out. Heard y'all had to take out six of them. Good riddance."

"Okay," I said, holding back my mirth. "You still haven't given me your name."

"Harley. Like the motorcycle. This here's Finn, Sadie, and Bruiser." Harley pointed to the two girls and the gangly boy who looked like he'd recently had a big growth spurt. They all seemed wounded and only briefly met my eyes when each heard their name. I wondered if Hannah's special skills extended to adolescents or children.

"Nice to meet you. I'm Lise. For the record, I'm going to save every one of the fruit trees we brought back. Want to make a bet on it?"

"I don't have anything to bet except my knife, and I'm not giving that up." Her stance grew rigid.

"Fresh fish," I answered. "I'm guessing you're quite an accomplished fisherwoman."

"I am." She grinned. "I hate working in the gardens."

Well, damn, there went my hope for a garden buddy.

Harley continued without noticing my disappointment. "Sometimes, Daryl or Trina will let us work on the generators or vehicles. I'm good with engines. Fishing allows us to contribute. Plus, we're good at it. I'm the best fisherwoman in our camp. There wasn't anyone to accompany us today, so we went on our own. It's better to ask for forgiveness than permission. I've gotten in trouble before. Trina's bark is a lot bigger than her bite. You don't gotta bet to get fresh fish. We bring them back for anyone who wants them. What were you planning to put up for the wager?"

I grinned. "Fresh apple pie, of course."

"Confidence. I like that. Here." Harley held up two large trout. "You can have these. Don't forget about us when you harvest those apples and make the pie, okay?"

I took the fish she offered and nodded. "I'll remember. Next time you go fishing, will you take me? I'd like to learn how to catch a fish. Em, my wife, is much better at it than me, but she'll be busy improving the systems in the compound."

"Won't you be busy saving your pitiful trees?" Harley asked.

I laughed. "Cheeky. You guys better scoot and ask for forgiveness before the rest of the fish rot. You're sure it's okay for me to take these?" I gestured with my head at the fish in my hand.

"Yup. There's plenty of dried fish in the stores, and most people prefer eating that versus bothering with cooking and cleaning the fresh fish."

"Thanks." I lifted the fish in the air, and the small group started toward the main house.

I heard Finn say, "I think she'll save those trees. I can't wait for the pie."

"Ha, you just have a crush on her. She's cute though, I'll give you that," Harley responded.

"She's too old for me. I heard she can make her own liquid fertilizer. I'm just saying she's a genius with plants. Everyone is talking about them. I don't hate the gardens like you, so maybe she can teach me. My mom was a gardener." Finn's voice trailed off, and I heard the sadness. They were now too far away for me to hear Harley's response.

I wondered if these were the only kids in the compound. Maybe there were more orphaned by either the bombs or the squabbles, and I hadn't seen them yet.

Leaving the unplanted tree next to the hole I'd dug, I returned to our tiny house and began preparing the fish. On the way was the greenhouse where I planned to harvest some vegetables to go with the fresh trout. As if by magic, someone had already stocked our pantry with canned goods and homemade condiments, including the best salad dressing I'd ever tasted. I wasn't bothered by a stranger entering the cabin while both Em and I had worked in different parts of the compound. I saw the gesture as kindness and not an intrusion into our privacy.

The compound had a massive storeroom and cold cellar. I was going to make it my solemn duty to fill the cold storage with fresh garden foods that someone skilled in canning could make good use of. For now, the compound was adequately stocked, and nobody was on the verge of starving, that was for sure.

✝

There was still plenty of light left in the day when Em entered the cabin, trailed by Sonny and Cher. I wondered if they could smell the fish I had placed on the makeshift grill. Gas grills were an unnecessary luxury considering we had plenty of wood and large rocks to fashion a camping grill. I'd ducked inside to finish preparing the vegetables, which I would also grill, a mere minute before Em returned. Neither would take long. I hated overcooked fish or mushy vegetables.

"I see you ran into Harley and gang," Em said.

I laughed. "Yeah, I did. How do you know them?"

"After you left this morning, I spied this kid hovering on the perimeter while I worked on one of the old trucks. I called her over, and then the rest of her troupe emerged from wherever they'd hidden. She's a bright kid."

"Sassy, too."

Em laughed. "Yes, Trina and I ran into Harley and her entourage when they tried to sneak by Trina to put the rest of their catch in the storeroom. Harley never altered her path, but the rest of them did their best to avoid Trina. I didn't wish to diminish Trina's authority, so I stifled a giggle when Trina sighed and patiently lectured Harley about taking the necessary precautions. Harley argued like a pro, insisting she could protect her fishing buddies and was smart enough to avoid *the others*. Did you know it was Harley who suggested that Hannah and her team climb trees?"

"Uh, huh. She was quick to point that out to me. That kid has guts."

"She does. She proceeded to cross her arms and stare down Trina, who relented with a request that she grab Trina the next time rather than have the kids going out alone. I get the sense she has a soft spot for Harley and tried to allow her a modicum of respect while she lectured her in front of me. Trina insisted that would give her the perfect excuse to satisfy her favorite pastime—fishing."

"I wonder why she acted like it was a big deal if I told Trina. I told her I wouldn't rat her out."

"Harley doesn't seem like the type of kid to trust easily. I would guess she came clean on her own, thinking you would betray her trust." Em looked contemplative as her brow furrowed.

"I would never," I insisted.

"I know that, but she doesn't." Em stole a kiss and smiled at me.

"Do you think there are more orphaned kids?" I asked.

Em shrugged. "I don't know. I haven't seen any. Why?"

"I hope there aren't. That would mean the kids have lost their parents. Finn, Sadie, and Bruiser looked a little adrift and severely damaged to me."

"We're all a little damaged. Some more than others, but I sense this camp is the best place for them. I'd hate to imagine what would have happened had they ran across *the others* first." Em slid her hand down my arm and then squeezed my hand.

"I better get these vegetables on the grill and check on the fish."

As I tended to our meal, I thought about what Em had said about us all being a little damaged. I wondered how much more trauma we'd all have to endure. I wasn't wired to accept violence in my life. Would that drive me to the brink of insanity, or might I adapt and allow this to become the new normal?

†

Earlier in the day, I had stumbled across a middle-aged woman who made bamboo furniture. She insisted I take two handcrafted bamboo chairs to our cabin. They were the preferred furniture for sitting outside and enjoying the evenings. This furniture was her contribution to the compound because other chores had not suited her.

"Come on, let's sit outside in our new chairs," I suggested. "It's such a nice evening, and the sun won't go down for at least another couple of hours."

"Sounds perfect to me." Em grinned. "I've got something special to share."

"Oh?"

Em opened the refrigerator and pulled out a brown bottle. "Mead. Apparently, Sam used to own a winery. Since grapes aren't prevalent in these parts, he's adapted to making mead. I had a small nip of Trina's stash this afternoon, and she showed me where I could grab a bottle. We have to respect the limited supply, but a nip here and there of this and the other offerings won't demolish the stash."

"I love mead. Damn, we didn't even find that very often before the world went to shit."

"I know, right?" Em swung the bottle in her hand as she joyously made her way to the front of the cabin where I'd placed the new chairs.

Her relaxed demeanor was rubbing off on me. Although I tried to control myself, I'd been on edge since our trip to the nursery, wondering when the next attack would happen. Ironically, it was my interaction with the kids that had calmed me to a small degree.

Harley was still so innocent and young, yet seemed unaffected by the threat. While the others were clearly suffering from trauma, they weren't nervous or unsettled in the same way as someone living their life in fear.

Sonny and Cher remained on their cushy bed in front of the woodstove. They'd already snagged a few pieces of fish earlier, and now it was nap time again.

I lowered myself into a chair and moaned in delight. The chair's curve allowed my body to mold to the contour and give my tired lower back a much-needed repose. Em set the bottle between us and flopped into the other chair, matching my groan. She picked up the bottle, flipped open the Grolsch-style swing top, and handed the mead to me.

"Oh my God, this is so good," I exclaimed.

Em made a gimme motion with her hand, and I offered her the liquid gold. I heard soft footsteps before seeing Trina and Hannah walk down the path in our direction.

"I see you've decided to share Sam's mastery with Lise. That's good. Lise definitely deserves a bit of this treasure." Trina held up a bottle. "We came to bring you another. Sam insisted. He thought you might need it after yesterday's adventure. I know it was hard on you, Lise. Hannah filled me in."

"I'm okay. Why don't you join us instead? I think there were some camp chairs inside the closet I could drag out for you." I started to stand.

Hannah waved her hand in the air. "No need, we'll sit on the ground. Thanks for the offer. I love this stuff, and it's been a while since we relaxed and enjoyed the simple pleasure of visiting with friends over a drink or two. Sometimes it's essential to enjoy the contributions others give to the community and relax for a few minutes. Not having to be on guard twenty-four-seven is encouraged for all of us. Any little thing to keep our sanity."

"Can you really? Relax, I mean. It seems like attacks happen randomly. How do you feel comfortable letting go? We've only been here a few days, and already..." I let the words dangle.

"Trust. It all comes down to that. I rely on our patrol to keep us safe tonight. We are far more organized than *the others*. Now that Em has helped us secure the perimeter with new technology, that should alert us to an attack well in advance. We have extra time." Trina sat and crossed her legs in front like a pretzel, then patted the space next to her, gesturing for Hannah to sit.

I smiled lovingly at Em. I was so damn proud of her.

"A busy beaver, I presume. That's my Em. What will you do to occupy your time once you get everything squared away? I've no doubt the improvements in the systems won't take too long to accomplish. I'm not suggesting we go on another scouting mission, but it would be nice to commandeer a tiller or auger versus digging holes or turning the soil by hand. You could convert them to solar power or something?" I offered hopefully.

"Is that a serious suggestion?" Hannah asked.

"Um, maybe, but not if it's going to put anyone in harm's way. Those are luxury items. The shovel and other hand tools work just as well." Suddenly I felt guilty for such a selfish recommendation.

Trina and Hannah shared another of their private looks, and then Trina spoke. "We've spent most of our time salvaging the most important items needed for survival. I suppose I'm leery of becoming too industrialized. Simple has served us well, but I'm open to reconsidering."

Normally it took me a while to warm to people, but there was something about Trina and Hannah that disarmed my tendency to let Em carry the conversation. Alcohol also helped to fuel my confidence. I took another swig of the mead before clarifying. "No, my gut says to keep things as they are. It was my sore back talking, and she's a big whiny baby. More exercise will not kill me. Hey, are there other kids in the camp beside the small troupe I met today?"

"Who did you meet? Wait, let me guess. I still smell remnants of fish. You must have met Harley, Finn, Sadie, and Bruiser." Trina's look of affection was evident on her face. "There are two other children, but they're younger and extremely fragile. Our resident furniture maker cares for them. I see she insisted you take two of her bamboo chairs."

"Yeah. I didn't even ask her name. That was rude of me. By the way, why do they call the tall, gangly kid Bruiser?"

"When we found Harley, Sadie, Finn, and Bruiser, he was covered in bruises. He took a beating, allowing the rest to escape. Harley was beside herself and insisted we go back to save him and the rest of the kids. I told her we needed a better plan of attack than to go off half-cocked with emotion. Fortunately, as we were carefully making our way back to the compound, Bruiser found us. He helped Cam and Maddie escape as well." Trina's face pinched as if she were reexperiencing a trauma.

"Cam and Maddie?" Em asked.

"The other children. One is seven, and the other eight— beautiful little girls. Their mother was raped and killed in front of them. She kept fighting to the end, and they made an example of her. Daria is the furniture artesian, and she's about the only one who can soothe Cam and Maddie," Trina added.

That answered my question about the name of the furniture maker.

"They live in her cabin. She doesn't have a partner and seems content to be their adoptive mother."

I was almost afraid to ask. "Were other kids left behind?"

Trina and Hannah shared another private look, and I could see the discomfort in their expressions.

"There were. It has taken everything in my arsenal of tricks to keep Harley from taking matters into her own hands. Even though Bruiser told her they didn't want to leave," Trina explained.

"*The others* sound barbaric. Why would anyone want to stay?" Em asked the question on the tip of my tongue.

"Like a cult, the leader is very charismatic. At first, the kids felt protected. Harley was always wary and not as susceptible to his rhetoric. I don't think she garnered as much notice as some other girls who developed more nicely. Looking like a boy has worked to her advantage. She'd decided long ago that religion was not her cup of tea."

"Cults are very hard to combat. Not too many people are successful at reprogramming someone who is ensconced in their teachings," Em noted sadly.

"Harley also knew she was a lesbian. There was no way in hell she would be married off to a man twice her age. She was smart enough to lie about her age and told them she was fourteen. She also suspected that some men were taking liberties before the girls came of age." The pained expression flashed across Trina's face before she remolded her countenance, and the lines disappeared.

"How did they even find their way to that camp?" Em asked.

"Good question. I suspect each has their own story to tell. They're all a little tight-lipped about that. I get the sense that Harley was on her own before arriving. It's possible Harley's parents kicked her out of their home. It wouldn't be the first time that happened to a queer kid. Anyway, she formed a bond with Sadie and Finn, who had an epiphany about themselves, realizing they were both lesbians. Bruiser had a different idea of what it means to be a faithful Christian, and he didn't like what was happening in the camp. He took on the role of protector. None of their small gang wanted any part of the cult. Sneaking around at night, they learned enough to know it was time to go." Hannah tipped her bottle of mead and took a long pull, as if that would sterilize the story she'd just told.

My mouth ran before I realized my ass didn't have the capital to pay up. "We have to rescue the kids. I'm assuming that when you say come of age, you mean they are under fifteen." I almost couldn't form the next words. "Is fifteen considered a proper marriage age?"

The disgust on Trina's face was clear as she nodded once. "I have to worry about the safety of those in our compound. If what Bruiser tells us is correct, the brainwashing is complete. We won't be able to free them. Even if we were successful, they might sabotage this camp and run back to *the others*. I can't take that risk. I'm sorry."

"They're kids, for shit's sake," I implored.

"Don't you think I know that?" This was the first time I heard even a hint of anger in Trina's voice.

Em laid her hand on mine. "Hon, you have to let it go. Everyone can't be saved, especially if they don't want to be liberated."

I tried to keep my unkind thoughts in check. A sixteen-year-old kid seemed to have more chutzpah than Trina. I didn't want to think less of her, but I did. She was a commanding leader, and if she wanted to lead a rescue mission, others would follow.

"Lise, this issue has not been entirely resolved. For the moment, this is the best course of action. We've discussed this before, and there may come a time to reassess."

Hannah's soothing voice calmed me. Besides, what was I really offering? I had no fighting skills. It wasn't like I was going to charge into battle to save those kids. I had suggested that others take the risk. I was nothing more than a self-righteous prig willing to put others at risk for my personal sense of right and wrong.

"I'm sorry. I'm acting like a spectator, yelling at the quarterback to do something I've no skill at myself." I leaned back in my comfortable chair and sighed.

"It's all right. If it helps, I've vacillated over the months regarding this dilemma. My gut tells me the time to act will come. Today is not that day. I hope we can still be friends," Trina offered.

"Of course," Em answered for both of us.

CHAPTER TEN

The sweat dripped uncomfortably down my face as I tried to wipe it away with the sleeve of my T-shirt. Finally, I gave up and made my way to the spigot to wash my hands and throw cold water on my face. I needed to drink more water before I passed out. I reassessed my comment that more exercise wouldn't kill me. It felt like I was on the verge of death by aching muscles. Lifting my T-shirt to wipe my face, I was startled by Harley, who had snuck up on me.

"Hey, Garden Gnome."

I squinted at Harley. "That's not a very appealing title. I think I prefer the Garden Virtuoso."

"Whatever." Harley's lip curled in adolescent protest. "Wasn't sure if you would rat me out to Trina, so I came clean."

"I heard."

"Thought you might. Your wife's not only hot, but she's cool and really smart. Like a genius or something. Trina lets me hang out with her and help sometimes, and in just a few hours, I learned so much from Em."

I laughed. "Yup. She's all that and more."

"You're smart too. I agree with you. We should rescue the kids. I've been working on Trina ever since they found us. Don't get me wrong, I respect Trina. Probably more than most other adults, but a lot of damage can occur while we're dicking around. Trina doesn't know the half of it. Finn and Sadie won't speak up. They're afraid that everyone will judge them."

"You shouldn't sneak around and eavesdrop on adult conversations." *That was the best I could come up with?*

"Why not? That's how I educate myself. I knew exactly what my parents wanted to do with me before they sent me away. I ran right before the war started. Ironic, huh, that I ended up in a place that would have been perfect in my parents' eyes? Pray the fucking gay away." Harley spit on the ground in apparent disgust. "Doesn't matter now because soon enough, I plan on being part of those conversations you all seem to think I'm too young for."

"Sounds like you already are. I'll bet you've had plenty of discussions with Trina about this issue."

"I have." Harley puffed out her chest. "I have a plan. It's a good one. I just need her to listen to me. You could talk to

Em, and then Em could convince Trina. She respects Em. I've been watching."

I didn't like the sound of that. "Does that mean you don't believe she respects me?" I pounded my hand against my heart. "Ouch, that hurts."

"I don't mean to be rude or anything. You have passion, but not the kind of brains that Trina will listen to. I'm not saying you aren't smart." Harley stuck her hands in her pockets.

"Okay, just for shits and grins, what's your plan?" I decided not to let her assessment hurt, even though I constantly had to work at not feeling inadequate compared to my brilliant wife.

Harley shot me her cocky smile. "Wanna take a break and sit on your porch? Maybe you can share some of that mead?"

I chuckled and beckoned her to follow. "Nice try. I'm guessing Trina has a no underage drinking rule. I'm surprised you haven't asked forgiveness when breaking that rule."

Harley shrugged. "Y'all seem to need it more than us."

As we sat in the chairs, I prodded Harley, "So, tell me about this plan of yours."

"Lise, have you ever played chess before?"

"When I was younger. I wasn't very good at it because I didn't have the patience nor the foresight. What does that have to do with your plan?"

"I used to be an exceptional chess player. It didn't win me friends or girls, but it taught me strategy. Anticipating your opponent's moves is the key to winning. Every single contingency must be accounted for. How will they react to an aggressive approach? When is it worth sacrificing your queen? When should you retreat or sit back and wait for the perfect moment? Those are all the questions needing answers. Trina's a good chess player, but she's a bit too cautious."

"What about her concern that the kids will present a risk? They may have been indoctrinated and are beyond reach."

"You know Hannah, right? And, you've met Daria. I trust in their skills."

"Why did you stay so long? Surely you figured out the camp long before leaving," I asked.

Harley shrugged. "There were a lot of vulnerable kids in the camp that needed someone to protect them. We were a lot stronger together. I couldn't leave them so unprotected."

I nodded. My respect for Harley was growing. "I got the sense that Trina is biding her time and will be on the same page when she deems all the stars in the universe are aligned. I watched this show once about chess. Isn't there something called the end game or the long game?"

Harley frowned. "Yeah, but I used to demolish my opponents before they played the long game. Surprise attacks work."

"I suspect they sometimes do until they don't."

"*The others* with the black bands always celebrate with their moonshine after a wedding. That's when they're most vulnerable. One girl turns fifteen soon. At least that's what they believe because she lied about her age. They'll marry her off on her birthday. That will give us an edge. Those celebrations get out of hand in a lot of ways. It's dreadful. Gave all of us nightmares. Trina doesn't know the grim details. We haven't told her. I know we should have, but..."

Harley choked up before gaining strength in her voice. "We have to stop them. Please?"

"Why haven't you been honest with Trina about everything?"

"She already feels guilty about her decision to wait. Even though I don't always agree with her, I respect her. She's a good leader, and I don't want to cause her unnecessary pain. I'd rather appeal to her logical side. Em can do that for us."

"So why not ask Em yourself?" I turned to look Harley in the eye.

"She's kind of intimidating, you know. She's even more intense than Trina."

"After you get to know her better, you'll see a different side, but I guess I understand that perception. You would have laughed your ass off if you'd seen me when I first met Em and how I acted around her. With far less bravado than you possess in your pinky." I held up my hand and wiggled my finger.

"Bruiser was wrong, you know. Not everyone that was left behind wants to be there. My girlfriend only stayed because her older sister is completely brainwashed by them. Her sister was married off, and at first, the asshole was decent to her. It didn't take long for him to convince her she needed to take care of the other men's needs. He's nothing more than a post-apocalyptic pimp. I begged her to come with us, but she wouldn't leave without her sister. She lied about her age too."

"She's the one who is getting married, isn't she?" I asked. I didn't want my guess to be right.

"Yeah, we've got to save her. Even though she's going to be sixteen and not fifteen, it's not right what they're doing.

106

It's not too late. At first, I thought they had already violated her, but then Silas, the leader, warned that anyone who touched his virgin bride would face a death sentence. I wanted to slit their throats for even thinking about doing that to her, but she made me promise not to do anything. She was worried they would punish her sister." Harley angrily swiped away a tear.

I put my hand on her shoulder. "I'll talk to Em, I promise, but you should tell Trina what you told me. I think she has broader shoulders than you think, and it might make a difference to know there is someone in the camp who doesn't want to be there. Come on, kid, I could use your help in the orchard. Go get the rest of your gang. I'd love to exploit your young backs to help me dig the rest of the holes for the trees."

†

The more I thought about what Harley had shared with me, the greater my agitation. I paced in our tiny house, and that's how Em found me when she returned that evening. I hadn't started dinner yet because my agitation had slowly grown like a cancer spot on my skin. It wasn't like making dinner each night was solely my responsibility, but since I worked in the garden, I knew it was a lot easier to gather the vegetables and begin. The snick of the door caused me to look in her direction. I imagine she could see the crazed look in my eyes.

"Lise," she started gently, "I thought we settled this last night. You can't save someone who doesn't want to be saved."

I stopped pacing. "What if that's not entirely true? Harley says her girlfriend is still in that camp, and she only stayed because her sister wouldn't leave. Trina doesn't know that. Maybe it would make a difference. I should have called social services on that bastard when I had a chance. They didn't want to stay. I saw it in their eyes." I looked at Em, imploring her to pardon me for not taking action.

Em slowly approached and gathered me in her arms, stroking my back to calm me. "They might not have wanted to stay with your brother-in-law, but they wanted to be with their mom."

While in her embrace, I shook my head. No matter how many years had passed, I still felt guilty about not doing more to get Kim, Rylee, and Brook away from Kim's abusive husband. I'd left that day and never tried to make contact, nor did I ever make that call to social services. It was an idle threat, but probably what I should have done.

"It's all a moot point right now, anyway. The chances that your family survived are low. You know that, right?" Em soothed.

I pushed away from her, not because I didn't need her arms around me, but because I wanted to wallow in my anger.

"Doubtful. Men like him are like cockroaches. They always survive. If there was even a chance there's a God in this pitiful world, he would have been the first to go." I could almost feel my blood pressure rise. "On the other hand, that son of a bitch might have actually saved Kim, Rylee, and Brook. He bought into that survivalist militia crap—hook, line, and sinker. They could very well be a part of some group that's still alive. In fact, I heard he took them to a remote place in these very mountains. Karma would exist if he picked a fight with the wrong guy and survived only long enough to get his ass shot off." I briefly wondered if now was the right time to broach the crazy notion of looking for them.

Em grabbed my hand and led me to the small love seat. "Come, let's talk about this."

"I can't get the look of pleading from Rylee out of my head. Brook just clung to her mom as if she could protect her by holding on. I broke my promise to Rylee."

"You haven't seen Kim for nearly ten years. Maybe she got out. You said you heard he'd started to hurt the kids. I don't think your sister would have put up with that. No mother allows someone to hurt their kids," Em reasoned.

I looked at her with incredulity. "You've never lied to me before. You know that isn't true. Plenty of mothers fail to protect their children. I don't like thinking that Kim could be one of them, but the evidence on that day when she wouldn't come with me was pretty convincing."

"These stranded kids remind you of your nieces, don't they?"

I nodded. I knew I needed to push my guilt aside because we had the more pressing issue of rescuing Harley's girlfriend and any other kids left behind. "What if these kids are waiting for someone to save them?"

"Okay, you're right. Do you want me to talk with Trina?"

"I want all of us to talk with her. Harley included. She has a plan. She knows things about the camp that are helpful. I'm not saying it won't be a risk, but it's worth it."

"Wait, you aren't suggesting you plan to join them on this raid, are you?" Em stopped rubbing circles on my hand.

"Harley trusts me. I can't let her down."

"You're a gardener, Lise, not a warrior."

"Yeah, I know I'm just a lowly gardener and not some brilliant scientist like you," I answered bitterly and then added, "but I did fine the other day. I can hold my own."

"You know that's not what I meant." Em sighed. "I call bullshit. The fact that you woke up several times last night tells a different story. You're still having nightmares after your excursion. I should have said something then. Making the liquid nutrients was absolutely doable, and you know it. You were hoping to find fruit trees and berry bushes. You're not fooling me, Lise."

I let a small smile form on my lips. "Maybe. I can train, learn to use a gun. I need to do this, Em, don't you understand? It's my absolution for not acting when I should have."

Em took an exaggerated breath and turned away, avoiding my eyes. When she twisted her wedding ring, I knew how agitated she was. I let her work through her emotions, keeping quiet for what seemed like an hour but was probably only a minute or two.

"Okay, you win. I don't like it, but I have to respect your decisions. Can we wait until tomorrow to talk with Trina and Hannah?"

I nodded. "I haven't started dinner yet. How does a simple stir-fry sound?"

"Perfect. Let me cook while you relax."

"I won't argue with you. My back is killing me. Even with Harley and gang, finishing the orchard was hard work. The true testament to my skills will show itself in the next couple of weeks while I baby them back to health."

"My Garden Virtuoso. That's your new nickname around the camp."

I snorted. "Nuh-uh. My new nickname is Garden Gnome."

"Who called you that?"

"Harley." I laughed. "Right before she pleaded with me to help rescue her girlfriend."

"Harley is a little delinquent. She's too young to have a girlfriend."

I raised my eyebrow. "Harley is almost seventeen. I'll bet you already had some unsuspecting girl's panties around her ankles by the time you turned seventeen."

"Maybe, but she wasn't my girlfriend."

I busted out in laughter. "I'm glad I met you after you toned your wild ways, or I would have been another notch on your bedpost."

"Never. I fell in love with you the moment I laid eyes on you."

"Sweet talker." I pushed on her arm. "Go, make dinner, wench, before I decide you're too irresistible and drag you to bed."

"Well, if that's on the menu, I'll take door number two, please."

My stomach growled on cue. "Raincheck?"

CHAPTER ELEVEN

The next morning, I forced myself awake, not wanting to see Rylee's beseeching eyes anymore as the scene with my sister played out again in my dreams. Slipping carefully from the bed, I dressed quickly. I planned to gather enough eggs for breakfast to bring to the main house.

My stirring must have woken Em because one bleary eye, and then the other, popped open. "What are you doing?"

"Shh, go back to sleep. You have a few more minutes. I'm going to collect eggs."

Em tossed the covers aside. "I'll come with you."

The crisp morning air was almost as good as a shower and a cup of coffee to wake us. I sniffed the air, and the distinct odor of wood smoke filled my olfactory glands. I loved that smell in the morning. The chatter of birds had combined with the melodious sounds of the early morning. The rooster added his voice to the mixture in the same way that individual musicians contributed to jazz fusion. The different hues of orange, yellow, and red in the morning sky faded to blue. The only sense left untapped was taste as we ambled along to the chicken coop, hand in hand.

"I feel good this morning," I stated.

Em narrowed her eyes, trying to decipher if I was telling her the complete truth or fudging a bit. "You had another nightmare. Want to tell me about it?"

"No, I'm good. The morning air is like nature's spa for me. I'm trying to appreciate everything in the here and now."

"Well, it's the simple things like snuggling in bed with you each night that do it for me," Em stated as she squeezed my hand. "So, I'm going to stick with valuing the then and there. I haven't completely woken yet. Do you think Trina and Hannah will have coffee by the time we arrive?"

I nodded before opening the door to the henhouse. After quickly filling the basket, we headed to the cabin where Harley and her gang lived. It was a cramped space for the four of them, but I suspected they didn't want separation from their notion of stability.

I set down the basket and knocked three times on the scarred wood door. Harley rubbed her eyes when she answered in a set of warm sweats.

"Morning, Hurricane Harley," I stated in my most chipper voice.

Harley scowled and blinked her eyes at the same time. "What are you doing here so early? And don't call me that."

113

"Don't call me the Garden Gnome, and I won't call you Hurricane Harley."

"Fine. How come you're here?" Harley casually rested her body against the door frame.

"Time to discuss plans to get your girlfriend away from the black bands." I smiled at her.

"Really? You mean it?" Harley pushed away from the door, almost vibrating with renewed energy. "Uh, Em, are you going to help us?" she shyly asked.

Em chuckled. "I'll join the conversation with Trina and Hannah. We'll see about working out a plan. What's my nickname?"

I covered my mouth to keep from laughing when Harley blushed as she answered, "Sexy Savant."

"I'll take it. You know my Garden Virtuoso is a virtuoso in many aspects of her life." Em winked.

"Yeah, I know, we all heard that first night," she replied cheekily.

I coughed. "Come on, let's go. I have eggs."

"I'll put on my shoes." I heard stirring inside the cabin and muffled voices. Harley turned around and whispered, "Shh, go back to bed. I'll be back in a few hours. Don't go fishing without me." She leaned inside the cabin and grabbed her boots, carefully closing the door behind her. "Is there a reason we have to do this at the ass crack of dawn?" She dropped on the ground and began lacing her boots.

"Trina gets distracted by all the happenings in the camp as the day progresses. Her attention is more narrowly focused in the morning. While she's relaxed at night when sharing a pint of mead, that isn't the best time to talk about plans that require laser focus," Em said matter-of-factly.

"Oh, that makes sense." Harley stood and started walking. "You coming?" she challenged. "Best to do this while you still have the nerve."

"Us? I seem to remember you confessing your nervousness around—"

"All part of my plan." Harley cut me off. "Awkward teen who needs the support of adults to make her case." She grinned as she walked the path with confidence.

"You do need our support," I insisted.

Harley shrugged. "I would have eventually convinced Trina to act, but I wanted to do it sooner rather than later. Our window of opportunity will close if we don't get on this."

How was it possible that I was more unnerved about the impending conversation than Harley? I'd always let my emotions dictate my actions, except for the one time I should have acted rashly and called the authorities on my brother-in-law. That mistake would haunt me for the rest of my life. I'd never looked back and checked on my sister after she kicked me out of her house and told me to never return. Em would be our steady, logical voice. I knew it, and so did Harley, even if she wanted to present an unflappable image.

†

I shouldn't have been surprised that Hannah and Trina answered the door quickly and looked like they'd been moving around for hours.

"This is a pleasant surprise. Although, I should be wary about Harley leading the pack," Trina said with a smile.

"Hopefully, you haven't had breakfast yet." I held up the basket of eggs.

"No, we haven't," Hannah answered. "I was getting ready to walk to the hen house. How do scrambled eggs with smoked trout sound?"

"Perfect, I'll help," I offered.

Trina waved us inside. "Come in. Coffee?"

"Yes, please," Em answered quickly.

Harley and I nodded in agreement.

I kept my ear metaphorically to the ground as I followed Hannah into the kitchen. After Trina guessed the purpose of our visit, I strained to hear what was being said.

"I'm assuming you want to talk about the stranded kids at the other camp. Except for a few feeble attempts to broach our territory, they've kept their distance. Why would I want to start a war with them?" The tone in Trina's voice wasn't accusatory, merely curious.

Harley took the lead and jumped into the conversation. "I didn't tell you everything because I didn't think you would take me seriously or place enough value on my relationship. You think I'm just some dumb kid."

"Not true," Trina answered. "I know you're a thoughtful, fiercely loyal young woman who wants to do the right thing, but I have this entire camp to think of. Why don't you tell me what you've left out?"

"Bruiser wasn't completely honest about those left behind. He didn't know, so it isn't his fault. My girlfriend stayed with her sister, but I know she wanted to leave with us. She told me she needed more time to convince her sister or to let events unfold that would make a case for her."

"What events?" Trina asked.

"When she turns fifteen in two weeks, they're going to marry her off. She isn't really fifteen, but they don't know that, and it doesn't matter anyway because sixteen is still child rape. Her older sister married the minute they arrived at camp. Her father approved, but his wife wasn't sold on the idea at first. Silas, he's the black-band leader, picked up on the rancor between the two. Silas stepped in one night when the asshole was beating on his wife. Played the fucking hero. He wanted her for his own. There are more men than women in the camp, and he didn't like his choices. Rylee's mom was beautiful. She looked a little like Lise, only kind of softer."

My head snapped up, and I ran into the living area. My voice wobbled as I asked, "Did you say Rylee?"

Hannah had followed me after I abruptly stopped whisking the eggs. Her brow furrowed as she looked at Trina.

Trina turned her attention to me. "Lise?"

"What's her sister's name?" I ignored everyone but Harley, who had the answers I did and didn't want to hear.

"Brook," Harley answered.

At that moment, the room swam, and I stumbled backward into Hannah, who led me to the loveseat, where Em stared wide-eyed and appeared as shell-shocked as me.

Harley seemed to put the pieces together more quickly than Trina or Hannah. Em recovered quickly, placing her arm around my shoulder and pulling me to her.

"God, I should have known. You're like the adult version of Rylee. She has your eyes, her mother's eyes," Harley amended.

I almost couldn't push out the next question, but I forced myself to ask, "Is my sister still alive?"

Harley looked at her feet and wouldn't meet my eyes. "No."

I lost my fight to stay in the present as a kind of wailing noise overwhelmed my overstimulated senses, and my heart beat too rapidly in my chest. I later learned that the wailing noise was me.

†

It felt like an out-of-body experience, and not in a beneficial way. Eventually, what hovered outside returned to my body, and I croaked, "I'm okay."

Hannah had rushed to the kitchen and come back with a glass of water, setting it in front of me on the coffee table. Trina shared a look with her wife, waiting as Em tended to me.

Em's concerned hazel eyes met mine as she searched for the truth in my words. Ever the logical one, Em reached for the water and brought it to my lips, encouraging me to drink. She kept making circles on my back as I trembled while taking small sips of the water.

"Right, okay, I suspect the facts laid out have changed the landscape. I'm not suggesting that Lise's nieces or Harley's girlfriend are more important than any other life in the compound, but family is one of the few things left that's worth fighting for. I'm not merely talking about blood relatives, but Rylee means a lot to Harley, and that should hold greater weight for us all. You said on the first day of our arrival that this compound is a refuge for the LGBTQ+ community." Em set up the argument to rescue the kids.

Trina put her hands on her thighs and leaned forward. "It is."

"They'll kill her if they ever find out about us. She swore that Brook would never say a word. I'm not so sure. Every day their brainwashing burrows inside more thoroughly than I thought possible. Brook was so enamored with her new husband, even after he started dropping hints about the men's needs. Eventually he spelled out what was required of her, and convinced her she would need to make herself available to his friends—for the good of the camp. He called it her God-given duty." Harley's voice took on a hard edge.

I heard myself ask the question, even though it sounded far away to me. "How did my sister die?"

"I don't know." Harley wouldn't look at me.

"Yes, you do. I need to know." The hatred was growing inside, and I couldn't do a thing to stop it.

"I only heard the rumors. Honest, I can't say for sure," Harley answered.

"Please tell me what you heard," I pleaded.

"Bruiser told me he overheard one of the men say it wasn't fair for their leader to have such a fine woman all to himself. The unrest splintered the group, and he was afraid of losing control, so he agreed to share her until they could find more women. He used all his charms to convince her the solution was only temporary, but when she also learned about her daughter being passed around, that was the final straw." Harley nervously licked her lips. "She poisoned herself. Silas told everyone she fell ill from tainted food. Without proper medicine, she didn't make it."

The tears I'd held at bay slipped effortlessly down my cheeks. It wouldn't be the only time I would cry for my sister or myself for failing to prevent her fate.

CHAPTER TWELVE

I remained on the periphery as Trina, Em, and Harley formed a plan. In the end, we decided a small group would slip in and out as quickly as possible.

I argued that Brook might be more inclined to come with us if I went along. My resemblance to her mother worked in my favor. It would be easy to convince Brook that I was her aunt. The last time I'd seen the girls, they had been only six and eight, but the family resemblance was too strong to ignore.

Em and Trina grudgingly admitted I'd made a good case for being a part of the extraction team. That was what Harley was calling us, as if we were some highly skilled elite army unit.

We had two weeks to train and prepare the grounds against the black-band camp. The south side of their base had a large fallen tree that Harley's gang had hollowed out as their means of entering and exiting the compound without being seen. The tree was too large to move, so the black band built an electric fence around the massive obstacle, not realizing the tree had decomposed inside.

Harley was sure that Rylee covered Bruiser's tracks after he escaped by camouflaging the tree that led into the camp. Harley suggested setting a dozen traps around the perimeter of the hollowed tree in a random pattern.

It was a calculated risk to prepare booby traps before Rylee's wedding night, but that would give our team the best chance of escape, should a few members remain sober enough to cause real harm. There was also the perimeter patrol to worry about. If we had to, we would take to the trees and wait them out for days. That's how Harley and gang had made a clean getaway in the past. I wasn't so sure my old body would survive sitting in a tree for that long.

†

When Em came home two days later with a distressed look on her face, I had to ask, knowing I wouldn't like what she had to say. "You're worried we won't be able to rescue them, aren't you?"

Em shook her head and implored me not to ask any more questions. "No, I'm not concerned about that."

"Then what is it? Come on, spill. Em, you've never sugar-coated anything before, so please don't start now."

Without saying a word, Em pulled a bottle of mead from the refrigerator, walked outside, and sat in one of the bamboo chairs. She knew I would follow her.

After taking a swig, she gave voice to her concern. "If you wait until after the men have passed out, it will be too late for Rylee. Harley won't talk about it, but I know it's eating her alive. Harley told me that after your sister died, Silas set his sights on Rylee because she looks so much like your sister. The only good thing is that he wants her pure before the wedding. Harley believes Silas will control his followers. For now."

"I know. Harley told me that before I knew that her girlfriend was my niece. We have to get her out before he has a chance…" I couldn't finish my sentence.

"That wouldn't be the wisest course of action. Harley knows that, and so do you. She said something strange to me today."

I didn't want to hear anymore, but I kept quiet until Em filled in the blanks.

"She said she was sacrificing her queen, but a pawn would resurrect her."

I thought that Harley didn't give herself enough credit if she thought she was only a pawn, saving Rylee, her queen. "A chess analogy. She's envisioning all the potential moves."

"Well, then there is one that maybe we haven't considered. If Harley can provide forewarning, maybe Rylee can help on her end and stave off the inevitable for one night. That's all that's needed."

"That means slipping inside the camp before the ceremony."

"Yes. It's risky."

From the shadows like the little delinquent Harley was, she appeared and said, "I'll do it. I know how to send a message without anyone else finding out."

"Shit, Harley, you need to stop sneaking up on people and eavesdropping on their private conversations," I chastised.

"You need to stop talking about me behind my back and not including me in the plans."

"Harley, you should know I would have talked with you about this tomorrow," Em responded. "Are you sure you have a way to send her a message?"

"I do. I used to leave a special flower that grew in the woods when I wanted Ry to meet me by the tree. I promised her we would be back for her. She'll understand. The garden is close to the tree, so I can be in and out in minutes. Ry is real smart. She'll hold him off. She has to." Harley's voice hitched with emotion.

"If you tell me where to leave the flower, I can do that," I offered.

"No offense, Lise, but I'm a lot smaller than you and can crawl through the hollowed tree much faster. We have to set the traps, anyway. I'll do it the night before. She'll figure it out because Ry knows chess and that's all about strategy. I taught her to always have several options to get out of an attack. I'd draw a board in the soil and use the pieces of wood I carved." Harley looked wistful.

It saddened me to think the memory of playing chess in the soil had created such a look of longing. They should have been stealing sips of alcohol and making out in their rooms instead of doing homework like normal teenagers, not creeping around, playing a game of chess in the soil while tending to a garden.

"Okay." What else could I say? "Will you help me with the hydroponic garden tomorrow?"

Spending time with Harley in the garden would give me a chance to ask about my nieces, and I desperately needed to know more about both of them. Harley had described Rylee's appearance, but I knew little about how she'd grown as a person. I knew even less about Brook.

"Sure thing, Lise, but don't wake me at the ass crack of dawn." She flicked her bangs aside. "I need my beauty sleep."

I laughed. "Nine too early for you?"

"Nah, that should work. Although I expect a cup of coffee when you come to the door. You want Sadie, Finn, and Bruiser to help, too?"

"No, just you. Is that okay?"

Harley looked closely at me like she was trying to figure out her next chess move, with her head tilted to the side and one eye squinted. Her features relaxed, she smiled and said, "Sure."

†

As directed, the next morning I arrived at Harley's door with a to-go cup of coffee in my hands. She looked raring to go, in cargo shorts and a hoodie that was probably covering a plain blue T-shirt. Blue was clearly a favorite color. All her T-shirts were various shades of blue.

She grabbed the coffee and muttered, "Thanks."

I led the way to the greenhouse where I'd started on the hydroponic garden. With Trina's help, Em built several tanks and an irrigation system, allowing recycled water to flow through the gutters. I'd cut evenly spaced holes in the gutters where the mature vegetables would grow to harvest-ready size. Mature plants weren't yet part of the gutter system, but they would be after the starters reached a particular phase. Coco peat wasn't readily available, so we had to fashion our own peat moss for our seedlings. Since our compound was in the woods, I'd experimented with decomposed wood and moss, finding the combination worked almost as good as some starter trays I might find in a nursery.

I was explaining the hydroponic system to Harley when she interrupted and cut to the chase.

"Lise, I know you didn't ask me to help you today because you want to make me some hotshot hydroponic gardener. Ry would love that, but it isn't me. I only volunteered for garden duty to get closer to Ry. She figured that out on the first day we met. So why am I here?"

"I wanted to ask about my nieces. What they're like? What kind of people have they grown into? Will they accept me as their aunt?"

"You mean because you're a lesbian?" Harley laughed. "Well, duh, you know that Ry will. The jury's still out on Brook. You know they grew up with Bible-thumping parents, right?"

"Yeah. So did I, but I escaped."

"They're both quiet. Well behaved. But I could tell right away that Ry had a little fire inside. She would do little things to buck the system. Nothing that most people would notice, but I did."

"Like what?"

"Well, underneath the hideous dresses they made us wear, she wore boxers. I guess she stole them from one of the men. She had a stash of clothing that she hid next to the hollow tree. She dreamed of ways to escape long before I ended up in their camp." Harley grinned.

"What else?" I was so curious to learn more.

"She read a lot, and when she found this plant, deadly nightshade, she told me she'd already experimented with it to see if it would work. She slipped a small amount into the moonshine her sister's husband and friends were drinking. The plant has atropine and scopolamine in it. Ironic that assholes use those chemicals as a date rape drug. I think Ry reveled in the irony. They all thought they'd had a bad batch of moonshine. That's why I believe Ry will know what to do. If she gets my message, she'll slip some in his drink."

"Most people don't grow deadly nightshade because atropine and scopolamine in the plant can cause paralysis. I'm surprised she knew how to find the plant."

"Like I said, she was quiet but had this kind of underlying fury. Ry told me she read everything she could get her hands on because she'd need it one day. She hated her father. At first, when Silas killed him, she thought Silas might not be so bad. He'd protected her mother. They don't pay much attention to kids, especially the boys. Bruiser was able to hang around and learn things. Rylee started paying close attention. Bruiser taught her how to sneak around without anyone knowing. It was a crushing blow when she found out what was going on with her mom and sister."

"And Brook. What's she like?"

Harley frowned. "Like a perfect cult wife. Brook does whatever her husband tells her to do. She doesn't look like you or Ry, and she doesn't act like either of you. She told Ry she was lucky because Silas had chosen her, and it was an honor to serve him. Brook was sure he could 'straighten' Rylee out." Harley sneered.

"Brook might not look like her mother, but the acorn did not fall far from that tree. My sister was devoted to her beliefs. Unshakeable. Kim believed a man had the right to strike his wife to keep her in check." I started grinding my teeth as my jaw clenched in anger. "She got that asinine notion from our mother. For good Catholic girls, divorce is out of the question. According to dear old Mom, the women are responsible for doing everything in their power to keep the marriage together. My sister Kim learned that important lesson."

"Well, Brook never stepped out of line, and still he beat her." Harley shoved her hands in her pockets and shuffled her feet. She sounded so unsure when she asked, "What'll we do if Ry won't leave without Brook?"

"We won't give Brook a choice. I'll gag and blindfold her if I need to. We're getting them both out. I promise."

"I believe you. I know that you have this false bravado, kind of like me, but you also have that same fire that Ry has, also like me. When backed into a corner, we fight like hell, and we win."

I hoped Harley was correct. Losing wasn't an option. I had a chance for a redo, and I wasn't about to walk away a second time.

†

Trina asked Em, Harley, and me to dinner three days before Rylee's birthday. I spent two hours every day climbing trees. I would have laughed if anyone had ever suggested I would do that in my late thirties. Hannah had gently proposed I learn to shoot, but I'd flatly turned her down. I would never become a warrior. That wasn't ever in the cards for me.

I continued to distract myself in the garden while Harley and Em finished building the homemade traps. Hopefully, the snares would give our extraction team the time we needed to make it back to the specially engineered scooters. We planned on taking them as close to the compound as reasonable to stay undetected. When I'd first seen them, I thought they looked more like a miniaturized motorcycle made for a grandmother, but at least the seat was long enough to fit two people—comfortably. The imperceptible whine of electric motors with the lithium batteries Harley and Em had fashioned to the scooters gave us an edge. It was both a blessing and a burden that *the others'* black-band camp was at least twenty-five miles away.

After inspecting each tiny shoot in the hydroponic garden to ensure they were growing as expected, I took a stroll in the compound and checked the other gardens I'd been neglecting. Not that I was the only gardener in the camp, but I felt an intense responsibility for a robust harvest, needing to establish my worth in our new home. Approaching the storage unit made me realize I didn't have a good sense of how much food was available or the storage capacity we would need to take advantage of an increased bounty with the new garden.

I was delighted to find the frozen blackberries left over from the previous season. I had to trust that the radiation hadn't affected last season's berries on the plentiful wild bushes all over the compound. I seriously doubted that anyone would have taken the chance to freeze the berries if they had worried about contamination.

I figured that since we were only a few months away from a new harvest, grabbing a few bags wouldn't be an issue. I knew how much Em loved blackberry pie. She deserved a treat. I headed back to our cabin, hoping to surprise Em and our friends, who I already appreciated far more than anyone else I'd let into my life before.

I opened the front door and found Em tinkering on a trap with a nasty-looking metal device that looked like dentures for a monster. The jagged edges were pointed like finely chiseled canines.

"Hey." Em looked up. "What's in your hand?"

"Frozen blackberries. I'm going to make a few pies. It was supposed to be a surprise."

"Yum." She returned to her device, and I worried about her hand getting caught in the contraption as she tightened one of the screws.

Retrieving the precious sack of sugar, I mixed the blackberries and other ingredients for the filling. I felt Em sidle next to me. She peered over my shoulder and reached around my waist. I lightly smacked Em's fingers as she attempted to taste the filling.

"Hey, stop that. It's gross," I chastised.

"Don't you need a taste tester? Maybe there isn't enough cinnamon or sugar in the filling. I'm just trying to help." Em pulled a spoon from the drawer and dipped it inside the bowl.

"If you really want to help, you can make the crumble topping."

"Needs more cinnamon."

I grated the cinnamon bark sitting on the counter into the bowl and shot her a questioning look. "Happy?"

Em smiled, and then her look turned contemplative. "Yes, but I'll be a lot happier when everyone returns safely to the compound. I like it here. In fact, I like our life much better now than I did when I spent half my nights in a lab. I would not wish another apocalypse onto this world, but this simple life with good friends is downright utopian."

"It is, isn't it? Harley's a good kid, isn't she? She'll never have to fit into a world that only pretends to accept you. As if tolerating her choice of who to love is such a magnanimous thing for us to celebrate," I said with a fair amount of bitterness.

My thoughts drifted as I remembered what it was like for me as a young lesbian. Growing up in a deeply religious family, I found life incredibly hard in my teens. The constriction sucked the vitality from me until I'd finally left and made my own way in the world. I wasn't much older than Harley when I'd done that. Not exactly by choice. Railing against Catholicism didn't earn me any brownie points, but getting caught kissing a girl was the cherry that put me over the top. Being a lesbian was strictly forbidden. However, beating the shit out of your wife was tolerated.

Kim had already moved out of the house, but she heard about my "indiscretions" from Mom. She'd offered to take me in, but I refused, crashing on a friend's couch until I'd saved enough money to get my own place. I'd been working part time at a nursery, and they offered me a full-time job the minute they'd learned about my circumstances. With only one month until graduation from high school, I stayed until I graduated and then never looked back, finding my calling with plants. Kim had welcomed me into her home until the big fight. She was one of those who "tolerated" my choice by choosing never to talk about it.

Shaking my head to remove those old memories, I tuned back into our conversation.

"She's very bright. I talk to her as if she were one of my former colleagues. She's like a sponge, sucking everything inside until she's ready to try new things on her own." Em rinsed the spoon in the sink. "Did you know she's the one who tweaked the scooters so they not only would travel well on uneven ground, but they'll exceed the top speed of any similarly manufactured motorized vehicle?"

"Hmm, that's impressive. I know they're only kids, but I hope Ry and Harley stay together. I can't think of a better partner for my niece. I worry about Brook. Who will she find to love?"

Drying her spoon and setting it back inside the drawer, Em answered, "I'm placing my money on Bruiser."

My nose scrunched in confusion. "Why? Because he's the only straight boy here?"

"No, of course not. You haven't paid that much attention to anyone outside your garden domain, have you?"

I hung my head. Being a social butterfly was never a skill of mine. "Not really."

"There are plenty of eligible young men, but Bruiser would die for your niece. He confides in Harley. She's not the only one with expert eavesdropping skills."

I laughed. "God, you're wicked. Such a little snoop."

"Well, there isn't any mindless TV to sink into. What else can keep me so occupied? Adolescent angst is quite entertaining."

"He's a good kid, too. If we can deprogram Brook, maybe I'll play matchmaker."

"Oh, no, Aunty Meddlepants, you should stay out of it."

I chuckled. "Aunty Meddlepants. Harley is definitely rubbing off on you. Do you have a nickname for Hannah or Trina?"

"Not one that I'll share with you. You'll rat me out in a hot minute."

"What a terrible thing to say. I will not."

"You can't help yourself. When someone asks you a direct question, you don't know how to be evasive. It's why you aren't good at sneaking around, either."

"Whatever, Snoopity Doggy Breath." I stuck out my tongue.

Em breathed into her hand and sniffed before grabbing me around the middle and pulling me to her. "Now that's mean." She rested her forehead against mine, and I watched the crinkles around her eyes grow as she grinned at me.

"God, if my work colleagues could see me now." She placed a kiss on the tip of my nose. "You know that's what I love best about you. You've never given in to propriety. I hope we'll both continue the silliness until the day we die. In each other's arms, if I have my wish." She dipped her finger into the bowl as she let me go, a wicked twinkle in her eyes.

I didn't express the nagging thought that death might come sooner than either of us desired.

†

The pie was still steaming when we reached the main house. Harley jogged to us and sniffed the air.

"Mmm, pie. It smells delish. Did it just come out of the oven?"

I put my hand over the pie protectively. "Yes, and don't be rude like Em and try to stick your finger in the middle for a taste."

Harley pushed out her lips and pouted. It wasn't hard to understand how she'd passed for much younger than her seventeen years. Her smooth skin with a roundness that highlighted the baby fat of youth had not transformed yet into a more angular version that I envisioned was in her future. I'd nearly forgotten she was still a kid. We continued on the path until we'd almost reached the front door. Harley was now in step with us.

"I say we eat dessert first. Life's too short to let a pie cool completely. It's so much better warm, and I know for a fact that Trina has ice cream in her freezer. Besides being a great doc, Taylor also knows how to make ice cream," Harley said.

"Taylor?" I wrinkled my nose. I didn't remember meeting anyone named Taylor.

Em chimed in. "She runs the clinic. I was going to send you to her that night your back hurt so badly, but apparently, my golden fingers were the medicine you needed."

Since I was holding the pie, Em knocked on the door.

134

Hannah opened the door at the same time I asked, "So, do we have good drugs here? I'd have settled for two Tylenol or ibuprofen."

"Did you hurt yourself, Lise?" The crease between Hannah's brow deepened.

I shook my head. "No, I'm a baby. Digging all those holes for the orchard was hard on my middle-aged back."

"How old are you?" Harley asked.

"Thirty-nine. I'm an ancient to you."

"That's not that old." As we walked through the door, with Harley close behind me, she continued, "You know that some women have relationships with people twenty years older than themselves. It's called a May-December romance. I'm not attracted to old folks, but Finn has crushes on older women all the time. She thinks you're hot."

I almost dropped the pie with that last remark, and I heard Em laughing.

I turned to face Harley fully and watched as Harley's nose wrinkled in distaste, "But I think it's wrong what's happening at the black-band camp."

Em moved beside me, wrapping an arm around my waist and giving me a squeeze before stating, "You're right, Harley, there's a big difference between a consensual romance where there is an age difference between two adults, and when adolescent children are being offered to men like they are prized heifers. I'd feel the same if the girls were married off to older women."

"That's why I wanted to talk to everyone tonight." Trina strode into the kitchen, Hannah towering behind her. "Frankly, I haven't slept well for so long, I was starting to accept it as my punishment for not acting sooner." Trina had such a pained expression on her face, I wanted to jump in and tell her I understood. Guilt was a powerful emotion.

Hannah must have felt the same way as she rested a hand on Trina's shoulder, and I could see Trina visibly relax under the touch. Hannah turned to us all. "Come on, let's go into the living room. Dinner will hold for a few minutes, but I don't think what Trina has to say will remain inside her for much longer." Hannah began making small circles on her wife's lower back as she expertly led her to the couch. It was almost as if they had switched roles, and Hannah was the immovable force leading us all.

Trina sat heavily on the sofa as Hannah continued her light touch. "We have enough scooters for each of you to take one. That should allow you to free others besides Rylee and Brook," Trina stated with renewed authority.

The light in Harley's eyes shined brightly. "Really?" Almost as if someone had stolen her ice cream cone, her face turned somber. "If we take all of their future wives, they'll come after us."

Trina nodded. "That's why we are going to have a gathering tomorrow. I'll lay out the risks, and unless the majority overrules me, consider this your new mission."

I frowned. "That's only four scooters. It's a small team. That won't leave much room for many other children besides my nieces. Besides, I thought Bruiser said they didn't want to leave. Won't it be hard enough for us to get Brook to come with us?"

"He was talking about Brook and Ry. There are three more. One is only about six or seven, and the other two are ten and eleven. I wouldn't be surprised if they move up or rather down the age of marriage." Harley had an icy glint in her eyes, the rage barely staying below the surface.

"You never said anything about more kids. Why?" I asked.

Harley shrugged. "The minute Trina heard Bruiser say they wouldn't leave, I knew she wouldn't want to risk it. Bruiser felt so guilty he couldn't get the rest out, so I promised I wouldn't say anything about them. I thought I could convince you without betraying his trust. I knew we were running out of time. I figured after we got Ry and Brook out, we'd tell you about the other girls." Harley narrowed her eyes. "How d'you know?"

Trina shared a brief look with Hannah, then answered, "Educated guess." Shifting her focus to Em, she asked, "Do you have any more ideas that would add protections to the perimeter? I'd like to be as prepared as possible for whatever comes our way."

"I have a few ideas that should help," Em responded.

"Would you present your ideas at the gathering tomorrow?" Trina asked.

"Absolutely. We'll need to mark the traps unobtrusively, so our own patrols aren't affected. I know Taylor is bored, but I don't think she wants to be swamped by a slew of casualties of our own making." Em grinned.

The pain seemed to ease a little from Trina's pinched features as she smacked her thighs. "Right, then. After this is all resolved, maybe a small group can see about adding to our pharmacy. Taylor's been grumbling about not having enough supplies. I'd prefer we find more natural alternatives, but some medicines can't be substituted for the same effect."

Setting her hand on Hannah's thigh, she said, "The sooner we eat, the sooner we can have pie. Let's eat."

CHAPTER THIRTEEN

Under cover of darkness, Harley and I shared a scooter while Hannah led the way. Initially, Harley wanted to drive and take the lead, but Hannah quietly responded that she knew where to go. The way Hannah said it led me to believe there was a story there. One she didn't want to share. Harley had caught my eye, and I could tell she wanted to ask her about it, but I shook my head. I still let Harley drive, which was probably a good thing since she was an expert at weaving around the many obstacles in our path.

When I offered to accompany Harley and Hannah to position the traps and sneak in to give Rylee Harley's message, I wasn't dwelling on the danger. I figured that if I was there to place the traps, I'd be less likely to inadvertently

139

set one off in a panic. Em didn't like it, but she wouldn't try to talk me out of it. I was placing my life in the hands of a teenager and a model. The camp nickname for Hannah was Runway Warrior.

Hannah slowed her speed and veered to the left, dismounting and walking the bike into the heavily wooded forest. She found a dense thicket and concealed the scooter with the surrounding brush. Soon I wasn't able to see any part of her bike. For good measure, she plunked down one of the noiseless traps, if you didn't count the scream that might ensue if set off. Harley found a spot to conceal our scooter and laid down her own unpleasant surprise.

Hefting our packs, we hiked through the forest. I wasn't as quiet as Hannah and Harley, but I had become more stealthy over the past couple of weeks of training and hoped the odd snap of a twig here or there wouldn't give away our location. Caution adds a lot more time to a hike than I thought possible, but we finally reached the old tree after walking for nearly an hour.

Harley began frantically searching the area, and I wondered what the hell she was doing. I was close enough to see the near panic on her face.

"What's the matter? The tree is right there." I pointed to the old Douglas fir.

"I can't find our flower. I need our flower," Harley whispered.

Hannah touched her on the shoulder. "What does it look like?"

"It's purple and sort of looks like a small crown." Harley dropped to the ground, crawling around and pushing leaves and other debris aside in her search.

"Sounds like a Fairy Slipper." I began searching the forest floor.

It was difficult to see in the dark. We needed the moon to help. But she was stubborn tonight, hiding behind a cluster of clouds.

I felt like a treasure hunter who'd finally come across the elusive chest of gold when I found the Fairy Slipper. Gently, I plucked the flower from the earth and snuck back to Harley, who was still focused on her own search. I touched her shoulder, and she jumped.

"Shit, you scared me."

"Here." I offered her the prize. Harley sighed in relief and tentatively smiled back at me when I squeezed her shoulder.

Hannah turned from her position, looking into the compound. "Alright Harley, you're up. Lise and I will set the traps while you leave the signal for Ry. Don't forget to look for us before exiting the tree so we can guide you out safely."

Harley removed her pack and placed it on the ground before tucking the precious flower inside her hoodie. She disappeared quickly into the hollow of the tree, crawling like a commando in one of those old World War II movies.

In a zig-zag, almost random pattern, we set our traps in the dark, marking each place with a pile of small rocks and a pine cone. They would be tricky to see in the dark, but I tried hard to visualize the pattern in my head, as if I were planning where to place individual plants in a garden. That was the only way I knew how to keep myself from inadvertently tripping one of the nasty devices.

Before we finished setting the snares, Harley's head had popped from the end of the giant fir.

"Careful, five feet to the right is the first trap," I whispered. "We used pebbles and pine cones to mark the spots."

Hannah reached into her pack, pulling out an extra trap and holding it out to Harley. "You can help us dig a few holes and lay the rest of the traps." As Harley stepped up beside her, reaching for the round disc, I heard Hannah ask quietly, "Everything go ok?" In the faint light, I barely made out Harley's head nod.

Harley was quicker than either Hannah or I, and in less than ten minutes, we had laid an impressive number of nasty traps. We remained low to the ground, carefully navigating our way through the maze of surprises we had deposited in case things went to shit.

"Put them on a chessboard," I whispered.

"What?" Harley lifted her head in my direction.

"The traps. Envision a large chessboard and try to remember where on the board we set the traps."

"You're fucking brilliant, Lise. Thanks."

We stood for several minutes, memorizing the maze in our own ways. Hannah stood behind us, quietly keeping watch before gently touching us both on the arm and nodding her head towards our hidden scooters. As we ducked under branches and across dried creek beds, I gathered enough breath to ask Harley the question that had bothered me ever since she said she would leave the flower as a sign. "Why not bury a note under the flower? Wouldn't that give her more information and help her gather the other girls?"

"I used to leave notes until Brook found one hidden beneath the flower. That's how she knew about us. I couldn't take the chance. I stopped writing notes after that, but not leaving flowers."

I frowned. "Do you really think Brook would risk her sister's life?"

Harley shrugged. "She's pretty entrenched in their society. I don't know, but I wasn't willing to take the chance."

Harley climbed on the scooter, and I settled behind her for the trip back to our safe space in this new world. As we turned and headed toward home, a massive wave of relief hit me, almost causing me to lose my hold on Harley. I couldn't believe our mission had gone without a hitch. I wasn't sure if that were a good or bad omen. Either it was the calm before the storm, or we were that good.

✝

It was after midnight when we returned. I should have known Em would wait for me. She jumped into my arms the minute I opened the door and crushed me in an embrace.

"Come to bed. Don't get up early tomorrow. Everyone expects all of you to sleep in and get a good night's rest. Lack of sleep isn't a recommended way to prepare for tomorrow, or technically tonight. It's after midnight." Her rapid-fire statements, I knew, covered her concern and subsequent relief. I squeezed her to me tighter and placed a kiss on her head before turning us toward the stairs.

"By the time we reach their camp, it will be tomorrow. We were hoping to make our move after midnight," I quietly relayed.

Em nodded. "I know." Her finger grazed her wedding band before reaching for me almost frantically. Skimming her fingers down my arm, I felt goosebumps. Em could start my motor with a mere look, but my arousal went into overdrive when she barely touched me. I wasn't sure who needed this connection more, her or me. In the end, it didn't matter, as long as we had each other. I knew where this was headed, and I was a willing participant in her seduction. She knew I still had too much energy to fall asleep. Adrenaline had powered me on the return journey and hadn't released its hold on me yet. She paused at the foot of the stairs, halting my progress. I was sure she sensed my need to wind down.

Putting both hands on the sides of my face, her kiss was unhurried, leaving me with a hint of what was just around the corner. "I love you so much. I am so proud of you. You're turning into quite the badass. Time for you to relax and relish in your success. I can do quick if that's really what you want..."

I shook my head and let my heartbeat return to normal, wrapping my arms around her waist for a quick hug before entering our bedroom. Breaking apart, I allowed one hand to inch down her arm, slowly, before grabbing her hand to lead her up the stairs.

Neither of us was in a hurry. After many years together, our lovemaking had lost that frantic, tear each other's clothes off in desperation vibe, but it was not any less satisfying for either of us.

Although I wasn't the type to put on clean clothes every single day, I tossed everything into the basket in the corner of the room. After crawling around on the damp ground, both knees were wet with small clumps of mud. A chill in the air caused a shiver before I disturbed our cats and climbed under the covers. Sonny and Cher meowed in protest but padded down the stairs. They were undoubtedly headed for their second favorite spot in the cabin where they would nestle together like they did when they were kittens.

Em was slower than me as she removed her clothes and set them on top of the small dresser. She was languid in her movements when she approached the bed, and I was incredibly thankful for that as the moon reflected off her silhouette.

Over the years, her body had rounded. She was no longer the rail-thin woman whose ribs were on prominent display. Mostly, her stomach remained flat. There was only a hint of roundness to her belly, just below her waistline.

My favorite pastime was running my hands over the softness of that tiny protrusion. Em felt the same with my own rounded belly. I was the first to name mine, Buddha belly, which she promptly stole.

"Stop worshiping my Buddha belly and lie on your back so I can help you relax. You're still keyed up from tonight," she stated.

I settled onto my back as Em crawled on top. My hands naturally rested on her behind, and I stroked her as she kissed the pulse point of my neck.

Along with all her other impressive credentials, Em had a doctoral degree in the art of making love. She could bring me to the edge and keep me there for what felt like an eternity. When I finally tumbled to the other side in bliss, I would swear it was the most satisfying orgasm of my entire life, until the next time she would kiss and lick her way down my body.

"You little tease." I pushed out the words between my rapidly growing arousal.

She halted her progress to capture my eyes as her chin rested on my much rounder belly than hers. "Would you prefer fast and efficient?" she taunted.

"Maybe," I answered.

"You little liar. For that, I think I'll take my time."

I chuckled. We both knew Em was planning on taking her sweet-ass time tonight. The way my body reacted was as familiar to her as the contours of her wedding ring.

She placed butterfly kisses on the inside of my thighs as her fingers played with the tight curls surrounding my swollen clit. I held my breath in anticipation of her tongue. When Em finally lazily let the tip of her tongue connect with my clit, my hips lifted in response, seeking a greater contact. I could feel Em's smile before she removed her mouth from my clit, denying me a stronger connection.

I sighed as I let my body relax on the bed. I knew Em would not let me control the rhythm, so I might as well sit back and enjoy the ride.

"After all these years, you would have thought you'd learned by now," she teased.

"Involuntary response. Science of the human body. You know I can't control myself when you lick me like that."

Em continued to let her tongue sweep my clit and lightly stimulate the area around the opening to my vagina, readying me for her fingers. She continued to tease me until she knew I couldn't take it anymore. I felt her fingers push inside while she gently sucked on my clit, and this time she let me move my hips to the rhythm of her thrusts.

The slow in and out movement of her fingers brought me to the precipice. "Don't stop. God, Em, I'm so close."

"I know, Lise," she murmured with her mouth still on my clit.

She let the vibration of her words stimulate the area before continuing to suck. Her teeth grazing my hood was my final undoing. I let the waves of pleasure wash over me.

After making love with Em, I knew why some people talked about the earth moving similar to an earthquake. I always experienced those tiny aftershocks, and Em would wait until they all subsided before pulling her fingers out and crawling up my body to kiss me.

I pushed my hand through her hair and whispered, "Just give me a few minutes, and then I'll do my best to make you feel as good as I do right now."

Em kissed the tip of my nose and said, "I'm good. Close your eyes. Turn over and let me be the big spoon tonight."

I wanted to protest, but she was already gently pushing me on my side and draping her arm across my body. I clasped her hands and permitted my eyelids to close. It didn't take long to let sleep overtake me.

CHAPTER FOURTEEN

The next morning, I stretched, but Em's side of the bed was empty when I turned over. I didn't enjoy waking up alone. I listened closely and heard stirring downstairs. I couldn't make out the whispers, but there was definitely someone else in our cabin. I must have been exhausted because the light filtering into the room was so bright, I guessed it was midmorning.

After throwing the covers off the bed, I yanked on one of the dresser drawers for a clean pair of shorts and a T-shirt. Em must have caught the creak of the drawer because I heard her call out.

"Lise?"

"Yeah, I'm up. I'll be right down," I called.

Before I was ready for whoever was in our cabin, my bladder yelled at me to pay attention. Clomping down the stairs, I glanced at Harley, sitting in one of the chairs with a cup of coffee in her hand. I waved before ducking into the bathroom.

When I finally emerged, Em explained, "Harley had a thought about the traps and wanted to run it by us."

"Okay." I turned toward the kitchen, looking to see if there was more coffee.

Anticipating my needs, Em said, "There's an empty cup on the counter. It's fresh. I've only been up for about half an hour. When I went outside to breathe in the fresh air, I saw Harley slinking around."

"I wasn't slinking around. I was waiting until the old folks woke up. I can't believe you slept in so long. I'll bet you got some last night."

Em reached over and lightly smacked Harley on the arm. "Don't be impertinent."

"What? I applaud your stamina. I was exhausted."

With coffee in my cup, I ambled to where Harley and Em relaxed in the living room. Sonny and Cher were absent, and I suspected they were out hunting. Harley had helped Em install a cat door, so they could come and go as they pleased.

"So, what's on your mind, Sassafras?"

"Funny, Garden Gnome."

Em laughed. "Okay, are the two of you done needling each other?"

I probably looked sheepish, but Harley simply smirked at me.

"So, what about the traps?" I asked.

"It's too much of a risk that one of us or the little ones will stumble on what we set or break an ankle in a hole. It'll be so dark, and even with the vague picture in my head, I'm not sure I'd be able to avoid them," Harley admitted.

I ran my fingers through my hair, pausing before saying, "I'm not going to like whatever you have to say, am I?"

"We have some neon paint and can use that to create markers. It'll be easier to find each trap at dusk. Then we can climb the trees and wait until the camp is passed out."

"What about the patrols? Won't they find them and alert *the others*?"

Harley lifted her shoulders in a familiar gesture I recognized as her attempt to toss aside any angst she might feel. "Calculated risk. For whatever reason, they rarely patrol around the tree. As we move through the traps on our way out, I'll collect the small rocks so anyone following won't see them."

I groaned. "So, I guess that means we'll be crouched in the trees for several hours."

Harley shrugged again. "Bonus. We'll have a good idea when to strike. Several large trees allow for a perfect view of most of the camp. We might even be able to time it when the patrols are on the other side, giving us more time and space."

"What do Hannah and Trina think of your idea?" Em asked.

"Don't know. I haven't talked to them yet. I thought I would run it by you, then we could float the plan to the rest of the team and Trina."

"I think it's a good plan. I was wondering how you would avoid the traps you set. To be honest, that had me worried," Em said.

Not that I didn't believe Harley was smart or had a good enough scheme to achieve success, but I admit hearing Em more or less bless the idea was enough for me.

†

When Trina answered the door, she shook her head and smiled. "You know, we love having visitors, but the last-minute meetings are becoming a habit. What new wrinkle has emerged on the day you intend to execute a plan to rescue the kids?"

"Harley identified a hole in our strategy, something I was wondering about myself," Em said. "I assume you've had breakfast already, but maybe we can share another cup of coffee." Em held up the carafe.

"How did you know I would be here?" Trina asked. "We were still working on the solar conversions."

"Educated guess. You wanted to pamper Hannah a little today," Em answered. "That and I already went to the shed to look for you." She grinned.

"Well, come on in." Trina waved us inside. Hannah lounged in a pair of workout shorts and a skimpy T-shirt.

"We have company, love. I guess our day of debauchery is blown." Trina winked at Hannah.

"I see that." Hannah stretched her arms above her head.

The outline of Hannah's breast strained against her shirt, revealing her flat stomach. No Buddha belly there. Harley turned beet red and looked away.

Trina caught Harley trying not to gawk and telegraphed her observation with a subtle gesture to her wife. "While

Hannah is getting dressed, why don't you tell me what has you concerned."

"Harley, go ahead. It was your idea," Em suggested.

Shifting in her seat, Harley began, "You know that neon paint that Lise grabbed to mark the sections of the garden?"

Trina nodded.

"I thought we could spray paint small rocks and place them by the traps at dusk tonight. I'm worried someone will trip one while making our way through the gauntlet. We were pretty random when we set them. I did what Lise said and imagined each one on a big chessboard, but in the heat of the moment tonight, well, I just don't want to fuck up and miss something or worse, let someone else hit one."

"That's logical. Aren't you worried that they will be found before you free Rylee, Brook, and the other children? Their guards patrol the entire perimeter, don't they?" Trina asked.

Hannah stepped back into the room, dressed in what I considered her uniform of camouflage pants and a black T-shirt. "There's a cougar that seems to like the area where the traps are set. I've seen the men give a wide berth to the tree." She sat on the couch next to Trina before adding, "I imagine they're avoiding the big cat. Pussies," she added with a smirk.

"A cougar? Seriously?" My voice wobbled. "You failed to mention that tiny detail," I accused.

Hannah shrugged nonchalantly, a slight grin still tugging at the corners of her mouth.

"How are you aware of this, Hannah?" Em chimed in.

Hannah and Trina shared another private glance at one another before Hannah answered, "I've maybe been doing my own reconnaissance."

"Cougars can climb trees, you know." I said, my voice still shaking.

"She's just trying to survive, Lise," Harley assured me. "I used to toss food over the fence for her. I don't think she would attack me."

"Yeah, a little food goes a long way when establishing a friendship." Hannah leaned forward and grabbed the rest of her biscuit off of her plate.

"A cougar is nothing like Sonny and Cher," I emphasized as I stood from my chair, the adrenalin making me too agitated to sit still anymore. "It's a wild animal with big teeth and sharp claws." I began pacing the room. "It's not like we're in a movie titled, *Dances With Cougars,*" I mumbled, swinging back toward the rest of the room.

Harley laughed. "That's funny, Lise." She edged forward on her chair and reached out for my arm. Looking up into my eyes, she quietly revealed, "Honestly, I'm more worried that Cora or one of her cubs will trigger one of our traps. That would be an unfortunate byproduct. I don't want to see her hurt."

Harley looked so sincere. I wasn't sure how to react. Harley tried to be so tough on the outside. But in moments like this, I could see the kind and thoughtful young woman she truly was.

I stopped pacing. "You named her?"

"Ry named her. Right before we escaped, Ry crawled through the tree and offered Cora a sizeable piece of meat that she'd stolen. Ry was like ten feet away from her. She wasn't scared at all. Normally Cougars stay clear of humans, but there used to be a big cat sanctuary not far from here, and I suspect Cora is used to people tossing her meat." Harley looked like she was reminiscing as a small smile formed on her lips.

"Alright, well, the markers aren't going to help Cora avoid the traps." Trina frowned. "I'd rather not leave evidence of a coordinated mission."

"Oh, I won't leave the rocks there. I'll gather them on our way out."

"How many were placed? Do you estimate that she will have enough time to get them collected without jeopardizing the time schedule you have?" Trina turned slightly toward Hannah.

Hannah took a moment before nodding. "Yes. I think it will work"

Harley picked at a thread on her T-shirt before speaking again. "Um, I'd like to fill in the holes and remove the traps after everyone is safely on their way. Ry and I can wait in the trees and then do it when it's all clear."

Em was always the voice of reason and spoke Harley's language. "Harley, you know that's not a solid move. Relinquishing your queen to save a pawn is not the right move."

"But Cora is innocent, too," Harley argued.

"Sam and I will take care of it, but not that night." Hannah spoke with finality, and again I was amazed by how her external beauty belied the strength and leadership she innately commanded.

"Reconnaissance on our neighbors has been one task we've incorporated into ensuring the safety of this compound. Knowing ahead of time what your enemy might have planned is solid insurance against a major attack. Every couple of weeks, we spy on their camp," Trina added before looking around the room. "All settled then?"

Everyone but me nodded. I couldn't shake the image of the cougar lunging at me with Cora's enormous jaws locked on my neck.

Chapter Fifteen

Harley was already attaching her pack onto a scooter using bungee cords when I entered the shed. My body didn't seem to belong to me as my senses went into overdrive. Instead, I studied the scooters, stored in perfectly straight lines along the back wall and wondering who, in our camp, had a touch of OCD. Had they ventured outside of the camp boundaries and found the enemy encampment in need of organizing? Did they itch to get inside and bring order to chaos? Or did they find it difficult to breathe with the thought of actually penetrating their haphazard fence line and stepping into danger? As I tore my gaze from the scooters, I focused on Hannah as she secured her backpack to her bike. I figured that Harley's pack had the painted rocks, but I wondered what Hannah was carrying. Weapons, maybe? Sam strolled into the shed with his own rucksack. It seemed like I was the only one not carrying a bag.

"Did I miss the memo on the *bring your own backpack*?"

Harley laughed. "You really are a funster, Lise. Now I know where Ry gets her sense of humor."

Hannah glanced in my direction. "If you really want to be one of the gang, I can hook you up with a few knives and guns to stick inside a bag."

"No, I'm good," I answered.

As I closed the gap between Hannah and myself, my nose wrinkled. I brought my face close to Hannah's bag and sniffed. There was no mistaking the subtle odor of iron that immediately brought a vision of blood to my mind.

"Fresh meat for Cora," Hannah answered as a huge grin spread across her face.

"Thanks for that visual, because I'm not freaked enough. Ew. She's likely to follow us all the way back to camp."

"That would be awesome," Harley exclaimed. "I kind of worry about her and her two cubs."

I shook my head and pulled a scooter from the clean line.

Sam smacked me lightly on the back. "Don't worry, Lise. We've got your back."

After we rolled our bikes onto the path that would take us away from our safe compound, we climbed on board. Hannah gave the thumbs-up gesture, and we followed her lead. Like before, we traveled along the forest, avoiding any major road. Hannah, Sam, and Harley were much more adept at avoiding the low-hanging branches, and I yelped a few times when one struck me in the face. As we moved closer to the black-band camp, I knew I needed to control my outbursts and not yell out anymore, even though I still caught a random branch here and there.

We stopped at the same location that we'd stored our scooters before, but we had four to hide this time, which proved more challenging. Grabbing as many fallen branches and brush readily available in the area, we covered each scooter. Our efforts to camouflage would have to do because we wouldn't have enough light if we didn't hurry to the spot so that Harley could mark each trap with her painted rocks.

When we reached the clearing in front of the old fir tree, Hannah stopped us with hand signals before turning to whisper to Sam and me. "Sam, make sure Lise has a solid tree and then choose one at six o'clock." She nodded her head behind her. She pointed to two substantial trees further along the edge of the clearing. "Harley and I will take those two trees over there at nine o'clock and twelve o'clock." As if dismissing us and knowing we would follow her orders, she turned to Harley. "Harley, let's go. You start closer to the fence and work your way to the exit. I'm going to make my way to the other end and work back toward you."

Not wanting to be seen too easily, Sam and I half crawled, half ran toward our trees. That's when I made the mistake of glancing at a spot in the mud. The massive cat paw was clear as day, and it looked fresh. I pointed to the neon sign that Cora was definitely nearby. The squeak that left my throat was out before I could stop it. I couldn't tear my eyes away from the large print that dwarfed my hand lying next to it. I felt Hannah next to me as she gently touched my shoulder, as if concerned that she might spook me further.

She pointed to the closest tree with a stable hanging branch low enough for me to grab hold of and start climbing before she reached into her rucksack. I didn't hesitate, preferring to climb and hope that Cora would not follow since Hannah was about to place a peace offering on the ground.

When I reached high enough to remain hidden amongst the massive trees' bushy pine needles, I straddled the thick branch and chanced a look into the camp and surrounding forest. That's when I saw her. Cora. She looked healthy with her thick tan coat and distinctive markings. I had to admit she was beautiful. Crouching on the forest floor, she watched Hannah closely as she laid the meat on the ground. Hannah was a fair distance from the traps that Harley was methodically marking with her neon rocks.

Once Sam was clear of the forest floor, and Hannah had stepped into the cover of the bushes surrounding the clearing, Cora made her move toward the hunk of elk. Harley must have noticed her because she stopped in her tracks and waited. The big cat stalked the forest floor until she nabbed the meat in her powerful jaws and quickly disappeared into the forest with her prize. I squinted, trying to see where she'd gone, but she slithered beneath the foliage, and I couldn't see her tan coat anymore.

I continued surveying the clearing, hoping I could provide Harley and Hannah enough notice if Cora returned for seconds, but Harley and Hannah made quick work of marking the traps and soon were scaling their trees. I marveled at how like the mountain lion they both were as they silently moved from branch to branch until they were level with Sam and me. My attention swiveled to the camp, and I noticed there seemed to be a lot of activity. I assumed they were priming the camp for the wedding.

A sour note hit my stomach as I realized they were preparing to sacrifice Ry to Silas, who was not a great messiah but a disgusting old man who preyed on adolescent girls and vulnerable women.

Hannah must have noticed my distress because she gracefully hopped from the tree she was climbing to where I'd hunkered down. "Don't watch, Lise. It'll only make you crazy. Besides, without binoculars, you won't be able to see a lot."

"Is it horrible for me to want every one of them to suffer some ghastly disease?"

"No," she answered. "You might as well settle in. We have several hours before we can make our move."

I wrapped my arms around the trunk of my tree and took several deep breaths, pulling in the smells of fresh pine. Hannah sat easily on her branch, alternating her gaze between Sam and Harley, both of whom I assumed were keeping watch for the guards making rounds. Hannah looked so in control and natural sitting there. I couldn't believe she would have done anything else before the war.

"Tell me either a funny tale or an aw-that's-so-sweet story about you and Trina."

She paused in her scanning long enough to look me directly in the eye. I watched as a crinkle formed between her flawless eyebrows. "I met Trina on one of those organized hikes for lesbians. I needed to get away from the city and the whole fake bar scene. The toxicity that goes hand in hand with modeling changed me in ways I didn't like. I thought what could be more opposite than camping and hiking in the woods and not taking a shower for days?"

"I've never been a model or cared much about sprucing up, but honestly, I need a daily shower. I would not have survived one of those trips."

"Well, I was definitely a fish out of water. My tent fell apart and collapsed on me the first night. Trina heard me screaming as I squirmed around in my sleeping bag, fighting an invisible nylon enemy."

I chuckled, keeping my laughter barely above a whisper. "I can almost see that."

"She scared the shit out of me when I felt her hand on my shoulder, and I jumped and smacked her in the nose." She slowly shook her head, her voice taking on a softer tone. "She'd partially propped up my misshapen tent with a sturdy branch and was trying to get my attention as I struggled inside my bag." She grimaced as she turned back toward me. "The poor woman! Blood poured out of her nose and was going everywhere, including my brand-new down sleeping bag, which at the time, I was very indignant about." The grin that hit her face was catching, and I felt my lips turning up to mirror hers. "Who knew, but, apparently, I have a wicked right hook." Hannah's gleaming white teeth reflected off the full moon.

"Oh my God, did you break her nose?"

"Nah, I wasn't that fierce." She shifted on her branch. "Once I realized it was Trina, the woman I'd been lusting after as I listened to her speak on our first hike, I froze. I mean, how does someone make explaining hydration sexy?" She shook her head as she continued to grin at me. "I, of course, apologized profusely while offering my T-shirt. Yup, the one I'd worn to bed. I didn't even think. I pulled the shirt over my head and pushed it into her face."

"I don't suppose you wear your bra to bed, do you?"

"Nope. I was naked from the waist up."

Hannah's engaging story relaxed me, and I felt myself release my death grip on the tree and lean closer to her.

"Eventually, she thrust my now bloody T-shirt back at me and said, 'Um, you better put this back on. I'd like to think I have enough self-control to avoid kissing you and gawking at your beautiful body, but damn, Hannah, I'm only human.' I didn't even think she knew my name." Hannah stopped for a moment, and I could almost see her returning to that moment. "I must have looked like a fish gasping outside of water as I sat there and blinked at her, my mouth opening and closing. When I finally responded, I lamely said, 'No, you keep it, I'd rather not wear your blood. I'll grab another.' Then I turned my back and rummaged into my bag for a new T-shirt."

There was a long pause, which she didn't seem ready to fill as she scanned back toward Sam and then Harley. I couldn't tell if she did that intentionally, but I finally had to ask, "So, that must have given you a clue she was interested, right?"

She uncharacteristically scrunched her nose before replying, "Not really. I'd had plenty of women who only saw the model and nothing underneath. I assumed Trina was one of those. I wasn't looking for a one-night stand, but I wanted so badly to talk with her. Do you know what I'm talking about? When you can't understand the *why* you just know it's almost a need?"

I nodded my understanding.

She continued her story. "I offered to tend to her nose because I wanted to spend more time with her. God, I would have tossed out any excuse to get Trina to remain in my orbit." She clenched her fist and lightly banged it against her knee. "She has this presence that people are attracted to. I knew I was merely one of many, but I had to try."

I saw movement out of the corner of my eye and pointed to Harley moving closer to our tree as if she was a spider monkey. She seemed so natural, ducking beneath the branches and pulling herself higher on the tree. She'd chosen to relocate to the tree next to ours and gave us both the thumbs-up gesture when she reached the sturdy tree limb adjacent to the thick branch we were sitting on. Straddling the rough bark, she skootched closer and grinned.

"Now, we wait. Who brought the mead?" Harley asked. "I think Trina should reduce the drinking age to seventeen, kind of like when we used to have a lower drinking age, figuring if someone could die for their country, they could certainly have a beer."

"I'm sure we could talk Trina into letting you have mead after we've successfully brought everyone home safely," Hannah answered.

Harley thrust her fist in the air, signaling victory. I wondered if the joviality of our whispered words blended with the wind that moved around the branches. Harley and Hannah didn't seem concerned. Although we kept our voices low, it was hard for me to relax.

Sam had apparently decided he was missing out and progressed to a tree also close to ours. He kept his voice low when he asked, "So, can I join this party, or is this like some kind of hen gathering where roosters aren't welcome?" His boyish grin appeared.

"Hannah was telling me a funny story, so shush while I hear the end."

"So, where was I?" Hannah asked.

"Half-naked, offering your nursing skills to the broken nose that you caused," I answered.

Hannah held back a laugh. "I wasn't half-naked anymore. Remember I rummaged in my bag for another T-shirt."

"Ooh, can you go back to the half-naked part?" Harley asked.

"Reader's Digest recap: we were on a hiking slash camping trip. I didn't correctly set up my tent, and Trina came to my rescue. I was only half-naked because I accidentally smacked her in the nose and gave her my T-shirt to stem the blood flow. Can I finish now?" She grinned.

We all nodded.

"After I untangled myself from my sleeping bag and crawled from the mess that was my tent, I followed Trina to her tent. She had a lantern. I didn't. After we wriggled into her tent, I began to attend to her bloody nose. She closed her eyes and leaned into my touch. Well, let's just say swooning was the only way to describe my reaction. Her eyes popped open, and there was no mistaking the want. She smiled and sort of half chastised, half asked me why I had avoided talking to her for the first part of the trip."

"Sounds like Trina," Harley said. "She doesn't beat around the bush, but I'll bet she knows her way around one." Harley started laughing, then covered her mouth to dampen the sound.

"Shush. Don't turn this into some raunchy story. She kissed me for the first time that night. I gathered whatever small confidence I had to respond to her, telling her she was always surrounded by women and who could get a word in edgewise when women were swarming her and demanding her attention. Besides, if she wanted to talk with me, all she had to do was mosey on over and ask me to take a moonlight walk." Hannah shook her head. "Cheesy, I know. I'm not sure how moonlight walk popped into my addled brain, but Trina was charmed by my sudden awkwardness laced with a jolt of confidence. Which, to be honest, was lacking the minute I met Trina."

"Get to the good part already." Harley rolled her eyes. "I'll be a grandma before you finish telling the story."

"Trina is the epitome of cool, calm, and collected. She reached out and lightly brushed my jaw with her fingertips and said, 'I'm going to kiss you right now, before our walk in the moonlight, but only if that's okay with you.' I barely responded with, 'Very okay.' And that, my friends, is the story of our first kiss. I'm sure it was a lot more pleasant for me than it was for her. The next morning, she had two black eyes from the smack to her nose, so I've no doubt kissing me hurt a little. We packed my tent the next day, and I spent the remainder of the trip in her tent. The rest is history."

Harley grinned when she asked, "Did you fuck her that night?"

Hannah squinted at Harley. If I didn't know Hannah as well as I'd come to know her, I would have been terrified.

"Harley, we have never once fucked, only made love. Because that's what adults who love each other do," Hannah chastised.

165

"Sorry." Harley started picking at the bottom of her shirt. "Ry and I never had time to, uh, you know."

Being the cool aunt I am, I responded, "You will, hon, you will, and then we will expect to hear your story, like Hannah graciously told us hers."

†

I couldn't make out anyone's features in the black-band camp, but I knew instinctively the girl in the simple long white dress with flowers in her hair was Rylee. There were a few other women and girls in simple dresses that reached the ground. It was like I was watching a wedding celebration from the 1800s.

Sparks from the enormous bonfire floated into the air until the tiny fleck of orange twinkled out of visibility. Someone had a fiddle and started playing tunes that many in the camp began to dance to. A slight scuffle arose when one of the men tried to intrude on a couple already dancing. There weren't enough women and girls for the men to dance with. The mix of alcohol and scarcity seemed to increase the number of squabbles. A tall, broad-shouldered man settled most of the fights when they reached a certain level. I couldn't be sure, but I thought I saw Rylee set out three new jugs while the large man, whom I assumed was Silas, broke up an altercation that had gotten out of control. It seemed like he was becoming exasperated by it all, and through angry gestures, he sent all the women, along with most of the men, into their cabins before leading Rylee into the largest house. Most were having a tough time walking, except for the tall man.

The remaining men seemed to pass out beside the fire, while others staggered to their cabins with considerable difficulty. The fire had already shrunk to barely smoldering ash.

As I readied myself to scramble down the massive trees, Hannah touched my shoulder and then held her finger to her mouth. She pointed to the ground, where I could barely detect the red tip on the man's cigarette. Two young men were slowly making their way to the area right beneath the trees, where we remained frozen. Their patrol path was at least twenty feet away from where we'd laid our traps. I held my breath, hoping they wouldn't stray closer to the fallen tree and subsequent snares. A scream of pain would undoubtedly alert the camp. I could hear their conversation as my hands began to shake.

"I don't like coming to this side of the camp. Look, there's a fresh print. Fucking cougar is fast and mean."

"You pussy, shoot the damn thing."

"If they'd get us some night-vision goggles, we'd have a chance. You know cats can see in the dark. We can't. You can't shoot something you don't see."

"I bet I could."

"Bullshit. You know we're out here patrolling because we're low men on the totem pole. He always chooses losers to patrol on wedding nights."

"I'm no loser."

"Whatever, it's not like there are many choices for us to survive on our own."

I'd never been so relieved and terrified simultaneously when I heard what almost sounded like a woman shrieking. And then I saw her. Cora had made her presence known with her nighttime scream. I wondered why these men threatened her and her cubs, but we didn't. Could it have really been as easy as tossing her meat? I watched in horror as both men ran, and she gave chase. As she closed the distance, one of the unfortunate men found one of our traps. He probably twisted or broke his ankle as he fell to the ground, and Cora jumped. His screams were sure to wake the camp, but he was quickly silenced. I said a small prayer as I envisioned Cora wrapping her powerful jaws around his neck. I shuddered. Maybe he was our enemy, but he was someone's son. They both sounded so young that it was hard for me not to feel like he didn't deserve that fate.

I watched the camp for any sign that they'd heard the young man scream. His patrol partner had continued to run through the woods. I wasn't sure if he would wake the rest of the camp or not, even if the men hadn't stirred.

"We have to stop him from alerting *the others*," Hannah stated loud enough for Sam and Harley to hear.

"On it." Harley scrambled down the tree so fast that I didn't have a chance to beg her not to kill the young man.

Hannah touched my arm. "Come on, we need to follow in case she requires our assistance."

"Okay." My voice quivered with that one word.

I followed her and Sam as we descended from our sanctuary in the trees. I wasn't sure what I was more afraid of, Cora or the men waking in the camp. Following in Hannah's footsteps, she held her hand up and stopped. Carefully pulling her pack from her shoulder, she unzipped the flap and removed another large hunk of meat.

"Hello, Cora. Easy, girl." She placed the meat on the ground and stepped away.

Cora's low growl was a warning, but she wasn't moving in our direction. Her amber eyes stared at our small group as she warily watched the three of us give her a wide berth as we carefully navigated around the young man, whose blank stare sent a chill up my spine. Blood continued to leak from the wound in his neck. I looked away, afraid I would need to vomit in the woods. I did not wish to give the camp more reason to wake to the sounds of my retching. I glanced back once to see Cora cautiously approached Hannah's peace offering before following Hannah toward the camp entrance. I followed Hannah without blowing chunks as we passed the body.

Hannah's eyes continued to scan the area, looking for movement. She pointed to an area around a hundred feet to the west, and I tried to make out what she was pointing at, but all I saw were trees and brush in the darkness. "Harley's on the move. It looks like she's heading toward the old tree."

Sam nodded as we followed Hannah, carefully navigating the gauntlet. Soon we were near the old hollowed tree. The three of us squatted and waited.

I didn't hear Harley's approach until she was almost on top of me.

"Did he make it back into the camp?" Hannah asked.

"No, I reached him as he was looking around and calling for his buddy. The stupid kid probably thought Cora would hear him. Shit, I could barely detect his whispers."

Afraid to hear the answer but unwilling not to know, I asked, "Did you kill him?"

Harley shook her head. "No, I don't think so, but Cora might after he wakes up. He's a kid. I couldn't do it. I hit him with a thick branch from behind, so I don't think he saw me.

But he'll know this was a planned escape if he survives. I took his gun and stuffed it in my bag, then zip-tied his hands and feet and put a bandana in his mouth. If he's lucky, a new patrol will find him before Cora."

"Okay, are you ready?" Hannah asked.

Harley nodded, and I gulped before answering with a weak yes.

"You have thirty minutes to locate Ry, Brook, and the others. After that, Sam and I will head in and start looking for you both. In the meantime, we'll wait here and scout for more guards. If something goes wrong before you're able to make it back, try to give us a signal." Hannah checked the magazine of her 9mm while talking, and when she reinserted the magazine, she offered it to me grip first. "Better to have it and not need it than to need it and not have it."

I could feel my palms sweat with the realization of her words. I captured her eyes and shook my head. "I just…I just can't do it. I'm sorry I'll fight with everything I have, but I can't use that."

She stared at me for another moment before giving an imperceptible nod and sliding the gun into her holster. I followed Harley as she crawled to the tree and disappeared inside. My body slithered through the rotten wood, much less gracefully than Harley. As the dew-soaked into the knees of my jeans, I found comfort in the smells of decomposing timber and rich soil beneath my fingers, but I was happy when I finally reached the opening inside the camp.

†

"Ry," Harley whispered.

Soft hurried footsteps added to the gentle sounds of the wind through the trees. "Harley?"

"Over here, by our tree."

A young woman in a floor-length nightgown hurried to Harley, and they fell desperately into each other's arms. "I knew you'd come back for me. I had to tell Brook you were coming. It was the only way to get her to meet me here. She thinks she'll be able to talk me out of leaving."

Harley kissed Ry, and the sweetness in their affection for each other brought tears to my eyes. I didn't want to interrupt their tender moment.

"I have a surprise for you. It might help convince Brook to leave," Harley said.

Not wanting to startle Rylee, I cautiously approached the young lovers. "Hello, Rylee."

At first, she didn't seem to recognize me, then her eyes grew wide. "Aunt Lise?"

"Yeah, hon. We're going to get you both out tonight." I placed my hand on her shoulder and let out a soft whimper when she wrapped her arms around me.

"Aunt Lise, I can't believe you're here." I could hear the catch in her voice, and I squeezed her closer.

"I won't leave you again, sweetheart. I won't leave either of you again."

She pulled away from my embrace and rubbed the back of her hand across her eyes. "The other kids, too?" she asked. "They're all in the last cabin with *the mother*."

Harley nodded. "Will she be a problem?"

Ry grinned. "I slipped her a cup of shine with a little extra added to it before Silas took me back to the main house. Fucking pig. I told him I was scared and asked if he would let me have a glass of moonshine to relax. He acted all kind and loving and agreed. Then I said, could we maybe make a toast and he could have a little with me, like a real wedding."

"So, uh, you didn't have to…"

"Hell no. I would have bitten his dick off before I let him touch me like that. I had faith in you."

"You should have come with us, Ry." I could tell Harley was covering her relief at having Ry safe within our reach with anger and frustration.

"Harley," I warned, giving her a slight shake of my head.

Ry seemed to notice as well and reached out and grabbed Harley's hand. "I needed a little more time with Brook. I was making progress. One of the men really hurt her two days ago. He got rough with her. It was bad. I need to grab my change of clothes and get out of this ridiculous nightgown," Rylee exclaimed.

She began pushing aside a collection of tree branches and pine needles to reveal a dark pair of pants, a sweatshirt, and a pair of shoes. After changing into the new clothing and lacing her boots, she grinned at Harley. "Much better. I fucking hate the dresses they make me wear."

"Ry?" A high-pitched voice called.

"Over here," Ry answered.

Even in the dark, the bruises on her wrists and arms were visible to me, and I felt such a rage that at that moment, I thought I could kill someone. Then I saw her split lip and black eye. I knew that an accidental arm flaying in the dark like what had happened between Trina and Hannah was not the cause.

"Harley, you shouldn't have come. Now that Ry is married to Silas, things will be better for all of us. He can control the men. He loves Ry like he loved our mother. You know how devastated he was when she died. Ry has to return to her wedding bed. It's the only way. If he finds his bed empty, we'll all pay for it."

I didn't want to scare Brook, so I stayed silent in my position behind Harley.

"Everything out of his fucking mouth is a lie. God doesn't preach punishment. Look what those animals did to you," Ry spit out. "He didn't love our mother, and he sure as shit doesn't love me. He just wants to fuck me. I can't, you know that. I love Harley, and she loves me."

"If you leave, I won't have anyone left. Mom's gone. I'll have nothing. No one."

As if all the stars aligned, Brook shifted her focus to me. "Who is that? Someone from the queer camp?" she asked with a healthy dose of disgust in her voice.

I inched closer, and the moon finally appeared after she had ducked behind a cloud a mere minute earlier. I stood taller before stepping between Harley and Ry. "Hello, Brook."

Like I'd done with Rylee, I reached out to touch her shoulder. Brook immediately recoiled as if my hand was a blast of fire intended to scorch her face. It took Brook longer than Rylee to recognize me. Although two years older, Brook had always clung to her mother, the shyer of the two with meeting strangers. Yet, I remembered how they would both greet me with excitement when I came to visit them.

"Aunt Lise? How? Why?" Brook cried.

"I'm so sorry it has taken me so long to find you both again. I never meant to abandon you. Please, Brook, please come with us. I know you're confused, but there are so many people in your corner who care for you—who would die for you." I wanted to reach for her again but held myself back, balling my hands into fists by my side. I'd made my plea, hoping that a tiny portion penetrated the constant brainwashing she'd endured.

She turned her gaze away from me and started looking behind us, scanning back and forth to the tree and along the fence. "Where's Bobbie? He got away, right?"

As I continued to study her face, I was having a hard time deciphering her expression between concern and indifference. I realized I may have overestimated my ability to sway her decision.

"After that night? Did he even make it?" Brook's gaze finally fell on Harley's.

I thought I glimpsed more fear and guilt than impassiveness. *Good. Maybe we could still make this work.*

"Yeah, we call him Bruiser now because he took such a beating…" Harley's voice trailed off.

"Bruiser," Brook said it like she was testing the name on her tongue.

"Look, Brook, I'm not saying this to be mean or anything, but if you'd come with us before and not alerted Peter, Bruiser wouldn't have gotten the shit kicked out of him. He's lucky to be alive." The anger Harley must have been feeling all these months leaked out as her whispered reprimand became more intense. Before I could step in, Harley muttered, "Your mother wasn't so fortunate."

"What do you mean?" Brook pushed into Harley's face, fists clenched. "My mother died from food poisoning. You can't blame Silas or Peter for that." Her voice had an edge, and I couldn't force myself to intervene. I looked desperately at Ry, but the concern on her face at this news startled me.

"Bruiser heard she killed herself right after Peter pimped you out to his friends." Harley wasn't backing down and pushed back into Brook's space. "It was the last straw for her," Harley vehemently whispered. Then she seemed to deflate before us all. "She couldn't handle you," she gestured to Ry, "and Ry having sex with all those men. It's child rape, and it wasn't right, Brook. It's *not* right."

"You're a liar." Brook turned around, and I thought she might return to camp, bringing attention to our presence. She swung around, and in a strong, clear voice, stated, "A liar, Harley Martin."

Rylee quietly stepped between Brook and Harley. "It's true, Brook. I swear, she's not lying to you. I overheard Silas talking to Peter. He was worried you would follow in her footsteps and told Peter to control his friends after that fucker beat you up. He said the camp couldn't afford to lose any healthy, breeding girls." Rylee crossed her heart. "I swear on Mom's memory, that's what I heard."

Brook looked unsure of herself and then asked, "Is Bobbie at your camp?"

"He is," I answered. "He's a terrific kid."

"Doesn't he feel out of place with the rest of you and the way you are? He isn't like that." Brook wrinkled her nose in confusion.

"Not everyone who lives in our camp is queer," Harley answered. "There are even a few devout Christians. They get together sometimes and read the Bible and pray. They follow the true path of Christ. Jesus never taught anger and hate. He taught love and acceptance. You'd like them."

"There's even a chapel you can go to. Every day, if you want," I added.

A grim line of determination formed on Rylee's lips. "I'm not leaving here without you, Brook. If I have to hogtie you and shove a rag in your mouth, you're coming with. I won't let you live like Mom did. She was always afraid, and then I guess the guilt at what she'd done was too much."

"What are you talking about?" Brook crossed her arms and looked defiantly at her sister.

"She blamed herself for how Peter treated you, Brook. It was the cycle of violence, and Mom finally got it." Ry touched her chest. "She felt it in here that it was wrong." She tapped her head with her fingers. "And she knew it up here that the cycle had to be broken." She took a deep breath. "But Mom wasn't strong enough to protect us from all of this, Brook. Don't you remember? Aunt Lise tried to talk Mom into leaving Dad. That's why we never saw her after that fight with Mom." Rylee glanced at me. What she was looking for, I wasn't sure. Confirmation? An ally?

"She wouldn't let me see you anymore, Brook. I thought of you every day, but she threatened to file a restraining order with the police if I ever tried to visit again." This time I touched her shoulder and squeezed it until she looked at me. "I'm not leaving you again, Brook. I'm with Ry on this one and will do everything in my power to keep you both safe and make us a family again."

Brook's face went blank, and in an almost robotic voice, she asked, "Are you going to kidnap the other girls not yet of marrying age?" The topic of her mother closed for now.

"Rescue, not kidnap. And, yes, that was the plan. But, if we don't hurry, everyone is at risk. They won't hesitate to kill Lise or me. They might save you and Ry, but both of you would get a beating. You can't want that to happen to your sister or your aunt. I know you don't care if they kill me, but think about your sister," Harley pleaded.

"Okay. I'll come with you. Someone needs to make sure the girls hear the word of our Lord. I think it would be best if Ry and I brought the girls to the tree. They'll be scared to go with strangers."

"I agree," Rylee answered.

I glanced at Harley, who nodded. I think we both realized this might be a significant risk, but we didn't have much choice if we wanted to free the girls without alerting the rest of the camp. We had to trust that Brook wasn't lying and cared more about her sister than her husband and Silas's distorted religion.

CHAPTER SIXTEEN

Harley and I crouched by the tree, hidden in the shadows, waiting for the two sisters to return with the other girls. To say the fifteen minutes we hovered beneath the veil of darkness were the longest in my life would be an understatement. I had to use everything in my power not to stand and start pacing. For the first ten minutes, neither of us tried to make conversation. I don't believe we knew what to say to distract the other. I could almost hear the clock tick in my head, every second sounding like a muted gunshot.

Finally, I couldn't take it anymore and asked, "You don't think Brook's suggestion was a ruse to get Ry to fall in like a good Christian soldier?"

"Even if it were a ruse, Ry can handle things. I have the utmost faith in her. I think maybe we got through to Brook, and I always knew she had a thing for Bruiser."

I raised one eyebrow. "He's just a kid. I know Em said he would die for Brook, but Bruiser is still so young."

"He's seventeen, almost eighteen. Only a few months younger than Brook. Em is right, you know. Bruiser would do anything for Brook. He already has when he took that beating."

Rylee might have had the skills to navigate the brush, but with three confused girls, we heard their approach well before they reached the old tree. I felt considerable discomfort to see their flowing white nightgowns act like a kind of beacon in the night.

When Rylee was close enough to hear me, I whispered, "You didn't happen to store four additional sets of clothes, did you? Those white gowns are way too visible, especially when the moon decides it's time to come out of hiding."

Rylee grinned. "I did."

"That's my girl." Harley beamed with pride.

The dark clothing that Rylee unearthed hung loosely on their small frames, and I wondered how they might move quickly through the hollow tree, not to mention the nearly one-mile hike back to the scooters. Brook and Rylee were efficiently rolling up the sleeves and bottoms of the sweatpants. Finally, they were pulling on the drawstrings and cinching the pants so they wouldn't fall off. Apparently, Rylee had decided their slippers would have to do, and she encouraged the three frightened girls to follow Harley through the tunnel. Brook took up the rear position to make sure they weren't startled by Sam and Hannah, who were waiting on the other side. Rylee went next to help form another anchor for the girls. I was the last person to crawl through.

The hard part was over, and I thought for a second we were home free—until I turned my head to look through the fencing. I saw a light flicker in one of the smaller cabins. It sounded like someone was trying to rouse the camp awake and not having much luck. A few men staggered from their homes but seemed too impaired to move quickly or comprehend what he was trying to say.

Once my body was entirely on the other side, I crouched and looked for the others. Sam, I learned, had a gift with children and had already enticed the smallest girl to climb on his back, and he was making his way through the gauntlet of booby traps. His soothing voice and short stature worked to his advantage.

Hannah's tense command made it to my ears. "Time to go. Quickly girls, follow my path and avoid the neon rocks."

"It'll be okay. We'll follow Hannah," Rylee added.

"You go ahead, I'll be right behind you," Harley whispered.

Brook took the hand of one girl, and Rylee crouched in front of the other. "Our aunt is going to lead you out, okay? You be a good girl and take her hand." Glancing in my direction, she gestured me over, and I smiled at the little girl.

She looked at me with her soft brown eyes. Even though she was frightened, her trusting gaze landed on mine, and she whispered, "You look like Miss Kimberly."

My eyes watered, and I responded, "Yeah, Miss Kimberly was my sister."

"She was nice to us." The little girl offered her hand, and I took it.

I kept looking over my shoulder into the camp but couldn't see anything in the dark. Then I heard them, the unmistakable barking of large dogs. I hurried my pace to catch up to Brook and Hannah while Harley methodically retrieved all the neon stones she'd placed as markers on our traps. Ry followed closely behind Harley, careful to step where she pointed.

As the barking grew louder, my heart pounded in my chest, and it took everything in my power to keep the panic at bay. I needed to keep my shit together. The little girl depended on me to lead her out of the maze of booby traps, and I couldn't afford to misstep or make an error now. I was never so grateful to hear Cora's screams as the growling and barking sounded not more than a couple hundred feet away. My money was on Cora, even if there were several dogs to contend with. At least I hoped she wouldn't injure herself. Knowing she had two cubs to care for, I was rooting for the big cat.

I heard the snap of a trap. "Argh, fuck. I'm going to kill those bitches," a man's voice screamed as he howled in pain.

We continued through the collection of fallen trees, branches, ferns, pinecones, and dense undergrowth. My charge clung to my hand, allowing her to keep up with me. It felt like an eternity, but finally, we made it to our scooters. The farther we had moved away from the camp, the barking, growling, and cougar screams had become fainter, and I slowly relaxed. As Harley broke through the tree's behind me, I felt a tremendous sense of relief that we'd made it.

Hannah had warned me not to panic if it took us longer to reach the site. She knew the girls would slow us down. We were no longer a small extraction team. One of us would have to put two girls on our scooter. Sam waved us over. At only five foot six, Sam was a small man. His muscular, wiry frame took even less room on the scooter than any of the rest of us.

Talking in a low voice to the smallest girl, he instructed, "We're going to take a little ride on this. It'll be as much fun as a roller coaster. I'm going to tie a rope around you, so you stick close to me and don't fall off because that wouldn't be fun at all, okay?" He waved me over, assessing that I held the hand of the next smallest girl.

I didn't know any of their names, but I hoped that because I looked like Kim, the little girl would trust me enough to let me bring her to Sam.

Crouching down to meet her at eye level, I explained, "Sam is a good friend, and he wants to take you on a ride."

The little girl blinked her brown eyes and looked skeptically at Sam.

"I get to take two of you on a fun ride, like at an amusement park. You have to hang on to me real tight, though. Can you do that?" Sam asked.

The girl looked at me, and I nodded.

She bobbed her blonde head of curls up and down. Once Sam had climbed onto his scooter and tied the rope around the first girl, I picked up my trusting little friend and put her on the back.

Placing her hands on either side of Sam's waist, I told her, "Hold on to his shirt and don't let go." I stroked her blonde curls and smiled before Sam slowly rolled away.

Hannah's tall frame squatted in front of our last rescue, and she smiled warmly at the girl. "Hello, my name is Hannah. Would you like to take a ride like your friends?"

Rylee moved to Hannah's side while the girl held tightly to Brook's hand, attempting to persuade the frightened girl to let go of Brook. "Miss Hannah is real nice, Chloe. You go with her, and we'll all be right behind you, okay?"

"Why can't I go with Miss Brook or you?" the little girl asked.

"I don't know how to drive a scooter like Miss Hannah, and neither does Miss Brook." Rylee picked her up, and the girl clung to Rylee's body, almost in desperation. "I know you're a lot braver than the other girls. Can you do this for me?" Rylee caught Hannah's eye and gestured with her head for Hannah to go to her scooter.

After Hannah climbed on her scooter, Rylee placed the little girl on the back. "You hang onto Miss Hannah as tight as you can."

I was becoming increasingly nervous about how long it was taking for us to exit the area. Visions of growling, foaming, rabid men and dogs popped into my head.

As soon as Hannah moved, Brook tentatively approached. "I assume Ry and Harley will be on the other scooter, and that leaves you and me, Aunt Lise."

"Yes, hon, I hope that's okay. I've become quite adept at driving one of these contraptions. Probably not as good as Hannah, Harley, or Sam, but I can do the job." I smiled at her.

"Chit chat at camp, let's roll." Harley jumped on her scooter, and Ry settled in with her arms wrapped around Harley's waist.

I was pleasantly surprised by Brook's lack of hesitation to join me on the scooter and wrap her thin arms around my thick middle. We were on our way. The quiet hum of the electric motors barely audible in the brisk night air.

†

Em and Trina must have been waiting for our approach because the gates flung open as we approached the compound. I saw them jog to the shed as our caravan of scooters rolled to the storage unit.

I put my foot on the ground and allowed Brook to step off first before swinging my leg across the seat. For a moment, I didn't know if my legs would hold me up as all the adrenaline of the past six hours drained from my body. I needn't have worried as Em flew to me, wrapping her arms around me and burying her head in my neck. I could feel tears forming in my eyes as my heart, mind, and body registered home with Em's embrace. Blinking to keep them from falling down my cheeks, my gaze caught sight of Brook standing behind Em, and I know Em could feel my body stiffen. Em, as always, understood my body language. She simply stood back after the hug before turning around to face Brook. I was thankful that Em kept hold of my hand before she addressed Brook, as that simple contact grounded me.

"You must be Brook," Em said, reaching out her right hand. "I'm Em, Lise's wife."

I had described to Em that Brook favored her father, while Rylee was the spitting image of Kim. Brook wrinkled her nose, but whether it was ingrained manners taught by her mother or the realization that this was her new home, Brook took Em's hand and shook it.

Harley and Rylee approached, and Rylee didn't hesitate to approach Em, initiating a hug. "I'm so happy to meet you," she said after releasing a surprised Em. "Harley just whispered to me you're Aunt Lise's wife and how incredible you are."

Em chuckled. "Well, I'm not sure about the level of incredibleness she described, but yes, I am Lise's wife, Em. You must be Rylee. I'd know those mischievous eyes anywhere. You're like a mini-Lise. The resemblance is uncanny."

"Yeah, Mom always said that people would mistake her and Aunt Lise for twins sometimes, at least when they were younger. I think the older they got, the more their individual styles diverged," Ry answered.

I'm sure my face registered confusion, learning how Kim had talked about me, and I wondered if this was before or after our fight. Em noticed my look and brushed my shoulder.

While we were having our reunion, Trina and Hannah had embraced. Trina let Hannah and Sam continue to develop a connection with the three girls. Trina's talents in leadership did not extend to a skill with children. It seemed as though Sam had already won over his two charges, but Hannah was still working on calming the suspicious little girl with wary eyes.

"We've moved Daria to a larger cabin. It'll be tight, but she is best equipped to handle all the children," Trina said with authority.

Harley and Rylee whispered to each other in the corner. I was thankful when they came to the rescue.

Addressing the frightened young girl, Harley said, "You'll like Miss Daria. I'll take you to her cabin. You must be tired." She held out her hand, and as if on cue, the girl rubbed her eyes and accepted Harley's hand.

The other girls had already each taken one of Sam's hands, and they all began walking to the next largest house in the compound.

"Where will you put me?" Brook asked.

Her voice quivered, and I wondered what she was thinking at that moment. Her question sounded like she thought she was nothing more important than a piece of furniture to move every few months to keep things fresh.

"For now, we'll have Brook and Rylee bunk with Harley, Bruiser, Finn, and Sadie. They've already blown up two extra mattresses," Trina said.

"Cool, a slumber party." Rylee grinned. "Come on, Brook, it's been ages since we had one of those. I've missed having you around. That asshole husband of yours barely let us hang out."

I felt encouraged by the tiny smile that formed on Brook's lips. Her love for her sister had survived the ordeal that both of my nieces had gone through. Even though their fundamental beliefs were as diametrically opposed as they could be, they were still sisters. Exhaustion finally made its presence known, and I greedily accepted Em's hand as she led me to our cozy cabin. I knew she would hold me, and everything was right in the world when she did that.

Tomorrow, we would face the challenges of the trauma I knew my niece had experienced over the past several months in the black-band compound. Instinctively, I understood Rylee was the stronger of the two and had narrowly escaped the same level of horror forced upon Brook.

I hoped Brook wasn't broken beyond repair after everything she'd had to endure while in the black-band camp. I worried so much about her ability to bounce back from the trauma, but I had no idea how to help her heal.

I watched as Rylee slung her arm around both Harley and Brook—the glue to bring the two most important young women together under a common denominator—their love for Rylee.

Em watched me closely and brushed the tear that had formed in the corner of my eye. "Come on, love. You can spill about your adventure when we return to our cabin. I love you so much and can't tell you how much of a relief it is that everyone is back safe and sound." She wrapped her arm around my waist and tugged me toward the path that would lead us to our home.

†

"Brook is wary. Based on her upbringing and recent brainwashing, she isn't going to embrace her lesbian aunt anytime soon. She couldn't be any more different from Rylee. And I'm not only talking about their physical appearance. I don't know what to do to reach her." My shoulders slumped in defeat as Em led me to bed.

We both quickly undressed before slipping inside the down comforter and soft cotton sheets. I turned to face Em, leaning into her soothing hand as it caressed my side.

"You'll find a way to connect. I have faith in you. There must be something you share in common."

"Maybe she picked up the green thumb from Kim or me. It runs in the family. Do you think I should ask her to join me in the hydroponic garden? The place is like Nirvana for people who love gardening. You should see how much the plants have flourished since you installed the system." As I continued to share my dream of working side by side with my nieces, my voice adopted that higher pitch I have when I'm excited about something.

"Hon, you have plenty of time to work that out. Tomorrow, we can start on project charm."

Em pulled me against her naked body, and I laid my head on her chest as she ran her fingers through my hair. This tactic never failed to send me into dreamland. There's nothing better than a head rub from Em. Before too long, I was fast asleep.

My dream started off lovely. Brook, Rylee, and I were in the hydroponic garden beaming about how big and healthy the plants were growing. Then their leaves lengthened, all the way to the floor, turning into vines that wrapped around my ankles. I watched in horror as they wove their way up Rylee and Brook's bodies, vines snaking around their necks. I reached out to stave off the vines that were rapidly choking off Brook and Rylee's air supply. Their eyes were so pleading, voices strangled by the fruits of our labor. The plants wouldn't let me move from the spot. I noticed the vines turned to solid thick roots, and I was literally rooted to the floor. Attempting freedom, I thrashed about wildly, looking for any weak spot in the live ropes constricting me in the same fashion as if I were a kidnap victim.

"Lise, Lise, wake up, hon."

I felt the small circles on my back, and my eyes flung open to Em's worried gaze.

"You had another bad dream," Em explained.

I rubbed my right eye with my fist. "It was a doozy. Talk about the saying, *reap what you sow*. Oh, boy, were we doing that. The plants turned against us." I chuckled to cut the tension and added, "An alternative version of *A Little Shop of Horrors*. These were like plants on steroids, and they wrapped around us like ropes, and then they were strangling Brook and Rylee, and no matter how hard I thrashed around, I couldn't save my nieces."

"You have the most imaginative nightmares, but it doesn't take a rocket psychologist to figure out this is concerning the guilt you still feel about how you left things with your sister."

"Rocket psychologist?" I chuckled.

"Well, it fits better than a rocket scientist. Wish we'd thought to keep some of those seeds from those marijuana plants you used to grow. You could benefit from a toke or two right now."

"What makes you think I didn't save some?" I grinned at her. "They are planted in the last row. I kind of hid them in the back. I know Harley will recognize them as soon as they sprout, but she doesn't enjoy gardening, so what isn't known doesn't hurt anyone. I hope Trina doesn't get mad. I suppose I should have asked first."

"She isn't as strict about things as everyone seems to think she is. I can't imagine feeling the weight of the camp on her shoulders. It must be exhausting. A little weed won't be the worst thing she has to consider. Like our state had in place before the bombs, reasonable rules are probably something she'd be okay with."

"Once Harley finds out about my small crop of cannabis, she'll undoubtedly argue for lowering the age of consumption."

Em smiled. "Yup, the whole 'if I'm old enough to patrol and fight, I should be old enough to drink mead and smoke weed.'"

"Drink mead and smoke weed. It rhymes." I lowered my voice and imitated, "Don't forget to drink mead and smoke weed responsibly. This is your public service announcement for today." I giggled.

"Go back to sleep and imagine us sitting in our cabin, smoking and drinking with our friends and family." Em continued rubbing my back and then moved her fingers to the nape of my neck, and off to dreamland I went again, but this time I didn't dream of people-eating-vines.

CHAPTER SEVENTEEN

The loud, incessant banging on the door startled me awake. I heard Harley and Rylee's panicked voices. Clambering from the bed, I began hopping around as I donned my sweats. I didn't bother to put a bra on and quickly pulled my sweatshirt over my head as I ran down the stairs.

I flung open the door and asked, "Now what?"

"Harley and I woke up this morning, and Brook was gone. We can't find her anywhere," Rylee said in a near panic.

Rylee's hair stuck up in all directions, and if she hadn't looked so rattled, I would have laughed at her epic bedhead. The look rivaled those mornings where Em and I had engaged in rather zealous sexual calisthenics.

191

"Did the two of you sleep together last night?" I tried to ask without condemnation.

If Brook's mattress was right next to theirs, that might have been enough to freak her out and cause Brook to flee. This was the last thing we needed.

"What? No. I mean, we didn't have sex, but we shared one of the blow-ups. Both of us were fully dressed. Honest, we cuddled together, but nothing else. I didn't even kiss Ry in front of her. I'm not stupid," Harley defended.

Thankfully Em came down the stairs and, in her soothing voice, tried to settle the young women. "Harley, no one is suggesting you're stupid. Lise was merely asking a question to see if we can discover why she might have left your cabin. It wasn't an accusation, okay? I doubt Brook went back to the black-band camp. It's too far away without transportation. The patrols would have seen her leave. Rylee, you know your sister probably better than anyone. Where do you think she would have gone? Was she upset last night?"

"She seemed fine last night. A little freaked, but we're all a bit unsettled. I saw her smile a couple of times. Bruiser was falling all over himself to make her feel comfortable, even pitched a tent for himself outside so she wouldn't be weirded out about staying in the same cabin with someone from the opposite sex who isn't your husband. Ironic, huh? Considering Peter made her have sex with all his friends," Harley explained.

I glanced at Rylee, who cringed when Harley casually mentioned what Brook had endured with her husband.

"She doesn't know the compound, but Brook always calmed herself in the gardens. It wasn't just because Mom taught her to be the good little woman who tended to the gardens because that's a woman's domain, either. She really enjoyed the peace of digging in the soil," Rylee said.

"Good, then before we all start losing our shit, let's take a walk around the compound and see if Brook found her way to any of the gardens."

I covered my mouth so I wouldn't laugh after Em had casually spit out the phrase, "lose our shit," that she probably thought was youth slang. Not that Em was stiff or a kind of pretentious intellectual who always spoke with perfect, proper English, but the phrase did not roll off her tongue. Each word was forced, exploding from her mouth, not unlike someone spitting sand.

"I'll check the hydroponic gardens. Harley and Ry, will you see if she made her way to the greenhouse? You two can check the orchard if you don't find her in the greenhouse, and Em, would you mind seeing if she's at the south garden?"

None of us started running, but our pace was definitely not a leisurely stroll. Em kissed me on the cheek before heading to the large open garden at as rapid a speed as I'd ever witnessed.

A few minutes later, I pushed open the door to the structure that housed our newly created hydroponic system. I saw Brook leaning over one of the tiny shoots that had broken through the small cluster of moss, sitting inside the water, and now soaking up the morning sun.

"Brook?"

Startled, she jumped before turning her attention to me.

"You have a hydroponic garden," she stated, a touch of amazement in her voice.

"We do. How much do you know about hydroponics?" I took a step closer, easing my way to where she stood. My movements were slow because I felt like I was approaching a skittish feral kitten, ready to bolt at any moment.

"A little. I wanted to build one, but Peter said that was fancy liberal talk, and there was nothing wrong with growing food in the earth like farmers have been doing for generations."

"Want me to show you what we've started here?" I asked.

Brook brushed her finger over the tiny shoot and nodded. "I'd like that. I could help you if that's allowed?"

The timid way she'd asked about helping nearly broke my heart. I tried not to go back to envisioning what horrors she'd endured while I was safely tucked away in a bomb shelter.

"I would be grateful for another green thumb to help with the hydroponics. I want to make sure we have the right blend of liquid nutrition." I walked to the table where I kept detailed notes on each plant food solution piped to varying rows of plants. "The trial-and-error approach has some method to my madness. It's all written here. I need someone who can inspect each plant to document the progress. We'll refine the solutions depending on what we're growing and how well they're progressing, both in the starter pods and after we transfer the starts to the irrigated gutters."

"You were afraid when you came into this greenhouse. Why?"

"Harley and Rylee banged on our door this morning. They were terrified that you'd left. Everyone is looking for you right now. We should probably find them before they start hyperventilating."

"They think I'll run back to my husband as soon as I find a way to escape." Brook looked to the ground.

"Will you?"

Lifting her head, she looked me in the eye and said, "No." Holding her hand on her belly, she revealed, "I'm pregnant, and I don't know who the father is. I'm no better than a dirty whore."

Taking a chance, I gathered Brook in my arms and implored her to hear my words. "Oh, hon, absolutely none of this is your fault. You are not beholden to the distorted teachings of Peter and Silas. Whatever you want to do with your baby, we'll figure it out together."

I looked at her slight frame and hoped that she wasn't very far along. She didn't look like she'd even come close to the second trimester, but it was hard to tell.

Brook pushed away from me. "I'd never give up my baby."

"If that's what you want, then I've no doubt your love and devotion, neither of which is bad, will easily be transferred to your unborn child. She or he is worthy. Peter and Silas are not."

"You're not telling me to kill my baby because of how she or he was conceived?" Her wariness was almost palpable.

"Of course not. I'm telling you you're the only one who gets to decide about your body."

"How can I raise a baby properly without a father for him or her?"

"A lot of women do that and have done that for ages. My definition of family encompasses more options than one man, one woman, and two-point-five children." I smiled to take the sting out of my declaration of a different way of thinking.

"So, you're married to that woman, Em," she stated, without her previous derision.

"I am. Legally, I might add."

"How come you don't have children? Don't people like you adopt or do in-vitro fertilization?"

I was surprised that her tone wasn't a rebuff. She appeared genuinely curious about my answer.

"Before we hid in our bunker, we tried. Eight times. None of them worked. We thought it wasn't in the cards for us. Now? Well, I suppose it's possible if one of the men in the camp donates their sperm, and we try the old turkey baster method."

"You're going to be, Great Aunt Lise. Maybe holding my baby will satisfy your maternal instincts."

"We'll be eager babysitters. Trust me, you're going to want to have those readily available. Even the best mothers need breathing room now and again." I reached out and touched her shoulder, and she didn't recoil from me. I took that as a good sign. "Come on, let's go find everyone, and we can have breakfast. I probably eat far too many eggs, but they're so good fresh from the hens."

"I haven't told Rylee yet. She'll want me to commit murder."

"She might surprise you. I don't think she will try to talk you into getting rid of the baby. Can I ask how far along you think you might be?"

"I've only just missed my period. Not more than two months."

I nodded. "At this early stage, none of us think it would be murder, but I understand that's what you believe. I don't know you or Rylee well enough yet, but I cannot imagine the young, mature woman I met last night would try to convince you to abandon all your convictions, especially the ones that only you have the right to decide on."

"Rylee and I do not agree on many issues."

"I don't suppose you do, but you still love your sister, and that's a start. Perhaps exposure to different ideas is not the worst thing to happen. To any of us," I added.

†

I led Brook out of the greenhouse. As soon as the greenhouse door opened, I saw Rylee running toward us.

She pulled Brook into a desperate hug. "Why did you sneak out this morning? You scared me. I thought you might have returned to Silas's flock."

"I needed to think. A brisk morning walk is always something that helps."

Harley and Em looked relieved as they approached. "Hey," Harley said.

"Who is up for some coffee?" Em asked. "How about we all head to our cabin, and I'll get the coffee going? Eggs, pancakes, or French toast?"

Out of the corner of my eye, I saw Bruiser. He looked like he wasn't sure whether to approach or hang back. My hesitancy to wave must have caused him to step away and return to wherever he'd come from. Later, I would ask

Harley to touch base with Bruiser. There was an almost pained expression on his face, combined with a kind of longing I hadn't seen before. I turned my attention to the girls.

"All three." I grinned. "We can have a feast. Harley and Ry can gather the eggs, and I'll start the pancakes."

I wasn't sure if Brook had already experienced any morning sickness, but I knew I would need to offer another beverage besides coffee—unobtrusively if possible. It wasn't my place to announce her pregnancy. I wanted to make sure Brook felt like she was in control of her pregnancy, including who to tell and when to make that announcement. I hoped that Taylor, the doctor in the compound whom I'd not met yet, would be capable of caring for a pregnant woman and delivering the baby when the time came.

The wariness had not left Brook, but she followed us to our cabin. I was thankful that Sonny and Cher had moved to their second favorite place to hang out in front of the wood-burning stove. Her innocent delight at discovering our affectionate felines allowed me to temper my worry for Brook and how she might meld into our camp.

"They let you keep pets?" she asked as she made a beeline for Sonny and Cher.

"We weren't about to give up our babies," I answered. "But honestly, Trina and Hannah spoil them more than we do."

"Hannah from last night?"

"Yes. Trina is the appointed leader, and Hannah is her wife." I wanted to get that fact out there quickly. The more Brook assimilated into a mostly queer camp, the better it would be for all of us.

"A lesbian is your leader? Sam can't be the only man who lives here." Brook started to pet Sonny, who had crawled into her lap.

"No, he isn't. When you meet Trina, you'll know why everyone looks to her for direction. Although, Em is undoubtedly gaining a lot of respect. Regardless, everyone's opinion counts. Trina is merely the person who ultimately makes the hard decisions."

"I can make the pancakes if you wish?" Brook volunteered.

She stood and looked wistful at leaving her new friends. I smiled when they trotted after her.

"That's okay, I've got it. You can feed Sonny and Cher." I pointed to the pantry, where we kept the homemade cat food of dried meat and fish. "Their food is in there. It's in a large plastic container. Don't give them more than a cup because even though we shouldn't feed them table scraps, I always catch people holding out treats for them on the sly. They've gotten extremely accomplished at begging."

The first genuine smile I'd seen formed on Brook's lips, and I felt a swell of hope and joy. If only we could show Brook we weren't the demons she'd learned to stay clear of. Would the contrast of kindness, freedom, independence, honesty, and love help create a new normal for Brook? Time would tell. One thing I knew for sure, I was never giving up again.

Em busied herself making the coffee. After the coffee had percolated, she poured three cups. I placed my hand over one of the empty cups and shook my head. I put my hand on my stomach, and she nodded her understanding.

"Brook, I shouldn't assume you're a coffee fiend like your aunt. I've made a special blend of herbal tea that you might like if you prefer," Em offered.

Brook lifted her eyes shyly to Em. "Thank you, yes, I don't drink coffee."

"I think I'll join you this morning. Sometimes a cup of tea settles me better than coffee when I don't wish to jolt awake and start the day, but would rather ease into it," Em said kindly.

I mixed the ingredients for pancakes and whisked the mixture into a smooth texture, ready for the flat griddle. The sizzle of butter before pouring the batter was a sound I loved, accompanied by the aroma of hotcakes.

Harley and Ry burst into the cabin, giggling with nearly a dozen eggs in their hands. They were pushing against one another playfully.

"Ry thinks she's the chicken whisperer. You should have seen Geraldine eye her with a level of suspiciousness that exceeds the disdain she has for me," Harley announced.

"I grabbed her eggs, didn't I?" Ry answered.

"Only after I distracted her because once she started pecking, you jumped and screamed like a little girl."

"I did not. You're such an exaggerator. But I did appreciate your gallantry."

Ry looked at Harley with such love in her eyes. It reminded me of how I mooned over Em until she finally put me out of my misery and made her move. Brook watched the two interact out of the corner of her eye while she filled Sonny and Cher's bowls.

Em pulled two more cups from the cabinet and poured coffee into them. She'd filled the teakettle with water for the loose tea that she'd already placed in the other cups.

After setting the eggs next to the stove, Harley asked, "Is that coffee up for grabs?"

"Oh yeah, I'd love a cup," Rylee chimed in.

Em pushed the two cups to Harley and Rylee. "Yup, these are for you. Fresh cream is in the refrigerator."

Most of us had adapted to coffee black or with a little cream. Sugar was a hot commodity that everyone preferred to save for baked goods. It was an unwritten rule that Em had picked up on immediately. Although Trina and Hannah always graciously offered sugar, no one seemed to accept that offer. When Ry didn't ask about sugar, I wondered if the black-band camp rationed sugar as well. She seemed happy to have cream to put into her coffee. At least Brook and Em would have honey for their tea. I'd never tried it, but Em said that she might try honey in her coffee someday, considering our resident beekeeper was doing very well gathering more honey for the camp.

A lull in the conversation occurred, and I wondered if the others, like me, were considering how to navigate the potential minefields any of us might trigger. I tried to tease my way out of the unease that had descended on us like a black cloud, ready to drench the entire group.

"Shoo, everyone. Get out of our tiny kitchen. I can barely breathe with y'all hovering around. Give us a few minutes to finish breakfast," I ordered.

After the kids moved to the small living room not more than a hundred feet from the kitchen, Em whispered too low for them to hear, "Is Brook okay with being pregnant?"

I shrugged. "Hard to tell. She's planning on keeping it."

Em nodded, then poured boiling water from the kettle into the cups with tea leaves. She added a spoonful of honey to each cup. The sweetness of the various spices added to the tea leaves, and the aroma filled my nostrils—the most prominent, cinnamon.

When Em brought the cup of tea to Brook, she asked the rest of the group, "I haven't tried honey in my coffee yet, but if either of you wants honey, we have plenty."

I glanced over to see their reaction. Ry wrinkled her nose. "Ew, that sounds awful. Even if I wanted a sweetener, honey in coffee wouldn't ever be something I'd risk trying."

Harley pushed against Ry. "Wow, so narrow-minded. I tried it once. It wasn't that bad. Sure, Em. You can hook me up with some honey."

Ry laughed. "You sound like Em is some kind of drug dealer."

Em couldn't hold back her roar of laughter. "I've had many titles in my life, but drug pusher was never one of them. Although, Lise used to say I was a pastry pusher."

"You were." I entered the conversation. "You never liked eating sweet treats on your own. You always felt so guilty without a partner in crime."

"You should talk, Lise. I saw those cannabis plants in the back of your greenhouse you were trying to hide." Harley leaned back onto the couch and smirked.

"Cannabis has great medicinal properties," I argued. "Besides, how do you know they are pot plants? The shoots have barely pushed through the peat."

"Duh, the fact that you had them almost hidden in the back was a major clue you were growing weed. Don't give up your day job as a master gardener. You'd make a lousy gangster." Harley snorted as she laughed so hard her coffee almost spilled in her lap.

I wondered how Brook felt about growing pot. Would she believe she'd landed in a hippy commune filled with queers and dopeheads? I chanced a look in her direction and was happy to see her expression hadn't changed. She'd lost a bit of the wariness I'd seen earlier, but that didn't mean she'd warmed to any of us.

The small things set her apart as an outsider, like politely listening but never participating. She took a seat in the single chair as far from the couch as was possible. Besides the quiet "thank you" when Em brought her tea, she hadn't said a word after Harley and Ry burst onto the scene, looking every bit the young couple in love.

Wanting desperately to bring Brook into the fold and move away from the conversation about my secret stash of cannabis plants, I took a chance and asked, "Brook, I was hoping you had time today to help me with my hydroponic garden? Things are at a crucial phase."

"Will there be others in the garden?" she asked when she glanced in my direction.

"Not unless Harley and Ry want to join us. The hydroponic garden is kind of my baby, and I don't let just anyone into my domain." I winked at her and held my hand up before Harley made an excuse. "Don't worry, Harley, you don't need to come up with an elaborate pretext to escape from garden duty. I know you'd rather work with Em on converting cars and trucks to solar-powered vehicles."

Before returning to sipping her tea, Brook caught my eyes, smiled, and said, "Okay."

"Um, Aunt Lise, I don't mind garden work, but I'd love to see what Em and Harley are working on. You won't be offended if I help them, will you?" Rylee asked.

"Nah. I'm sure her work is more interesting, but I want y'all to remember how crucial those gardens are when you're chowing down at night after Brook and I have harvested the fruits of our labor. Solar-powered vehicles you can live without, food is a whole other ball game."

"Ah, but solar energy allows that fancy-schmancy set-up in your hydroponic garden and a daily shower," Harley said.

"You have daily showers?" Ry asked.

"Yup. Compliments to Em, who fixed and enhanced all the camp's generators."

Ry looked wide-eyed at Em. "Wow, really? Are you some kind of genius scientist? How did you snag someone like that, Aunt Lise?"

"Beats me." I shrugged.

"Don't let her fool you. I had to work incredibly hard to woo your aunt. Besides her stunning good looks, she is the most generous, loving, and compassionate woman I've ever met. Not to mention, brave when it counts."

I noticed Brook shifting uncomfortably in her chair, nearly hiding behind her cup of tea. I was thankful that Em had completed a small stack of French toast while we were talking. My heap of pancakes was also high enough to serve the girls.

"Why don't we bring the food out to you while it's still hot? You shouldn't wait for us. We'll join you soon." Em carried her stack of French toast to the living area and set it on the small table in front of the girls.

Harley rubbed her hands together. "You don't have to tell me twice. I'm starving. I can smell the cinnamon. Load me up. Ry, try the toast with the homemade jam Hannah makes. It's delicious. Maple syrup isn't easy to come by, so we adapted. Hannah hooked you up with the good stuff, right?"

Em pointed to the small refrigerator, and Harley jumped from the sofa to grab the butter and jam. She was right. I didn't miss syrup after having tasted Hannah's berry preservatives one day.

Through the rest of breakfast, Brook remained subdued while Harley and Ry chatted animatedly with one another. My warring emotions were taking a toll on me, and Em noticed. Normally, she would shower me with affectionate touches, but she instinctively knew this would only send Brook further into her shell. Although I was delighted to see Ry so happy, I felt impotent to fix it when Brook visibly retreated from her new family. Ry and Harley's touches weren't so overtly intimate as to cross most people's lines, but it seemed anything that might reveal Ry and Harley as a couple was too much for Brook. I was both startled and relieved by the timid knock on our door.

†

Em and I shared a glance at one another before I made my way to the front door. "Bruiser, come on in. Have you had breakfast? We still have French toast and pancakes left. The bottomless pits haven't devoured everything yet."

"Um, no ma'am, I haven't. Thank you. I asked Trina if I could show Brook around the camp. I figured that Harley was gonna take Rylee around."

"Don't call me ma'am, Bruiser." I waved my hand for him to come inside. "It makes me feel old, and I am not old. There's still a lot of gas left in this tank."

"Yes, ma—Lise."

I ventured a glance at my niece, who seemed to perk up when Bruiser entered.

"Hi, Bobbie. I'm glad you're okay. I'm so sorry. I didn't want Peter to…"

"It's okay." He smiled. "I got a cool nickname out of it. So, um, would you like me to show you around?"

"I told Aunt Lise I would help her in the hydroponic garden today." Brook lifted her eyes to me.

I flicked my hand. "We have all day. The plants aren't going to grow roots in the shape of feet and walk away. I think it would be good for Bruiser to show you around. Just come to the greenhouse when you're done." I pointed to the food left on the table. Em had already discreetly brought another plate and utensils out. "Finish it."

"Do you need help with the dishes, or can we eat and run? I'm eager to show Ry the camp set-up, especially the projects that Em has been working on." Harley was already on her feet and ready to dash away. "I might take her to our favorite fishing spot."

"Not without an adult. Maybe Hannah, Sam, or Daryl will want to go with you," Em said.

Harley looked like she was about to argue, but one of Em's death stares was enough to get her to back down. It was remarkable to me that Em had the mom glare perfected, even though she'd never been a mother. Not for lack of trying. It was the one thing that had utterly unraveled Em over the past three years. Each time the test was negative, I saw her hopes melt away.

I wanted a child almost as much as Em, but Em seemed to take it personally when she couldn't conceive. Before the entire world went to shit, we'd decided it was time that I give it a go. I was approaching the age where I hadn't been as excited about carrying a child, worried that having a baby in my forties was risky. Besides, I thought Em's genes were much better, but I'd agreed. By the time I'd finished all the preliminary testing, Em's anxiety grew, and we'd started preparations for the bomb shelter. Our baby-making plans were abandoned. Pregnancy inside a shelter was not a wise idea.

With the kids touring the camp, that gave Em and me a chance to provide Trina with an update. I needed to tell her about the pregnancy and ask about how to access Taylor's services. So far, I hadn't needed to see a doctor for anything.

After we finished cleaning the mess in the living room, Em and I headed down the familiar path to the main house. We spent so many mornings and evenings with Trina and Hannah that it was unusual not to show up for breakfast.

Hannah opened the door before we knocked. "I wondered why y'all hadn't come by yet until Bruiser came to see us." Hannah chuckled. "He acted like he was asking for Brook's hand in marriage. I know you've already had breakfast, but would you like a second cup of coffee? We were having a lazy morning."

"That would be lovely," Em answered. "I think we all deserve a lazy morning. Not to interrupt your sloth fest, but there is an update to provide."

Em and I took our traditional place on the loveseat while Trina laid two cups filled with coffee onto the table.

Trina sighed. "Please tell me this is not something so catastrophic I have to make another tough decision."

"Brook is pregnant," I blurted. "She doesn't know who the father is because they passed her around like a jug of their moonshine." I could feel my mouth form a grim line.

Anger was the only emotion I could allow myself. I tried very hard not to envision what those bastards had done to her. If I let guilt or grief take hold, I could never help my sweet, innocent niece through the trauma. Em always knew when I played the what-if scenario in my head. What if we'd emerged from the shelter before they defiled her? It wasn't fair that we'd been able to keep terrible things from happening to Ry, but not Brook. I'd have to live with those uncomfortable feelings for the rest of my life. Hopefully, with time, they would lessen.

A pinched look returned to Trina's face as the line in her forehead deepened. "I see. I suppose she wants to keep the baby."

"She does," I answered. "I was hoping that Taylor could monitor her and make sure the pregnancy goes well."

"It'll be the first baby born here. I think that's something to celebrate." Hannah brushed her fingers over her wife's back.

"How much of an impact did the other camp's teachings affect your niece?" Trina asked.

"You're wondering if she'll try to make her way back," Em stated.

"The thought has crossed my mind. Who else knows Brook is pregnant? Did she share her suspicions with her husband at the other camp?"

"I don't know. I was surprised Brook confided in me," I answered.

"They will have several reasons to come after us now," Trina stated. "Perhaps your other niece, Rylee, will have useful information to help us prepare. I don't want Hannah going on any more surveillance missions now that we've whacked that hornet's nest and split it open."

"Can we let them settle a bit before bringing them in for an interrogation?" I didn't like how this discussion was advancing. They were kids.

Em placed her hand on my knee. "Hon, it's not an interrogation. If Rylee or Brook have inside information that will help protect us, we need to talk to them."

"Brook is fragile. Pushing her too far may cause exactly what you don't want." I needed them to see what I'd been observing. If we had any chance of undoing the damage from the other camp, we needed to tread lightly. "Talk to Rylee, not Brook. I want to spend time with her and gain her trust. Let me do that in the greenhouse. It seems we both have an affinity for digging in the soil. But I want to take her to Taylor sooner rather than later."

"I don't know if Taylor has experience with obstetrics, but she's all we have. Do you know where the clinic is?" Trina asked.

"Yeah, isn't it near the south gardens? I think I saw someone limping into a large building a few days ago. I figured that had to be our medical facility."

"I'll go with Lise to see Taylor. Sometimes she can be a little prickly with new people. As a former surgeon, her bedside manner doesn't track with a small-town family practitioner. She's getting a little better but has her moments," Hannah explained.

Trina chuckled. "Diplomatic as ever, Hannah."

I wondered what persnickety troll I was about to meet and if she would be the best person to manage Brook's pregnancy. Since the dawn of time, women had been having babies. Maybe I could help Brook with her pregnancy without going to a prickly pear for assistance. Brook was young and healthy. As if reading my mind, Em shook her head and chuckled.

"Nope, Brook should see Taylor. I'm no expert with the human body, and neither are you." Em's logic to the rescue again.

†

"How the hell do you always know what I'm thinking?" I asked Em on the way to the clinic.

"Don't ever play poker for money, hon. You have a very expressive face. I knew you thought you could play doctor for Brook."

"It'll be fine," Hannah assured me. "She hasn't bitten off my head in over two months now."

"Not reassuring." I glared at Hannah.

Hannah reached for the door, and when she opened it, the small, stout, ginger-haired woman announced, "Unless you're bleeding to death, we're not open yet."

"Stop reinforcing the picture I've already painted of you to Em and Lise," Hannah said with a smile.

"Em? Which one of you is Em?" Her steel-blue eyes looked between Em and me.

Em raised her hand and met the woman's penetrating gaze. "That would be me." She stuck her hand out. "You must be Taylor."

"Heard you were the one who got the generators purring like a litter of kittens nursing. Thanks. Do you know anything about biomedical equipment?"

"A little," Em hedged. "Do you know anything about babies or, more specifically, pregnant young women?"

"A little." Taylor smiled and didn't look as fierce to me. "It's been a while, but I believe I could navigate a woman's vagina. Just because I didn't choose that specialty doesn't mean I can't oversee her care. Who got themselves knocked up?"

Hannah quieted her voice. "Taylor, you need to tread lightly with Brook. She's one of the girls we rescued last night from the other camp. The way she was impregnated isn't pleasant."

"It won't be a problem for me to perform an abortion," Taylor stated matter-of-factly.

"My niece doesn't want that. She wants to have the baby," I answered.

"Your niece?"

"Yeah, Brook and Rylee are both my nieces. Brook has been through a great deal more than Rylee, and she was a lot more susceptible to the black band's distorted teachings. I'm hoping with our love and compassion, she'll be able to adapt.

Living with a bunch of lesbians was not on the top of her to-do list."

"Got it. Brook will presume I'm a lesbian, and a lesbian doctor wouldn't be her first choice. Well, I'm the only doctor here. We don't have any midwives hanging around either, but I'll do my best to allay her fears."

"Thanks. Can I bring Brook by later today? I'd like to ease her into seeing you and getting prenatal care. I was thinking around four?"

"I suggest having Daria help. You can act like she's your assistant. She has a way with the fragile ones. I know Trina thinks I have a gift in that regard, but certain kinds of trauma are much harder for me, and Daria is the better choice." Hannah kept her focus on Taylor until she nodded her agreement.

"With that settled, everyone out while I check my inventory. I might need you to lead a group on another pharmacy raid. I'm not sure if I have any prenatal vitamins."

"We can do that," Hannah answered. "Make a list, or we'll empty the shelves and take everything. I'm hoping that not all the pharmacies have been depleted. Or if they have, maybe they left the prenatal vitamins alone."

I wasn't sure how well Taylor would deal with Brook, but it wasn't like we had any other options. Hannah, Em, and I left the clinic and heard a rustling behind the building.

"Mmm, God, I've missed you so much, Ry."

I held my laughter and placed my finger to my lips as we rounded the corner. Harley had Ry pinned against the wood with her hand inside Ry's T-shirt, and the two girls were enthralled in a passionate lip lock. It was as close to pornographic as two teens could get without crossing the line.

I cleared my throat, and the girls jumped apart. I tried to remember when I was a teen with raging hormones. Then I recalled how my mother had caught me kissing my girlfriend and promptly kicked my gay ass to the curb.

"Shit, Lise, you scared us," Harley said.

"Please tell me you don't act like this around Brook." I crossed my arms in front of my chest.

The last thing we needed was for Brook to come upon the two of them and scatter like a single dandelion seed in the wind. I wanted everyone to help Brook ease into her new reality.

Em touched my arm. "Hon, Brook will need to adapt at some point. Everyone can't walk on eggshells forever. She's going to have to learn that there is nothing wrong with Ry and Harley showing affection toward one another. Granted, there are more appropriate places to show this level of intimacy."

"We're not stupid. Of course we haven't hooked up in front of Brook, but we wouldn't have to sneak around if we had our own place," Harley argued. "You wouldn't want to do a girl a solid by letting us use your cabin during the day, would you?"

I was sympathetic to their dilemma, but they were still so young. I hesitated to answer Harley.

I looked to Em to step in, but she just grinned at me, letting me know I was on my own. *Traitor*.

"Um, we're not saying yes, but we're not saying no either." I glared at Em, signaling she wasn't going to get away with suddenly becoming mute. "Em and I will talk about it."

"I could have taken her to the creek, but I want our first time to be special, you know. And that means a bed, not on the ground with fallen leaves and pine needles getting into all our cracks." Harley grinned.

"Just be mindful of who is around, okay? Don't make this your go-to place. I'm taking Brook to see Doc Taylor later today, and she doesn't need to see two horny teenagers making out behind the building." This time my warning was delivered with less irritation because Em was right. Brook would need to learn to deal with a reasonable amount of affection between couples.

Ry furrowed her brow. "Why? Do you think Peter and his friends did more damage than she's letting on? Those bruises were hard to miss. I wish I'd fucking killed them."

I didn't know how to respond without lying to Rylee, and I didn't want to do that. It wasn't my place to reveal Brook's pregnancy. Fortunately, Hannah came to the rescue.

"We're going to get you all checked out. We can't very well send our young, fresh workers to the fields and streams to slave away for us if you aren't in tip-top shape," Hannah teased. "Now git and finish the rest of the tour without stopping for more make-out sessions. I'd like to get some fishing done sometime today."

Harley clapped her hands together. "Really, Hannah? You'll go with us today?"

"Yes, I will, and I plan on catching the biggest trout."

"In your dreams." Harley giggled. "It's on. I think if I catch the biggest fish, then I should be allowed a bottle of mead."

"And then you woke up," Hannah taunted before turning away.

The three of us continued on the path, and before Em and I parted from Hannah, she suggested, "Want to join us for a bottle of mead tonight after dinner?"

"Always. I could cook that massive trout you plan on catching if you want to add dinner to that invitation."

"Deal. Especially if one of you plans on cleaning the fish."

"Wow, Hannah, I didn't take you for a priss."

"I'm not a priss, but fish guts bring out my gag reflex."

I figured it was best not to remind her how casually she'd wiped the blood from her truck and dealt with the six dead bodies. That was not something I wanted to remember again. I must have grimaced because Em took my hand and squeezed.

When it was just Em and I walking along the path, I turned to her and said with a fair amount of sarcasm, "Thanks a lot for not stepping in when Ry asked to use our cabin as their own little love nest."

Em chuckled. "You were doing just fine. I enjoy watching Aunt Lise in action. Besides, I was as lost as you on how to respond. It's one thing to guess that they're having sex and quite another to know it's happening in our bed."

"Right, I know. But if we don't let them have the cabin, where will they go for privacy? It seems ridiculous to wig out about kids having sex and not concern ourselves with all the violence they've been exposed to and will most likely face in the future. I think we might have to give our blessing."

"Agreed. Can I be there when you tell Harley? I want to watch Aunt Lise in action." She shot me her most mischievous smile.

CHAPTER EIGHTEEN

Bending my head as I checked the tiny shoots, I hadn't heard Brook and Bruiser enter the greenhouse. When my head lifted, I saw clearly the marks on her neck and face in the bright light of the day. At that moment, I shared Rylee's earlier sentiments. I wanted to demolish the men who had done that to my niece.

"How was the tour?" I kept the quiver from my voice.

"This compound is a lot bigger, with larger gardens, and you have an orchard," Brook said with excitement.

"*We* have an orchard. It belongs to everyone who lives here." I smiled, proud of what I'd planted for everyone to enjoy. "Hey, Bruiser, Hannah is going to join Harley, Finn, and Sadie on a fishing trip today. I assume you'll want to go with them. They're probably ready to leave soon."

I was hoping he would take the hint. Even in the short time I'd known him, his tall, gangly body was filling out, and he was transforming into a very handsome young man, whom I was not opposed to as a partner for my niece. But I didn't know if Bruiser was smart enough to pick up on subtleties. Turns out, he was.

"Yes, ma'am, I mean, yes, Lise." He looked at Brook and offered her a crooked smile. "I'll see you later?" he asked.

Brook nodded.

After Bruiser left, Brook surprised me by stating, "You didn't lie."

I wasn't sure what she was talking about and stared at her, waiting for more explanation.

"Bobbie showed me the chapel. It's nice. He said there's only one Bible, so they leave it in the chapel, but anyone can read it. He told me a group gets together to talk about passages in the Bible, and he would take me. He said he goes all the time. He doesn't care that Harley, Ry, Sadie, and Finn are the way they are because they're the best friends he's ever had. He would do anything for them."

"Yeah, Bruiser is a good kid. Loyalty is a wonderful trait. So is acceptance of differences. If everyone were exactly the same, this world would not be as astonishing as it is. Throughout history, the world has progressed because of our differences, not despite them. Em is a plant murderer, and I'm known as the Garden Virtuoso. But I can't do what Em does to make the camp run smoothly through generated power. Each of us has a gift to share with the world."

"I don't think the world is astonishing at all. It hasn't been for me." Her quiet words broke my heart.

"Give us a chance, and maybe you'll see the world the way I do." I pulled Brook into a hug, and she let me hold her. "You are not broken. Sometimes when you allow yourself to accept the glue that others offer to build you back better, those tiny cracks let the sunshine in. Without those cracks, there is only darkness."

Her tears fell. "I'm soiled. Nobody will love me now. Bobbie won't want me when he finds out."

"I don't believe that for one second. From where I'm standing, that boy would run through fire for a chance at being with you. Trust me, with my years on the planet, I know love when I see it. In Bruiser's eyes, you're perfect in every way."

After she stepped away and wiped her tears with the sleeve of her sweatshirt, she said, "Thank you, Aunt Lise."

Her quiet words let me know that maybe I had a second chance with my niece. I wasn't about to squander it.

"It looks like solution number six works best with the lettuces." I pointed to the tiny shoots. "See how these are much taller and wider than those."

She smiled when she asked, "Did you also use solution number six on your cannabis plants?"

I laughed. "Yup, solution six and seven. But in that case, I think seven is a little better."

†

I was running out of time to broach going to the clinic. We'd been working well together for nearly six hours with a quick break to have lunch. Many of the starter plants had been moved to the gutters where they would grow to full maturity, readying them for harvest. I decided honesty was the best policy. If I wanted Brook to trust me, I had to level with her.

"Brook, I went with Hannah to see the camp doctor today. I'm concerned about your health and making sure you and your baby remain healthy. You need good prenatal care. I was hoping we could visit her today. Would that be possible?"

Her eyes flitted to mine before she looked at the ground. "If I started spotting after, uh, the men were rough with me, do you think that means I could lose my baby?"

"I don't know, hon, but I'm sure Doc Taylor can answer your questions. If you're still spotting, all the more reason to have her check you out."

"Okay. Is she nice like everyone else I've met so far?"

I coughed. "Well, to be honest, Doc Taylor might not have the best bedside manner. She was a surgeon before. Let's just say surgeons aren't always the warm and fuzzy type of doctor. But she is very competent. That matters more to me than her disposition. I'll be right there with you every step of the way. I promise."

Brook laid her hand on her belly and said, "Okay. Can we go now?"

"Of course, honey. Let me clean up, and we'll head over right now."

I hoped that Hannah had arranged for Daria to be at the clinic by the time we walked over. We would arrive earlier than we'd initially discussed. I breathed a sigh of relief when we met Hannah on the path. She wasn't carrying any fish, so

I wondered if she'd been skunked or they'd finished their fishing adventure for the day.

My quick glance at the clinic and her subtle nod let me know that Daria was with Taylor. That left me free to tease her. "So, master fisherwoman, where's that biggest fish you bragged about? I certainly hope you caught something for us to clean and cook?"

"Oh, ye of little faith. Not only did I catch the biggest fish, I have four beauties on ice right now, waiting for you to get busy. I've invited the kids to a fish celebration. It felt only fair that they should join us since they also caught a mess of fish, but we're kicking them out before we pull out the mead."

"Sounds like a plan. I'll come by in a bit to get started."

With my arm around Brook's shoulder, I led her to the clinic and poked my head in, announcing our arrival.

"Hey Taylor, Daria, we're a little early…"

Daria's gentle smile greeted us, and she cautiously approached Brook. "Hello, Brook, you're in good hands with Doc Taylor. Don't let her brisk manner fool you. She's a teddy bear inside." Daria winked. "Why don't you come with me, and I'll get you situated in a room."

The smoothness and peacefulness of Daria's voice and gestures could settle the most frightened person. Daria truly had a gift.

"Can Aunt Lise come with me?" Brook tentatively asked.

"Of course, honey."

†

I wasn't sure what to expect, but an exam room that looked no different from those I used to go to for my annual checkup was definitely not what I had anticipated. Daria handed Brook one of those flimsy gowns, and I turned away to leave and give her privacy.

"It's okay, you don't have to go," Brook whispered.

"Are you sure?" I asked.

Brook nodded, and Daria left the room.

My eyes zeroed in on the deep purple generously displayed all across her upper body and belly. No wonder she was worried about her baby. I tried to control my anger at seeing her battered body. I needed to take my eyes and mind from the evidence of her mistreatment. After tying Brook's gown in the front, I gathered her clothes, neatly folded them, and placed them in my lap as I sat in the plastic chair in the corner of the room. I assumed the rolling stool was for the doctor.

Brook looked so small as she sat on the exam table with her hands clasped together. I wondered if I should wait in the chair or stand beside her and take her hand.

Two quick knocks and Taylor entered the room. "Hello, I'm Doctor Taylor. Let's see how far along you are. Can you please place your feet in the stirrups, and I'll take a look?" Taylor barely looked at my niece as she began washing her hands in the sink. So much for the pep talk from Hannah regarding her bedside manner.

Brook's eyes widened, and she looked to me before scootching down and complying with Taylor's request. I decided lending my support would not happen by remaining in my chair. I set her clothes on the chair and walked to the side of the table to take her hand.

Taylor donned a pair of gloves and, after performing an internal exam, announced, "It looks like you're about two months along. Does that sound about right?"

Brook nodded.

When Taylor removed her gloves and untied Brook's gown, Brook clenched my hand as I held on. I knew the minute Taylor registered the bruising that covered Brook's thin frame because her gasp was accompanied by a brisk question.

"Where did these bruises come from? Damn scooters. I keep telling the kids to stay clear of them."

I felt the need to come to her rescue. "Brook didn't fall from a scooter. One or more than one of the men at the black-band camp did this to her."

"I see. Have you been experiencing any spotting?"

Tears formed in the corner of Brook's eyes as she nodded. "Have I lost the baby?"

"No, but we'll need to monitor you closely. If the bleeding continues or you feel a lot of sudden pain, you need to come back immediately. No heavy lifting or excessive exercise," she added. "I wish I had a damn ultrasound machine," Taylor grumbled. "I want to start you on vitamins and no caffeine or alcohol. From your pale skin, you look like you might have a small iron deficiency. Add foods that are rich in iron to your diet. Actually, I'd like to see you gain a bit more weight. Don't be stingy with food."

"I'll make sure she eats well. Good thing we're eating fish tonight. I'll cut some spinach and broccoli from the greenhouse."

Taylor nodded, and before leaving the room, added in a softer tone, "We're going to work together to make sure you have a healthy baby."

"Not all the bruises are from Peter's friends. When I told him I was pregnant, he wasn't happy about the news. He suggested I get rid of it, and I told him I didn't think Silas would approve of that. I threatened to tell Silas about my baby. I thought Silas would protect me. Peter went crazy after that and said he was gonna beat that bastard child right out of my belly. Peter didn't want to care for a baby that might not be his. I was afraid he'd succeeded. I want my baby to live. I'll do anything."

I brushed her hair aside. "We'll do whatever it takes to keep this baby healthy. Are you going to tell Rylee about the baby?"

"Do you think I should?"

"Yeah. Ry will be thrilled for you. Being an aunt is about the best thing that can happen to a person, except for maybe having your own baby." I smiled at Brook.

"Did you tell Em?"

I wondered if being honest and confessing the truth to Em would ruin the tenuous rapport I'd established with Brook over the short time we'd spent together. But I couldn't lie to her. "I did. I hope that's okay. I also talked things over with Hannah and Trina this morning. I'm sorry if I broke your trust."

"It's okay. Can I have my clothes now?"

I grabbed the sweats that remained folded on the chair and handed them to her. "Of course. How about you come to our cabin, and you can take a quick nap while we prepare dinner? I'm sure Sonny and Cher would love to cuddle with you. I imagine our cabin is a lot quieter than the one you're sharing with Harley's gang."

Brook giggled. "She is kind of bossy sometimes, but she loves Ry, doesn't she?"

"Yeah, she does. So much that I think she would have stolen a scooter and come to rescue you all by herself if we hadn't agreed to join her."

"I might have initially agreed to come because I wanted to protect my baby, but I'm glad I'm here now."

"You have no idea how happy that makes me."

"I have to tell you something. It's about Silas and what I overheard…"

CHAPTER NINETEEN

After I settled Brook in our bed and encouraged Sonny, who was the friendlier of the two, to curl beside her, I marched to Hannah and Trina's. I needed to warn them. I didn't knock politely like normal and barged inside. Thankfully Em was already there and had cleaned the fish. Em knew me well enough to detect my high level of distress.

"What happened? Did Brook lose her baby?" Em asked as she quickly washed her hands in the kitchen sink.

Hannah stopped washing the vegetables and turned her body to me, but let Em lead the conversation.

"Brook told me something that has me worried. She knows what Silas is planning. And it does not bode well for us. In a very short time, he will have the armory to flatten our camp without breaking a sweat."

Trina had watched me make a beeline to Em and was now standing in her living room. Her face pinched with worry as she made eye contact with her wife. Trina gestured for all of us to take our place on the soft chairs in the other room.

Trina's face returned to a blank mask. "Why don't you sit and tell us exactly what Brook shared with you."

"They're planning on raiding a military base in Yakima to bring back a tank that was left behind. A recent recruit of theirs has experience with tank maintenance and repair. He's a military deserter."

"Unless the explosives we've placed on the perimeter hit the soft underbelly just right, a tank will crash through our gates and leave a massive swath of destruction in its path. We have nothing that can stop something like that, do we?" Em asked.

Em's voice was calm and steady. But I could tell by the way she wiggled around in her chair that this news was unsettling.

"You're sure her information is accurate?" Hannah asked.

"I am. Brook doesn't have a motive to return and has an excellent reason to stay. Her husband had his own barbaric way to cause a miscarriage. Our camp was the lesser of two evils for her, considering she desperately wants to protect her unborn child."

"Something seems off. From the small amount of intel Hannah collected on her solo missions, he wants to grow his flock. A baby would be a symbol of new life he would welcome with open arms. You're sure she's not trying to set us up? Perhaps they believe we'll be foolish enough to go on the offensive."

"She threatened to go to Silas about the baby that Peter had no interest in raising, and that's why her husband beat her. We haven't spent a lot of time together, but I know I'm getting through to her. I trust that Brook told me this because she doesn't want anyone hurt. They talked about attacking our camp as soon as they secured the necessary armory, which she believes is this tank. I assume the gunfire we heard on our first day was from the black-band camp. They're the ones who keep attacking, right?"

Trina nodded. "We're the closest organized group, and they consider everyone inside an abomination."

I squirmed in my chair before continuing. "Brook said they already have other arms that will prove difficult for us during a direct confrontation. She thinks that with us taking all the younger women and girls, they are more than a little upset with us."

"Hopefully, we have a few days to prepare. I need to think about this. I'll bring Daryl and Sam up to speed, and they can alert our skilled fighters. I'd rather leave the kids out of this. They already have far too much to worry about than I'm comfortable with. If Brook hasn't already told her sister, do you think you can convince her to keep quiet?" Trina asked.

I shook my head. "This is a whole new world. I'm not about to tell Brook what she can and cannot share. I don't want any of them in the center of a battle, but keeping them in the dark isn't right either."

Hannah nodded. "I agree."

"As do I," Em added.

Trina pinched the bridge of her nose and, in a rare outburst, raised her voice and asked, "Fuck, is it too much to ask that we safeguard a sliver of their innocence?" She lifted her head. "Don't answer that. You're all probably right."

Hannah clasped her wife's hand. "Why don't we enjoy our time tonight and bask in their youthful energy. I'm looking forward to watching young love in bloom. It reminds me of what we're all fighting for. I wish *the others* had never found us. We would have been able to live in peace. Instead, we've been forced to adapt in ways I never wanted."

†

I'd almost forgotten how fun it could be to have the bubbling energy of youth. Growing up, we always had large family gatherings. My cousins and I would run around the house, vibrating with excitement before my mom served the big meal. This felt like one of those family gatherings. I'd lost that when my parents kicked me out, and for a while, I could recapture a microcosm of that feeling when I visited my older sister, Kim. She hadn't completely turned me away yet. Not that she agreed with who I loved, but her faith was decidedly more compassionate than my parents'. Kim even continued to tease with me just like she'd always done during those gatherings. I missed that.

"Hannah cheated," Harley insisted.

Laughing, I asked, "How in the world can a person cheat at fishing?"

"I don't know. She just did. She probably has superhuman vision and saw the biggest trout in the stream.

Then she muscled her way to that spot." Harley leaned back in her chair and patted her lap for Sonny to jump into.

The cats had followed their noses and moseyed to the main house, knowing someone would slip them a few morsels. Both cats were filling out, and I worried they might have health issues with how much everyone was feeding them. Bruiser had unobtrusively carried Cher to Brook, placed her in Brook's lap, then sat beside her while we let our meal digest. Cher wasn't the friendliest cat, but somehow, she instinctively knew Brook was the one person needing her attention more than any other.

As we sat there joking and enjoying one another's company, I stiffened when Sadie and Finn seemed to snuggle against one another. I wondered if their obvious affection would make Brook uncomfortable, but she didn't seem to notice.

Em sighed. "I miss the lazy summers of my youth. Fishing and climbing into our secret treehouse. No boys allowed."

"If I had a secret treehouse, I wouldn't say no girls allowed," Bruiser quietly said.

I watched as Trina sat forward. It looked like she'd discovered the cure to cancer. "Treehouses, or at a minimum, several sturdy platforms built into our taller trees is an excellent idea. How fast do you think we can assemble them?"

Brook shifted her eyes from me to Trina. "You told them what I overheard?"

"I did. It wasn't something you expected me to keep in confidence, was it?" I asked.

"No. I haven't told Ry or the others. Should I have said something earlier? We could have been working on the platforms today instead of gardening." Brook looked distressed.

"What is she talking about?" Harley asked.

"*The others* will probably procure a tank and an impressive arsenal from the military base in Yakima." Trina began tapping her fingers.

"Shit. I thought all the working tanks were already commandeered by a militia group farther north of us." Harley stood and began pacing. "Trina, we need a plan. Tanks can do a lot of damage. We don't have anything to fight something like that. I was glad when I heard the other militia group got there first."

"I know how to build a treehouse. Putting up a few platforms for snipers will be a piece of cake," Bruiser offered.

"Finn and I can help. That will make the work go faster, and no offense, Lise, but a lot more fun than gardening," Sadie said.

I smiled at the two girls. "None taken. Not everyone appreciates the finer qualities of gardening."

"Ry and I could help, too." Harley stopped pacing.

"No, Harley, I need you for something else. And I require your brilliant mind to examine a few different scenarios. It's time I took advantage of your exceptional chess abilities. You can help me brainstorm every contingency," Trina said.

Harley beamed with pride. "Thank you for not treating me like a kid."

I was surprised by Trina's about-face. Earlier she hadn't wanted to involve any of the kids, and now she was inviting

Harley into the bowels of her planning strategy. I sent her a questioning look.

"I had a little time to think about this, and Hannah often has a fresh perspective. Plus, you know how she has this ability to suss out someone's value and character. She wasn't wrong about either of you, and I don't suspect she's wrong about Harley. Sounds like many of us will have a long day tomorrow. It's time to call it a night."

As the kids filed out and Em and I made our move to leave, Trina touched Harley's arm and asked, "Can you stay for a few minutes?" She glanced at Em and me and added, "I'd like the two of you to stay as well."

Ry's forehead creased in concern, but Harley kissed her cheek and said, "I'll be back in our cabin soon. Make sure Bruiser behaves himself with your sister. He better not get lucky before Lise and Em let us use their cabin," she teased.

Ry lightly smacked her arm. "Shush. Don't say anything like that around either of them. That kind of teasing will send both of them off the deep end."

†

Trina pulled open her refrigerator and grabbed several bottles of mead, handing all of us one, including Harley.

"Really, I can have a bottle of mead?"

"Your arguments about the drinking age being eighteen in some states because boys were sent to war have not landed on deaf ears. I know you recently turned seventeen, one year shy of that milestone, but I am going to ask something of you that will put you at significant risk. If I had a better choice…"

Based on Trina's pained expression, I knew this was tearing her up inside. I couldn't imagine having to decide to put kids at risk.

Hannah began rubbing her arm. "I was the one who made the suggestion."

"This is only one possibility, and hopefully a last resort, but if it comes down to it, we might need you. Sam or well-placed grenades will be our first option. We'll want to have more than one plan. If we're able to stop them before they reach our gates, that will be optimal, but I suspect our greatest chance might be a surprise attack."

"I agree," Harley responded.

"I regret not trying to determine what was wrong with that old tank when we had the chance. At the time, I honestly did not believe we would have to engage in an all-out war to secure our survival, complete with a military-grade armory. I wish I'd had the foresight to stockpile more weaponry." Trina sighed as she took a hefty gulp of mead.

Harley's eyes brightened, and she asked, "Hannah, will you teach me how to shoot one of those automatic rifles? Ooh, and I saw the grenades. I'd love to learn how to throw those."

"No, I'd rather you not engage in direct combat. Your mission will be dangerous enough. What I had in mind will require throwing skills, but nothing as dangerous as a grenade. And this will be the last resort. Em, I'll need some help from you to create something that would work inside the tank."

And with that statement, Trina laid out her thoughts to Em, Hannah, and Harley. I was simply a bystander listening to the plans but not having much to contribute. Their conversation gave me an uneasy feeling that lingered for several days, as it seemed everyone but me was preparing for battle.

Em's contribution was limited to creating tools for other people because she wasn't any more proficient or inclined to enter a war than I was. Even though I'd gone on missions, I hadn't once engaged another human in a fight. The gun Daryl had given me on the day we visited the nursery had remained awkwardly tucked away in my pants until I could push it away like a rotten piece of meat.

CHAPTER TWENTY

I tried not to dwell on the comings and goings in the camp. Brook and I continued to work the gardens, bringing forth life versus planning for death. My efforts to pull Brook from her shell were only intermittently successful. We had our love of plants and gardening as a common passion, but other than that, we were virtual strangers trying to understand each other's perspectives.

"Aunt Lise, do you believe in God?"

I should have thought more about my answer to such a loaded question, but instead, I blurted, "No."

Brook was kind enough to follow up and ask, "Why not?"

I fidgeted with the peat moss in my hands before setting it on the tray and turning to face my niece. "Honestly, hon, with all the things I've seen happen to good people and no retribution to those who are evil, I'd rather not believe in a God who could be so vengeful. Where is this loving God that Christians speak of? I certainly don't see evidence of him."

"He brought me to you and saved my baby."

I blinked back the tears. "You think that reconnecting with me is a good thing?"

Brook nodded. "Even after you left, Mom talked about you and how kind you were. She taught us to love the sinner even if we couldn't love the sin."

"How magnanimous of her," I spit out with a smidgeon of bitterness.

"I've offended you. I'm sorry. I only meant to let you know that Mom still loved you, and I think she regretted what she did to keep you away."

"One of my greatest regrets, too," I answered.

"Bible study was interesting yesterday," Brook casually tossed out.

"Oh, how so?"

"We read from the book of Ruth. Then we talked about other passages that have been interpreted differently. I didn't know that the term homosexuality had not been used until the nineteenth century. I guess I never thought about how it is not used in the Bible. Bobbie doesn't think that homosexuality is a sin."

I smiled. "Do you still believe homosexuality is a sin?"

"I don't know. Bobbie made some good points. He believes all those passages that condemn same-sex relationships are talking about lust, sexual exploitation, and sexual violence, not loving relationships. I haven't told him about the baby yet, or what Peter and his friends did to me, but I think Bobbie would view those behaviors as sins. I know Jesus Christ died for my sins, so I hope he will absolve me. I pray for that."

"Oh, hon, I hope you hear and absorb what I'm about to say to you. You did nothing wrong. You are not a sinner. Try to focus on the uplifting teachings of the Bible. I remember many passages from Sunday school that encourage loving one's neighbor and treating everyone with love and respect. Jesus did not judge those around him. He taught love and acceptance. If you search for those passages, I'm sure you will find them."

"You went to Sunday school?"

"I did until my early teens."

"Will you come to one of our Bible study sessions? We can look for them together."

"Sure, honey, I'll come. A little reeducation on the subject won't kill me," I joked. "But, I'm not sure I'm a suitable candidate for a conversion. I left my parents' church a long time ago."

She grinned. "If I'm able to keep an open mind, I think it's only fair you should as well."

"Well played, Brook. Shall we finish and see what everyone is up to tonight? Hannah mentioned that Daryl killed an elk the other day, but I can't seem to celebrate having fresh meat. It's hard for me to think about eating Bambi. Maybe I'll toss together a vegetarian option while the rest of you enjoy your meat."

"Bambi was a deer, not an elk."

"I know, but they're in the same family in my mind. Both animals are far too majestic for me to consider eating."

"Could I have the vegetarian option?" Brook rubbed her belly. "I've had a little nausea lately, and elk meat doesn't sound appealing to me."

"Absolutely. I think Taylor mentioned something about legumes being high in iron. I'll gather the beans and get creative for us. If you want to go back to your cabin and clean up, then come around in a few hours, we should have dinner prepared. Invite your sister and the rest of your cabinmates."

"Okay. Thank you for answering my questions about God."

"You're welcome, honey."

†

As I prepared the vegetarian chili with the canned tomatoes and other items from the garden, Em entered our cabin, smiling and whistling.

"What's got you in a good mood?"

"I feel like I've returned to my youth. It was kind of fun making the smoke bombs today. One of my favorite Christmas gifts as a kid was a chemistry set. I got to experiment with chemicals today to find the right mixture."

"I've invited my nieces and Harley and gang to dinner tonight. Brook and I will eat vegetarian chili while the rest of you savages gnaw on that elk that Daryl shot. Who needs in-vitro fertilization? We have an instant family now, complete with six new kids," I joked.

"Except they're all grown, and we never got to experience the terrible twos or the start of puberty. Oh, and don't forget endless nights without sleep and thousands of dirty diapers," Em added.

Em's sad smile let me know that while her words were joking in nature, there was a hint of truth to them. She wanted the whole motherhood experience.

"I'm sure Brook will let us take control when it gets too much for her. Being on the periphery should satisfy our maternal instincts." I turned up the heat on the large pot and stirred.

"Did it work for you when you spent time with your nieces before the big blowout with your sister?" Em asked.

I could tell we'd already traveled into raw-and-honest land versus jokester nation. Talking about having children again was an unavoidable topic.

"No. Em, you know we could try again," I suggested.

"I've always been a woman of science, and the best chance of success was with in-vitro fertilization. If we try intracervical insemination, our chances are reduced to somewhere between five and thirty percent."

"Oooh, I love it when you get all sciency on me. You know how sexy you are when spouting medical facts?" I set my large spoon aside and wrapped my arms around her stomach as I kissed the back of her neck.

Em leaned into me, but I could tell we weren't about to take a train to love town when she pulled away and turned to face me. "Are you prepared for a lot of disappointment? Besides, do you believe it's the most prudent decision to bring a new life into this screwed up world?"

"Honestly, where we are now, surrounded by a kind of family I desperately wished for while growing up, is a hell of a lot better than what we had before. Despite the danger, this is a loving, supportive place to raise a kid," I answered with a kind of passion I wasn't sure I had ever possessed before.

Em smiled. "So, whose sperm? Have you picked out your donor yet?"

"Sam is handsome. I like the idea of having a biracial child. He's good with kids, too. I wouldn't be opposed to him having a role in parenting, either."

"A little short, isn't he?" Em rested her hip against the counter.

I laughed. "Height? You're worried about how tall our child will be?"

"If we choose Sam, Daryl might want to be involved. They're together, you know?"

I frowned. "Yeah, I figured that out, all on my own. Not that I'm opposed to the whole *it takes a village* concept, but I'm not sure I want Daryl too involved. He still scares the shit out of me. Although, I see glimpses of the person I suspect he used to be. Give me a little time to warm to the idea of him rocking our baby."

"Are we having a serious discussion about this?" Em asked.

"Yeah, I think we are. Both of us are nearing forty, so we better get on this right away before all the good eggs shrivel and die."

"You know I'm not worried about that. A lot of women successfully have babies much later in life." Em looked at me with such love in her eyes she was hard to resist.

"Maybe Taylor can help. I know this isn't her area of specialty, but she's smart like you. It's a thought."

"I know you wanted me to be the one to carry our child, but before the shit hit the fan, it was your turn to be inseminated. Maybe we should consider both of us trying. That would double our chances."

"You just want my Buddha belly to grow because you love rubbing it," I teased.

"That's not all I love rubbing," she shot back.

"Do you think we have time?" I raised my eyebrow and glanced at the large pot of chili.

"I can be quick."

I wasn't about to turn down an invitation to make love with my wife. I promptly reduced the heat on the pot of chili and then ran upstairs, giggling the whole way.

†

"Damn, you're good. Even when we have to be quick." I remained on my back, basking in the afterglow as Em continued to draw tiny circles on my belly.

"I do love your Buddha belly."

The loud knock on the door startled both of us, and we scrambled to pull on our clothing. "Whoops, better answer the door and check on the chili."

"I'm right behind you." Em's voice was muffled beneath the shirt she was pulling over her head.

When I flung open the door, I wasn't disappointed to only see Ry, Harley, Brook, and Bruiser. Harley gave me an appraising look, smirked, and then whispered in my ear, "Got some this afternoon, huh?"

I patted down my hair and straightened my T-shirt, then glanced at Em, who followed my lead. I wondered which of the two of us looked more disheveled.

"Shush, you little troublemaker," I hissed.

Bruiser carried several elk steaks and held them out for me. "Brook mentioned that even though you don't want to eat Bambi, Em and the rest of us don't mind."

That Bruiser was willing to tease with me was an enormous step. His comfort level around Em and me grew exponentially.

"Thanks, Bruiser. Do you think you could light the fire and be in charge of grilling the steaks?"

"I can help," Harley offered. "Bruiser sucks at grilling."

"Do not. Quit showing off in front of your girlfriend," he tossed back.

"Ha, me showing off. Look in the mirror, dude." Harley grinned.

I sighed. Maybe having a baby wasn't such a great idea after all. I stepped between the two to redirect their squabble.

"Let me see a show of hands for who is having steak tonight? I don't want to assume everyone is comfortable eating Bambi." I winked at Bruiser.

Everyone raised their hands, except Brook.

"Okay, then, I'm having dinner with a bunch of savages," I joked. "Harley and Bruiser, you are both on grill duty. Try not to kill each other. Ry and Brook, you can help Em with the vegetables for the grill. I'll start on the salad."

I was happy our brief interlude in the loft hadn't ruined the chili. The spicy aroma filled our tiny home, combining with the smell of charred flesh. I had to admit that grilled meat always created an enticing scent. When I ignored what I was eating on special occasions such as Christmas, I enjoyed the taste of a thick slice of prime rib, cooked to a perfect medium-rare.

I'd set out the folding camp chairs that were stored in one of the small closets, so when it was time to eat, I suggested we take advantage of the mild weather and eat outside. Our place was way too small for six people to enjoy a meal when right outside the cabin offered open space and fresh air.

The conversation remained light. By unspoken mutual agreement, none of us would broach the topic of an inevitable confrontation with *the others*. That suited me just fine.

I wondered why Sadie and Finn had chosen not to join us, so I asked, "What are Sadie and Finn doing tonight?"

Harley was quick to fill me in with her usual impish grin. "Sadie's been trying to get Finn to notice her for ages. She's planning a dinner and is gonna spill the beans about how she feels."

"They looked pretty cozy to me the other day," Ry noted.

I glanced at Brook to see her reaction, but she seemed nonplussed by the statement. I noticed the initial discomfort with the affection shared between Harley and Ry had lessened considerably. I wondered if Bruiser's influence was making the difference.

I smiled. "Good for Sadie having the guts to share her feelings. I hope it works out for her."

"Yeah, me too, because Sadie can be a total bitch when she doesn't get her way," Harley said.

"A little like someone else we know," Ry teased.

"What? I persevere. There's a difference between how I react and how Sadie stomps around for days without saying a word, and then she explodes like a cannon," Harley defended.

"So, what's on the agenda for everyone tomorrow?" I redirected.

"Same old, same old. Maybe we'll be able to do more exploring soon," Ry answered.

And just like that, we hovered along the edge of talking about the impending danger.

"I have some random gadgets I've been working on if any of you would like to visit the workroom tomorrow." Em came to the rescue as she enthralled the kids with her futuristic vision for the camp.

CHAPTER TWENTY-ONE

It was unusual for Em to visit the gardens. When she entered, I quickly made my way to her, leaving Brook to finish mixing more nutrients. We were almost done for the day, anyway.

"What's up? You've entered my realm, which I know isn't your thing."

"Hannah asked if you wouldn't mind stopping by tonight. They're having a hard time with Trina's decision to involve Harley in the plans to combat an attack from *the others*. I think they could use a sounding board. I know that you and Hannah have a special bond. They could both use our support on this."

"Of course. Maybe we can plan for a late dinner, rather than wait until after. It's eating them both up, isn't it?"

Em nodded. "Harley might be gung-ho about the potential for her to be intimately involved in the fight, but Trina and Hannah are petrified there is a real possibility she'll be injured if it becomes necessary for her to enter the fray."

"I think the kids have their own plans for tonight, so this works out well. Apparently the discussion with Finn went well for Sadie, and they're doing a triple date tonight."

Em raised her eyebrow. "Triple date? Does that mean what I think it means?"

I grinned. "Yup, Bruiser got the guts to tell Brook how he feels about her, and she didn't exactly discourage his interest. She asked me what I thought about that."

"What sage advice did you give her?"

I shrugged. "I told Brook I was sure that God wanted her to be happy and that men who beat their wives don't deserve to have the marriage continue. It's not like she can go to a lawyer and get an annulment because good Catholic girls don't get divorced. I said that her leaving their camp was equivalent to annulment in these unusual circumstances. She seemed to consider that. I'm guessing she will have further discussions with that Bible study group that she and Bruiser attend every day."

"I've heard they have very liberal interpretations of the Bible. Good for them. I'm glad Brook found her way to that group."

"Bruiser had a lot to do with that. I sense he has a deep faith, but that faith must have originated in a liberal church. He doesn't seem uncomfortable around any of us."

"Aunt Lise, I'm finished," Brook called.

I walked to my niece and responded, "Okay, hon. Enjoy your evening. Don't forget what I told you. You deserve happiness."

She waved at us and exited the greenhouse.

†

We settled in the living room in the main house while Hannah made tea. If it was possible, it looked like Trina had aged ten years.

Em jumped right in and opened the festering wound. "Harley desperately wants to be a part of this. She has a score to settle—the amount of rage inside of her needs an outlet. Aggression is not a part of either Lise's or my DNA, but that doesn't mean either of us holds any judgment against someone whom we've forced to make the hard decisions. I know you both are beating yourselves up right now. Don't do that. It won't be helpful to you or the rest of the camp. Everyone needs your strong leadership. Now more than ever. I trust you."

"Me, too," I chimed in.

Trina's face relaxed a little, and I was glad we could lessen her hesitation. "Thank you for saying that. You two are good friends, and I'll never take your support for granted. I want your honest assessment. Should I pull the plug on our contingency plan and force Harley to go into the cellar with the other kids?"

"No." I was quick to respond, and Em murmured her agreement before I continued to share what I'd observed. "I've been watching Harley train while working in the

247

greenhouse. That kid is amazing. Considering I believe we are descended from monkeys, you'd think the rest of us could navigate the trees in the same manner. I wonder if someone slipped Harley a little simian blood to enhance her natural abilities."

Hannah smiled. "I ventured a quick peek as well. Ry set out buckets for her to toss balls into while swinging from a tree limb. It reminded me of the time I went to see Cirque du Soleil in Vegas. That was truly a thing of beauty."

Em sighed. "I never wanted to go to Vegas. Too much bling and crowds. I was waiting for them to go on another tour and make their way to Seattle or Portland. Now I'll never get to see them."

"Never say never. We're all young enough that maybe the US will dig itself out of this massive hole. Part of me doesn't want that to happen. I wonder how much I will miss going to my favorite sushi restaurant or attending another Broadway musical. I took for granted my ability to attend all those openings and swanky events that were part of my former life. That was the only perk to modeling." Hannah looked wistful.

"I won't miss anything from my old life, especially that life before Hannah. I used to be an engineer, working for a company that definitely did not value their female employees. I was constantly getting in trouble for speaking up. Engineering was a male-dominated profession with little tolerance for assertive women. After ten years of putting up with their crap, I quit and started an outdoor adventure company, leading tours for women. That's where I met Hannah, and my life began to look up." Trina smiled warmly at Hannah and kissed her cheek.

I smiled. "Yeah, Hannah told me your story when we were up in the trees, and she was trying to distract me."

"What are you doing for dinner tonight?" Trina asked warmly.

Before we had a chance to answer, I heard the low rumble of machinery off in the distance. Hannah and Trina turned toward the noise and were suddenly on high alert. The front door burst open, and Daryl's expression was grimmer than usual and filled the room with a sense of dread. I hadn't even felt this disturbed during the two dangerous missions I'd been a party to.

"We've got company," Daryl reported.

"Our neighbors?" Trina questioned.

"Yes, and they brought their tank," Daryl answered. "It looks like it's in perfect working order."

"Open the gate and let them in," Trina ordered.

CHAPTER TWENTY-TWO

"Daryl, are the snipers set?" Trina asked.

"Almost. By the time we open the gates, they'll be in the trees and ready for your signal."

"Make sure that Daria moves all the children to safety, including the older kids." For the briefest moment, I saw hesitation flash across her eyes before disappearing behind a mask of determination. "Tell Harley to meet me at the shed immediately," Trina directed.

"Will do." Daryl headed off in a trot. He looked almost resolute in his duty to engage in battle. Even though I could barely stomach talking about how we would handle an attack, I was grateful for Daryl, Hannah, Trina, Sam, and

Harley, who had less reluctance to do what was necessary to protect everyone they loved.

"I'm sorry, Em and Lise, but unless you intend to join the melee and see things you don't wish to observe, remain inside the house while we take the trash out. The first door on the left leads to the basement." Trina pointed down the hall. "You should be safe there."

"I wish we could do more to help, but I still think of them as human beings," Em confessed.

"Not anymore. What you've learned about how those animals treated the kids is only the tip of the iceberg." Trina shuddered and then stood. An immovable expression that reminded me of a granite slab replaced the warmth in her earlier demeanor. "I'm responsible for the survival of every person in this alternate society. There is nothing I won't do to protect the people I consider my family."

Hannah pulled open a drawer, retrieved a handgun, and handed me the Beretta. "I understand your stance on violence and guns, but you've insisted on being part of several other dangerous missions. I know you want to survive, or you wouldn't have volunteered, ventured out on your own, or stayed inside a bomb shelter for ten months. You, Em, and your nieces are a part of this family. Don't let *the others* cut your life short or, worse, take away the people you love. Living with that guilt will be far worse than killing another. Trust me on that."

I took the gun for the second time. It still felt alien in my hands. I wasn't sure I could use it, but the prospect of losing everyone I cared about loomed heavy on my mind. I remembered Daryl's quick lesson on the safety and prayed I wouldn't have to flip the lever.

A vow to adapt to this new world might require a tiny adjustment in my previous stance. I suspect Hannah surmised that I could muscle up the chutzpah to use the damn thing if forced to defend myself. This was the reason I held the foreign object in my hand and not my sweet Em. It was ironic that Em viewed me as the more unlikely of the two of us to alter our nature. I knew Em was the one who could never hurt another human being, no matter what.

Trina crossed the room with purpose followed by Hannah as they both exited the safety of their house, opting to address our enemies head on.

†

Warring emotions caused me to freeze before deciding not to crawl into the basement like a coward. I might not actively engage in battle, but I didn't want to literally keep myself in the dark. Knowing what was happening outside was too important.

I glanced at Em, who seemed to wait for me to make a move. "I don't want to hide in the basement. What if they need us? We can't just abandon our friends," I implored.

"I understand. I'd like to help, but I don't know how."

In an instant, our roles had changed, and somehow, I'd become the brave one. It seemed like a slow evolution to get me to this point, but I didn't want to live my life in fear anymore.

"Let me see what's happening." I jumped from the chair and looked out the window. If I didn't know any better, I would have believed Trina was opening her home to beloved friends as she waved the tank in smiling. Her stance was devoid of any aggression. This wasn't exactly the original plan, but I wasn't blowing smoke up her ass when earlier I'd said I trusted her. We had discussed various scenarios. My preference was the one that would render them impotent before reaching the inside of our camp. I tried hard not to think of all the lives that would be lost regardless of which scenario unfolded. None of this made me happy, but losing any of my friends or family wasn't an option.

Following the tank was a group of twenty men carrying what looked like assault weapons. Most of them bore the scars of war. I wasn't sure if the disfiguring marks resulted from infighting between the different militia camps, the new nerve agent Trina had told us about, or radiation burns. After that first day, when we'd received an infodump on what had happened while we sequestered ourselves in the bomb shelter, we hadn't returned to that depressing conversation. I supposed there was more to learn, but we'd avoided talking too much about it.

The men were lumbering behind the vehicle as if each step brought extra pain to their bodies. I felt an immense sense of empathy for the men, despite their aggressive demeanor and what I knew they'd done to my nieces.

Opening the window, I turned my ear to listen to the conversation. The tank halted. A large man with no visible scars emerged from the top and jumped to the ground. The hatch remained open, and I thanked a higher power I didn't believe existed that this would help our plan. He pulled a pistol from his waistband and pointed the gun at Trina. His arrogance was working to our advantage. Clearly, he didn't register the threat and probably thought his band of men would roll over our camp with little resistance.

"We've invited you inside and are prepared to offer whatever help or resources you and your men need. I don't believe the gun is necessary," Trina reasoned.

Hannah stood beside her wife. It was clear her acting skills were not as polished. She wore a grim expression and looked like a cobra about to strike. For an ex-model, with her height, she could transform from every man and woman's wet dream to an Amazon warrior in a matter of seconds.

"Your companion does not seem to share your view," he spat.

"I've made a genuine offer. If you choose to ignore the olive branch and start a war, I promise many of your men will not survive. I'd prefer to handle this with diplomacy," Trina's voice held steady with not an ounce of hesitation.

"We don't negotiate with dykes and fags. We want our women back, and we'll take the rest of the women of childbearing age, starting with your companion. You stole my wife, and you'll pay for that. I'll not waste my seed on you. Too ugly to pass on those genes," he sneered, and his troupe of men laughed.

"No one here is compelled to stay. Any attempt to force any of the women to join your camp will be considered an act of aggression, and we'll respond accordingly." Trina remained rigid as she stood in front of their leader.

I continued to watch in horror as the events unfolded.

The men appeared to respond to his cruel statement, lifting their guns. I saw a bit of movement in the brush. Trina nodded once, and then she tackled Hannah, pushing her to the ground when all hell broke loose.

Some well-placed sniper shots took out ten men before they scattered. The rat-a-tat-tat of machine-gun fire filled the air. Bullets flew everywhere as some men fell to the ground, while others attempted to find cover or provide cover for their colleagues. Trina had pulled a knife from her boot that landed on Silas's thigh. His scream of rage as he hobbled forward was terrifying. Instead of going after Trina and Hannah, Silas limped toward a building to take shelter and haphazardly fired his pistol. After emptying the magazine, he tossed it to the ground in obvious frustration.

The tank moved, and it was clear the large hunk of metal would inflict sizeable damage if we weren't able to stop its progress. The rolling menace would demolish every single one of our tiny cabins without genuine resistance. I could see a few grenades land in the path. It seemed like they were trying to launch them into the opening at the top, without success. There would be collateral damage from the explosions. Before Sam climbed onto the moving tank, I saw him grab his leg and fall to the ground. He crawled to safety and took cover behind a large tree.

I hoped all the kids were underground and remained unharmed. Everyone but Harley would be shuffled to the safe location. I had to trust that Daria knew what to do. The camp had several cold storage cellars that Daria knew were at least some level of protection against a major attack. I didn't know if Taylor could patch everyone who wasn't able to escape the barrage of bullets falling all around the people I'd grown to love.

Harley swung from the branch of a tree with a protective mask over her face. Her first few attempts at tossing one of the smoke bombs into the open hatch almost made it, but bounced off the rim. It looked as though she abandoned Plan A and switched to Plan B as she gracefully landed on top of the tank like a gymnast sticking her landing for a perfect ten. Pulling another bomb from her hoodie's front pocket, she removed the homemade pin that would release the chemicals, then tossed the object into the open lid at the top.

For the second time, I wondered why they hadn't closed the hatch on the tank after Silas made his dramatic appearance. *Dumbasses.* I was convinced that my notion about the men's arrogance regarding a confrontation with a camp full of queers was ultimately our saving grace. Smoke billowed from the hole beneath, and Harley raised her fist in the air. I saw Harley grab another one from her pocket, and then my attention returned to my wife. With the tank disabled, I knew the inevitable conclusion to the skirmish. The remaining men would not stand a chance against our snipers. I didn't want to see the men picked off like ducks on a conveyor belt at a cheesy carnival.

I glanced at my sweet Em, and she was holding her hands over her ears. I wasn't sure if she was blocking out the gunfire or screams. Both sounds littered the air. I thought of Trina's comment about taking the trash out. I wondered if that trash also entailed the sounds of chaos and pain. I didn't hesitate to rush to Em's side to comfort her.

When a grenade crashed into the main house through the broken window, I blinked once, and then somehow, my legs moved toward the intruding weapon. Without thinking, I picked it up and tossed it back outside two seconds before the horrible thing exploded.

I had focused on the tiny bomb and didn't realize one of the scarred men had entered our place of refuge. He leered at Em, reaching for his belt buckle. She was frozen on the love seat. I could see she was trying to keep from panicking.

256

She'd once told me she would rather die than have someone violate her. Her frightened eyes shifted to me.

My hand shook as I lifted the gun in front of me. I tried to duplicate what I sometimes saw on TV and what Daryl had said when I'd accompanied them on that first mission. I flipped the safety, then held the gun steady by placing my left hand on the bottom. By some miracle, the intruder hadn't registered another person in the room as he continued to unzip his pants.

"You will bear me a son," he declared. "And this time, I will know it's mine."

I took aim at the large target in front of me and prayed as I squeezed the trigger. The gun had a kick to it, but the bullet hit the large mass I was aiming for. The man crumpled to the ground. Unfortunately, he wasn't dead. As I stood over him and saw the murder in his eyes, I squeezed the trigger again and again until he wasn't moving.

Could this be Peter, the man responsible for my niece's distress? Had I killed Brook's husband? Would she judge me harshly for what I'd been forced to do?

Em began crying, and I tossed the gun on the floor. I was now a killer, but Em was untouched. I wasn't sure if Brook or Em would forgive me for what I'd done, but I was sure I'd do it again if it meant that I kept someone I loved from harm.

If this man was Peter, Brook was a widower at eighteen, and I was glad for that, even though I knew my inner demon might haunt me for what I'd done.

Em looked at me with her tear-streaked cheeks. I saw something in her expression that I will be forever grateful for—forgiveness and love. I expected her to condemn my actions. To look at me with disgust. But Em uttered two words before kissing me. "Thank you."

"I couldn't allow him to do that. I'd rather become a monster than let him take you away from me. I love you."

"I know," she said. "I love you too."

After we'd made our declarations, there was an eerie silence. I noticed the gunfire had ceased.

I turned around in time to see Trina limp inside the house and glance at the lump on the floor, staining the beautiful rug. She held her leg, and Hannah was helping her.

"Oh my God, you're shot," I exclaimed.

"Are you both okay?" Trina asked.

I nodded. "I couldn't let anything happen to Em..." I tried to explain.

"I'm glad," Hannah answered. "Taylor is outside tending to the wounded. As soon as she finishes with Sam, she'll be here. We need to stop the flow of blood. Can you help her to the couch while I get something to use?"

Em and I rushed to Trina's side and took over as human crutches. Hannah was back in the living room after less than a minute and held a cloth to the wound. "She'll be okay. We've not lost anyone yet. Thank God Taylor is used to working in a war zone."

The small, stout, ginger-haired woman came barreling into the house and yelled, "Jesus Christ, Trina, kill 'em with kindness. That was your strategy?"

"It worked, Taylor. Besides, the fencing material is expensive and hard to find. I couldn't risk those idiots tearing it down."

"You're worried about fencing material? Are you out of your fucking mind?" Taylor yelled.

258

Trina took a deep breath before responding. "Look, you know as well as I that if we had engaged them in battle before my little ruse, we would have nothing left to rebuild and no wounded for you to take care of. Our snipers are much more effective inside the camp. After careful consideration of the risks, I determined this was our only chance. Was it a calculated gamble? Sure, but it was one I had to take. I was prepared to accept the consequences. Trust me, the decision was not an easy one to make."

"Fine, let me see your leg. I should pull out this bullet and stitch you without anesthetizing the area for your insane need to be on the front lines."

"How's Sam?" Trina asked.

"He'll live. Daryl's with him now. Daryl is laughing at him because I gave Sam the good drugs. He's declaring his undying love for Daryl." Taylor chuckled.

Trina nodded. "Wonderful. Can I get those good drugs?" She grinned.

Taylor retrieved a needle from the small black bag she carried and stuck it into a small vial, pulling the liquid inside. Without warning, she jabbed the needle into Trina's leg next to the wound. Trina grimaced but didn't make a sound.

"I'll give the injection a few minutes to take effect. Then I can pull out the bullet and stitch you up. It doesn't look too bad. You're lucky." The doctor glanced at the lump on the floor with the blood continuing to spread on the carpet. Her head gestured to the dead man. "You or Hannah?"

"Neither. I believe Lise, the pacifist, took him out." Trina glanced in my direction.

"I take it he was about to violate her or—" she shifted her eyes to Em "—Em, by the looks of his hanging belt buckle and open fly."

Trina lifted her shoulders. "I don't know. Probably. It was another reason for the attack. They weren't too happy with our rescue mission. We've removed most of their childbearing women. They wanted what they considered their property back and thought they might snag several more women to fill their needs and act as breeders."

"Fucking animals," Taylor hissed. "Glad you took him out, Lise." Taylor looked in my direction before returning her attention to Trina. "How's the leg? Does it feel numb yet?"

"Yeah, sure, just get the bullet out and stitch me up. I want you to make sure no one else is injured. And don't let any of the children see the men's bodies, not even those held captive by Silas and his men."

Taylor worked on Trina's leg as she pulled out the bullet, irrigated the wound, and then stitched her up. "What about Harley's gang? Surely that will offer some closure to their nightmare and they're old enough. Seeing that Silas will no longer be a threat might give them some peace."

"No. Death is never a pretty sight." Trina shook her head. "I'd prefer to move the bodies and then give them all a proper burial. Anyone else hurt? I assume Harley and the snipers did their job and got to the rest of the men. Harley wasn't injured, was she?" Trina's look implored Taylor to give her good news.

A rare smile formed on Taylor's lips. "That girl is like a monkey. She was in and out within minutes. She looked like GI Jane with her precious knife in her hand as her head popped out of the tank. And yes, there is no one left to cause any more harm."

"Good, I know it was a risk, but I hoped the tank would roll under one of the planks in the trees. We'll have to finish the treehouses for the kids to use. Who knows, maybe I'll climb into one and enjoy a relaxing bottle of mead, toasting everyone who did what was required to save the day."

I knew this was Trina's way to tell me it was okay I'd taken a life. Even though earlier we'd basically agreed with Trina's decision to use Harley, I felt sick to my stomach, knowing what she'd done with her prized knife. She was a kid, but she'd probably taken more than one life today.

†

I was unusually quiet when we returned to what had become our place of refuge.

"Alone at last. Wanna get naked?" Em teased.

I knew this was her way to cope with a stressful situation. She wanted to act like everything was back to normal as soon as possible. She needed that to be the case. I admired her ability to do that. She could turn on a dime, refusing to let anything ruin the positive aspects of her life. I was safe, and so was everyone else. That was all that mattered to her.

"Funny." My thoughts drifted to something a lot less jovial. "I took a life today. He was a human being. He was the father of Brook's unborn child. I don't even believe in God, but I sure acted like I had the power to judge him and decide on the worth of his life."

Harley had confirmed that the man I'd killed was Peter. I didn't know why it was important for her to confirm my

261

suspicions, but it was. My body shook. The reality set in as if the concrete was hardening around a fence post.

Em grabbed my other hand. As if with a magnetic force, she caught my eyes and forced me to stay present with her. "You listen to me, Lise. That bastard might have taken away a lot more than either of our lives if you hadn't acted. I know for a fact I would have preferred death to what he was planning. I'm not suggesting anyone should ever make a choice to take another's life lightly, but I will always believe you made the right decision. This is a new world with a distinct set of moral standards. I hope to develop the fortitude to act with the same strength should a similar situation present itself to me."

"I don't want to have a cavalier attitude about life and death. Defending you and this place is one thing..."

"You won't."

"How do you know that?"

"Because of what you just said. You're strong, but not a cold-blooded killer. You could never be that. Nobody knows what they are capable of until faced with an impossible choice. You might think I would not have pulled the trigger if I was in your spot, but I'm not so sure about that."

"Maybe this will be the last time I face an impossible choice, and I won't ever have to fight again. Silas is dead. They can't have many fighters left, and we have the tank now."

"It's possible." Em's hesitant tone told me everything I needed to know.

She knew enough to suspect that while neither of us would take a prominent position on the front lines with the other warriors, everyone had to develop necessary fighting skills. Defending the camp was essential to survival. We knew that while the black-band camp presented a very personal reason for us to prevail, *others* were out there to worry about. Small militias were what was left of the United States of America.

I felt dirty in more ways than one, but tonight we would bathe. I knew it wouldn't be as simple as washing away my sins.

The new world wasn't what I had expected when we'd emerged from the bomb shelter, but I was glad Daryl found us before *the others*. As long as I had Em by my side and my nieces back in my life, everything else was whipped cream with a cherry on top.

EPILOGUE

Five months had passed, and my orchard had produced enough fruit for several pies, as well as jams and preservatives that we could use throughout the winter months. Hannah couldn't help herself and snuck out one night to see what remained of the black-band camp. She was delighted to report that nothing was left. It looked like they all had scattered in the wind. She surmised that most had probably sought another militia group to join. She felt confident that none existed within a hundred-mile radius of our location. That was good news for our sense of well-being. For now, *the others* would ignore us.

Hannah reported that Cora and her cubs had not gotten caught in any of our traps, and now they never would because she had removed them. Harley and Ry were delighted to hear that particular news, but they were banned from trying to entice the beautiful felines to make their home closer to our camp. I was glad Trina had put her foot down on that idea.

Brook had finally confessed to Bruiser she was pregnant, and he vowed to stick by her. I gave the kid big points. He'd essentially told her he would take on the role of a father before he'd barely emerged from adolescence himself. Of course, both Brook and Bruiser knew they would have the support of nearly every adult in the camp.

Harley pranced around like she was a proud aunt-to-be. She started calling the baby Peanut and would squat in front of Brook, whispering to her belly. I was more than a little amazed that Brook didn't seem to mind. Harley decided that she would take the Peanut fishing the minute he or she was old enough to hold a fishing rod.

The main house had such a lovely fireplace that we decided to visit Trina and Hannah for a cup of cocoa on a crisp evening that signaled the fall had arrived. The blood-soaked rug that was the evidence of what I'd done had long since been removed and burned, leaving no evidence for me to dwell on. However, that didn't stop me from suffering from occasional nightmares stemming from that horrible day. Em was worried the nightmares were affecting my ability to get proper rest. I'd been feeling fatigued over the last week, and the past two mornings, I felt so queasy, I thought I'd picked up a nasty stomach bug. The thought of a warm cup of cocoa sounded perfect.

"You still feeling a bit under the weather?" Hannah asked as she handed me a steaming cup of hot chocolate.

"Yeah, this morning, I thought I was going to blow chunks after breakfast, but I seem to be fine now. A little tired, maybe."

Hannah caught her wife's eye in that special way that they seemed to communicate with one another, and then wide grins appeared on both their faces.

"Em, I'm surprised you haven't asked this question yet, but Lise, when's the last time you had your period?" Trina asked.

"Wha..at?" I stuttered as the reasoning behind her question registered.

Em hadn't asked me about this, and her startled expression clued me in that she hadn't considered this possibility yet. Were we both so used to failure that the likelihood that one of us was pregnant hadn't occurred to either of us?

Em's expression turned to amazement, and she looked at me with such hope. "Can we go see Taylor right now? I know it's late, but…"

I nodded. "Yes, and I don't care if the grumpy goose yells at me! Sam and Daryl will be beyond thrilled. I just wish you'd been the one to succeed."

"I don't share that desire. I'm glad you're the one to carry our child."

"You two should hurry. There's new chatter on the radio. The president plans to make another one of his speeches from his cozy bunker. I doubt he'll say anything earth-shattering, but I find him amusing. It's one of the few things left to provide such entertainment," Trina announced.

†

"We're pregnant," I said with considerable awe in my voice.

Taylor, true to form, had been grumpy until she learned why we'd come to see her after clinic hours. Underneath her gruff exterior, Taylor was a giant marshmallow. She knew how much we wanted to have a baby, and she was rooting for us. Hannah had led a scouting mission to restock the pharmacy and obtain prenatal vitamins, so we were all set in case one of us also became pregnant in addition to Brook.

"We are." Em stroked my face and placed a gentle kiss on my lips. "I heard that hormone-fueled pregnancy makes a woman particularly horny. I plan on taking advantage of that."

"Um, I don't remember hearing any complaints about our sex life or the frequency."

Em chuckled. "Damn, I also heard that pregnant women can get touchy. I'll have to remember that too. You know, I think I'm already seeing that beautiful pregnancy glow. You look ravishing. Maybe we should skip going back to see Hannah and Trina. I'm not as entertained by the blowhard as they are."

I grabbed her hand and pulled her along. "You know they'll not leave us alone until they know for sure that we're pregnant. We might as well jog on over and give them the good news and then listen to the Imposter-in-Chief."

When we reached their door, it flung open, and we said in unison, "We're pregnant."

Hugs ensued, and then we took our usual places next to their fireplace.

"I've got herbal tea for you, Lise. I figure cocoa is as bad as coffee, but tea will be okay," Hannah suggested.

Trina began fiddling with the radio until the crackle and scratching had diminished, and the president's nasally voice bellowed from the speaker.

"We're rounding the corner, yeah rounding the corner. Our big military is restoring law and order. All media will go through this channel only. I'm going to build big, beautiful cities, better than before. I know more about building than anyone, and that's why I'll be your president for a long time, yeah, a really long time. Because, you know, you need me. I and I alone can make America safe again. Yeah, we're rounding a corner. The skyscrapers will soon be the biggest on earth, and they'll all have my name on them. America will be bigger and better than ever…"

Trina turned the dial and shut off the radio. "I guess we've had our entertainment for the evening. He sounds like he's at one of his famous rallies. Those are the same words he used two months ago. I think we're safe for now. I can't envision him getting anything done for a very long time. The rest of the chatter on the radio reported massive militia squabbles, mostly in other parts of the country. Nothing in our area since the black band attacked. For once, I'm happy for his incompetence."

"Maybe everything works out the way the universe wants it to. The massive destruction led us to this alternate society, and now we're going to have a baby surrounded by a community that is a true family. I couldn't ask for anything better. Tomorrow, I'm going to run to Daryl and Sam and give them both a big kiss," I joked.

"That's something we all want to see. Have you noticed lately how every time Daryl sees one of us, it's like he wants to ask but can't bring himself to intrude on our privacy? I almost feel sorry for him. Sam, too, but he usually asks. What a long way we've come to get to this place. It is exactly where I want to be," Em declared.

"The bomb shelter was fun and all, but being part of a community is priceless," I said.

Despite our challenges, I knew we would always have the support we needed to prevail over any obstacle placed in our path. I hoped I'd never see the inside of a bomb shelter again. Maybe, if my first kiss was with a girl, I might not think that way. A bomb shelter was the last place I ever wanted to return. I preferred the tiny home that we'd claimed as our own, filled with love and joy and, in about seven months, a new life.

ABOUT ANNETTE MORI

Annette is an award-winning author, published by Affinity Rainbow Publications, who lives in the beautiful Pacific Northwest with her wife and their five furry kids. With twenty-four published novels, three Lesfic Bard Awards, and one Goldie Award for her fourth novel, *Locked Inside*, she finally feels like a real author. Annette is as much a reader as a writer and is always looking for the next lesfic novel to queue up. She came up with the One Fan at a Time tagline, because it rolled off the tongue much better than One Reader at a Time. After pondering who she was at her core, she feels it was all about connecting to each reader on a personal level. Annette would be the first to admit she doesn't do well with the masses. If someone picks up her book and it touches them, she believes she has achieved what she wants with her writing by reaching each reader. It is who she is at her core. Drop her a line, she loves to hear from readers.

Email: annettemori0859@gmail.com.
Sign up for her mailing list: http://eepurl.com/cS7nr9
Check out her blog: Everyday Occurrences:
https://annettemori0859.wordpress.com/

The Others

Visit the Affinity Rainbow Publications website for her
books and many other outstanding authors:
www.affinityrainbowpublications.com

OTHER AFFINITY BOOKS

The Black Knight and the Lady JM Dragon

A lady faces the bleak loss of someone who had caught her heart but never known her love at the final battle where King Arthur Pendragon is returned to the Ladies of the Lake. A knight armored in black, in search of redemption, has a personal secret that at any time could ruin the reputation of the family name.

When the lady's father, a nobleman affiliated with King Arthur, asks the Black Knight to bring his daughter home from Camelot, the knight reluctantly agrees. Neither the lady nor the Black Knight could have expected what was to follow in this timeless romance of love battling secrets and treachery.

<u>Sculpting Her Heart</u> by Annette Mori

On the surface, it appears as if Zari Woods has achieved everything she set out to accomplish; fame, money, a supportive best friend, and loving parents. But to a person on the neurodiverse spectrum, a loving woman is elusive. When Frankie moves into her neighborhood, Zari starts her final quest, a happily ever after. Frankie is beautiful, kind and seems to genuinely enjoy spending time with Zari despite her quirks. Unfortunately, Frankie already has a girlfriend. Sort of. It's complicated.

Soul on Fire by Ali Spooner

A perfect summer ends with danger on the Appalachian Trail for Whit, Mitch and Brad. Once safely home, the relationship between Eli and Whit continues to strengthen as the boys return home and they grow as a couple. Eli falls deeper in love with Whit and North Carolina as the trees come alive with autumn color. The first Christmas at Cast Iron Farm is celebrated with Eli's family as a new chapter in all of their lives begins. Join the family for the third book in the Cast Iron Farm Series.

The Boss's Daughter by Samantha Hicks

Vivian Westfall, CFO of *Bridger Holdings*, meets her boss's estranged daughter, Lauren, when a disturbance at the company spring party piques her interest. Lauren is clearly drunk and making a fool of herself. To prevent embarrassment, Vivian forces Lauren away from the party. They have angry words, and things take an unexpected turn when Lauren kisses her. Months later Lauren pitches a proposal to her father to loan her the funds to start her own health club. Her father reluctantly agrees with a caveat; Vivian must go with her to Scotland to keep an eye on the money. It doesn't take long for the sparks to fly in all emotional directions. When Gregory Bridger finds out about their relationship, he does everything in his power to break them apart. Trust is at the heart of this love story, a fragile emotion that without it, things can and do fall apart.

The Ghost of East Texas by Ali Spooner

Agent Blair Cooper and her partner, psychic Tally Rainwater (Terminal Event), are back in a gripping new murder mystery investigation. When the serial killer Casper Caruso, known as The Ghost of East Texas, was sent to death row, Agent Blair Cooper was adamant that there were more victims of his killing spree. As his execution day approaches, Casper reaches out to Blair. If she agrees to a face-to-face meeting, he will give the whereabouts of 10 additional bodies left in his wake. Blair and Tally must piece together the clues to bring closure for some of the victim's families. However, when you bargain with the devil, there is always a price to be paid.

Terminal Event by Ali Spooner

Tally Rainwater was born with the gift of second sight, something she never understood. A near-fatal accident, at age twelve, makes her visions clearer, but not the reason for them. As she matures, Lisa, a spirit, enters her visions to guide her in using her gift, but still not the reason why. Can Tally and Blair's budding romance survive the possibility? Read this intense murder mystery romance and find out.

The Star Child by Ali Spooner

Eli and Whit are enjoying their life together on the mountain when Whit is called into action for a secret mission at the Pentagon. While she is gone, the Cast Iron Farm comes to life, literally, when Eli discovers a mysterious cave that has a connection to Whit's past. Younger brother Brad joins the gang. When Whit returns, she plans an Appalachian Trail adventure with Brad and Mitch. Join Eli and family as their adventure at Cast Iron Farm continues.

My Dear Vet by JM Dragon

Ava Lawrence, a research veterinarian, is thrown in the deep end when her uncle asks her to cover his country practice while he has a vacation of a lifetime. How could she refuse? His team shouldn't be any different than the crew at her parents' practice, oh, was she so wrong. What she now has to work with is a sassy nurse, an obnoxious receptionist, and an animal whisperer, or so it seems. Ava finds herself embroiled in taking care of animals in the area and local issues outside her experience, making her question her sanity. Throw in chickens, cats, dogs, and a donkey named Theo, along with various other animals. This turns out to be Ava's unexpected adventure with far reaching romantic benefits.

One Shot at Love by Annette Mori

Blair returns to her hometown after the death of her sister. Always an activist, she vows to use her voice to advocate for better gun control. She meets Maribel, an irresistible, sexy woman who proves to be an enigma to Blair. Maribel can't help approaching the weeping woman and learning the origin of Blair's grief, Maribel thinks she is the last person who should form a friendship with Blair. Ultimately, the allure is too much for Maribel, but how long can she keep her secret and continue to nurture their burgeoning feelings for one another. A committed left-wing social activist could never fall for the poster child of the

NRA. Unless taking that one shot at love matters more than anything else.

The Mountain Whispers by Ali Spooner

Arriving home and discovering the betrayal by her best friend and lover, Eli Fortner leaves to run off her anger and hurt. A chance stop at a convenience store and the purchase of lottery tickets sends Eli's life into a whirlwind of change. Able to now pursue her dreams, Eli heads off to see what else fate has in store for her.

Whit Brewer, Eli's neighbor, is everything Eli never knew she needed and wanted. But can she let go of the betrayal long enough to let Whit in? Thirteen black cats, a baby goat, and Cruz, her furry best friend, join Eli on her adventure, new life, and the possibility of real love.

Charlie by Erin O'Reilly

At fourteen, Hannah Garvin met 'the one,' Charlene Gaines, and her life was never the same. They were inseparable and spent every moment they could together. One day, Charlie left without a word and again, Hannah's life took a dramatic change. Hannah vowed to never fall in love again. When she meets Mick, a new arrival to the small Texas panhandle town near her family's farm, her heart remembers what being in love was like, and yearns for more. Will Hannah let the memory of Charlie go so she can start a new life with Mick? Or will her heart betray her and hold on to her love for Charlie?

Misha's Promise by Renee MacKenzie

Misha Wyatt has settled into a peaceful existence as a healer in Karst, New America. When an airplane crashes in the meadow outside of Karst, Misha hurries to help the pilot.

Misha is not expecting the pilot to be alive...or so beautiful. Will her uncontrollable desire to keep the pilot safe be her downfall? Can *they* survive their journey? The last book in the Karst series brings our characters to their physical and emotional limits. Don't miss the culmination of this exciting series!

Heart Strings Attached by Ali Spooner & Annette Mori

Socialite Remy has her world shaken. Bartender Chancy has her orderly life turned around. A mutually beneficial business agreement between Remy and Chancy turns into undeniable attraction. Will the two ignore culture norms to explore their intense desire for each other?

The Panty Thief by Annette Mori

Someone is stealing panties, but who? And why? Joey Hartford is a fourth-year medical student who insists she doesn't have time for a relationship. A new tenant in her apartment building is proving too tempting to ignore. Sabrina is in her final year of her doctoral program and focused on completing her dissertation. Meeting Joey is dangerous for so many reasons. Add a suicidal ex-girlfriend who suddenly reappears in Sabrina's life and Joey's jealous friend-with-benefits, and things get complicated quickly.

Country Living by Jen Silver

Peri Sanderson achieves her dream of moving from London to a cottage in the English countryside with her wife, Karla. Peri sees their future as pastoral while chatting with the locals in a quaint village pub. Sexy urbanite, Karla, has other ideas. Secrets are everywhere. Peri quickly senses something not quite right among her rural neighbours and also with Karla. Temptation, betrayal, and intrigue combine to change the lives of both women beyond anything they could have imagined.

Before the Light by Samantha Hicks

One year after her long-time partner Meredith's abduction and their subsequent break-up, Kathleen Bowden-Scott's life is spiralling out of control. She meets Bethany Jones and despite an instant attraction Kathleen shies away. In this fast-paced, romantic suspense, lies are exposed and hearts unite as Kathleen and Beth fight for their future.

Affinity
Rainbow Publications

eBooks, Print, Free eBooks

Visit our website for more publications available online.

www.affinityrainbowpublications.com

Published by Affinity Rainbow Publications
A Division of Affinity eBook Press NZ LTD
Canterbury, New Zealand

Registered Company 2517228